THIEF
OF
DREAMS

THIEF OF DREAMS

JP POWERS

CITIOFBOOKS, INC.
3736 Eubank NE Suite A1
Albuquerque, NM 87111-3579
www.citiofbooks.com
Hotline: 1 (877) 389-2759
Fax: 1 (505) 930-7244

Ordering Information:
Quantity sales. Special discounts are available on quantity purchases by corporations, associations, and others. For details, contact the publisher at the address above.

Printed in the United States of America.

ISBN-13:   Softcover   978-1-960952-84-4
                eBook   978-1-960952-85-1
                Hardback   978-1-960952-97-4

Library of Congress Control Number: 2023913584

CONTENTS

All Kyle Stone wanted was to build his business, make
good friends, and feel the love of a good family.

But corporate corruption, betrayal, and fate intervened.

Follow as his journey weaves together loss, war, and
the cutthroat playgrounds of the 1980s…

AUTHOR BIO

The story of the protagonist, Kyle Stone, is based on JP Powers' life experiences. Starting when he lost his father to suicide at a tender age. He lived with several families before he found his home in the Army. After a year of intense training in combat engineering, he earned his commission as an Infantry Officer at just eighteen years old. He served during the Vietnam war and received injuries that would later become crippling. After serving in the Army, Powers started a business alongside his family, his future looked great. What followed were some of the strangest events leading up to betrayal, greed, corporate corruption, witchcraft, paranormal activity, and much more. Those years were the craziest in his life. Thus Thief of Dreams had to be written.

JP Powers spent many years in the Entertainment business as a rock star manager, Concert, and Movie Producer, and was honored to be Producer of USO Entertainment, Bob Hope, serving our military delivering the best entertainment to those deployed throughout the world.

By producing a USO Show, he not only selected and negotiated with artists and management, formatted the show from music to comedy to dance, and organized the logistics of travel.

He saw sick, terminally ill children throughout his travels and decided to do something to help them. He chose the magic of moviemaking to reach out to them. The children became the stars of their movies. The results were amazing for these children, and it gave them a will to live again.

For over twenty-five years, JP founded 'The United States Entertainment Force,' a nonprofit charity serving the USA military and their families. In addition, they set up the 'Hopes and Dreams Project,' which was also for sick children and gave them life through the magic of moviemaking.

Looking back at his life, it seemed necessary to take the time to finish writing his story, Thief of Dreams, from his home in California with his wife Lynn and dog Duke. It weaved through a time in his life when he was surrounded by those consumed by greed, corruption, and deceit as they graveled for what they could steal as his life and business continued to unravel.

Today they keep looking for hope and love for everyone.

Vietnam Vet Kyle Stone starts fresh in the 1980s with a thriving business and a family that depends on him. But what begins with a celebratory roar turns into a decade of greed and corruption that tests Kyle's tenacity, wits, and, ultimately, his ability to survive. After a close friend betrays him, Kyle is forced to work for a violent crime family. The Family makes him carry out various tasks that endanger his life and lead him into wild and unwieldy paths. He leaves his wife, relocates, and becomes entangled in new relationships. His new life is, at times, harrowing and dangerous, yet it offers opportunities for him to learn valuable lessons. As he reflects on his past experiences as a soldier and, further back, to his father's suicide when he was young, Kyle faces down his traumas and emerges as a new man filled with hope and love.

Kyle's transformation is dependent on his willingness to face the past and embrace the true power of love, and this comes through clearly in a high-octane plot and through hard-driving exploits at every turn of the page. This fast-paced thriller is full of financial intrigue, criminal endeavors, and unscrupulous ploys. Kyle is thrust into unexpected circumstances that test his morals and resolve, but the flashbacks to his past help convey a fuller picture of him as a man seeking betterment with every experience he endures. Powers captures the exhilaration and excitement of the 1980s while refining a message about love in the midst of empty ambition and reckless living.

– Michelle Jacobs
US Review of Books

DEDICATION

This story, a story like no other, is dedicated to those souls of the eighties who found love to be as elusive as the pot of gold at the end of the rainbow. Kyle became immersed in the pursuit of love after losing his father at an incredibly young age. This void would continue to increase as the years and lack of replaced passion, compounded his search and wanting. As Kyle's life filled with chaos, he would always keep the faith that he would find love, the kind of love you would shout from the mountain top.

Thief of Dreams is reaching out to all those in love and traveling aboard the Love Train, following their hearts with the knowledge that love they want is just around the corner before the next tunnel. All aboard, destination: the reality of your imagination, where your true love resides. Come and fall in love!

CHAPTER 1

A STORY LIKE NO OTHER

A new decade, time to celebrate as the 80's were coming in with a roar. Kyle was at his favorite restaurant, sitting on his favorite stool at the end of a beautiful wood carved bar with a gorgeous large mirror reflecting the very busy restaurant.

"Will it be your usual?" Jim with a smile, asked from behind the bar. "No, just a cocktail today, I am not hungry." "You look down in the dumps Kyle, everything alright?" "I'm okay Jim thanks for asking. I am just overwhelmed with all that has taken place in my life lately. You know, finding it hard to balance everything." "Well I know what shared with me, your family and your business, and let's not forget the witchcraft that nearly burned your office down, and also, other unbelievable things that have happened to you, it would be enough to take any man down. I don't know how you do it?" Jim said. Kyle, looking down at his cocktail, "well not very well I guess if you can tell all the stress that I am under. Let's just hope with the decade of the 80's just around the corner, it will be much nicer to me, damn Jim it can't be any worse."

Jim walks back towards the register as he notices two gentlemen in black three-piece suits coming into the restaurant. They started looking around as if looking for someone. The Suit started pointing towards where Kyle was sitting. Jim watched as they made their way to the bar and walked behind Kyle.

"Kyle Stone?"

"Who's asking?" Kyle said as he turned around to see who was addressing him.

"Not important. What matters is that you are coming with us. We have a car waiting outside for you."

"If you don't tell me who you are, I am not going anywhere with you, got it?" Kyle said as he turned around to face the bar and glance at Jim who was watching intensely. Kyle was definitely not in the mood for any more drama in his life.

The Suit reached out and grabbed Kyle's shoulder. Kyle reacted quickly, "get your hand off me and don't ever touch me again." The Suit ignored Kyle and grabbed his shoulder again. Kyle stood up and landed a punch right in his stomach, bending the Suit over, as he tries to catch his breath. That was enough for his partner to see, he took his beretta from the holster and put it in Kyle's side. "Don't try anything stupid like you just did. Get up, and let's all walk out of here nice and gently."

Kyle had no alternative at this point but to do as he was told, as he was ushered out the bar to a waiting limousine. The suit with the gun opened the door and said "Get in." Kyle lowered his head and got in, he was now pissed off as the two got in the car, "who the hell are you guys anyway, the Mafia?" The limousine pulled away from the bar, heading to a destination he had no clue or control of, leaving Kyle with the feeling of fear in his stomach, similar to what he felt in Nam.

Vietnam 1971

He was thinking that all they had to do was get to the designated landing zone, and they would be on their way home, but he was wrong.

As the infantry squad approached the designated pickup point, they started to take on small-arms fire again and fell into defensive positions, establishing a perimeter. Kyle called in on the radio to change the LZ, landing zone, to a hot LZ. He hoped the chopper pilots would realize and take defensive measures while lighting up the area with their M-50 machine guns as they came closer to pick up the squad of men in trouble. The squad surrounded the LZ, listening out for the blades of the schnook coming in. The enemy fire increased. Bullets bounced off the ground. Mortar shells were sent in for maximum explosive damage. They were just young men trying to evade death.

San Francisco 1976

It was a beautiful night; the stars were extremely bright. The ships on the bay sparkled as their lights shimmered and bounced off the dark water under the Golden Gate Bridge. The hot tub was bubbling like champagne as the gentlemen sat near the pool. Kyle's thoughts wandered back to Vietnam. It seemed so far away now, he thought, as time continued to run though his fingers.

Their wives were inside with the children. Kyle had asked his friends and work associates to get together at Doc's house, the neighborly Heart Surgeon. David and Ron sat around the pool with Kyle, conversing about life and politics. They sipped their champagne, glancing at the night sky.

"Holy shit, did you see that?" Doc looked up to the sky in total amazement.

"Look, look, it's right there," David gazed as a bright light moved over the Bay. They all looked up. "Watch, there it goes, that is no plane, I will tell you that." The light flashed across the Bay and then disappeared into the night sky as quickly as it had appeared.

"That was crazy," Kyle said.

"That is what you call a UFO," said Ron.

The five men stared into space astounded, not sure of what they just saw flashing through the sky. Maybe Ron was right. Perhaps they were not alone after all.

Ron was Kyle's neighbor, and he was married to Donna. David was VP of Kyle's company and one of his best friends. As the men sat by the pool, laughing and having a great time, David's wife Linda stared out through the window. Her eyes fixed on Kyle. She always thought of Kyle as a stallion, an Adonis by most women's standards. She loved that he was rich, powerful, charming, and a war veteran. He could sweep any woman from her feet without much effort. The surgeon's wife, Donna, was also in hot pursuit of Kyle.

They were celebrating the tremendous success of Kyle's endeavors, a national financial investment firm that now had 26 offices, and each was producing $175,000 a month. He had just signed several franchise agreements hoping to double his financial gains. Money was pouring in, and there were smiles all around.

Kyle looked at the window and saw his wife, Suzette, talking with Linda. He thought back to when he just started and finally felt the fun of having some riches from his hard work. He remembered when he stood outside on his front porch and threw five- and ten-dollar bills to the neighborhood kids who could not believe his generosity. When he saw Suzette driving down the street, he stopped feeding the children green love. He knew she would not appreciate his offerings.

Suzette was with Kyle when he was building his empire, but the only thing she seemed to have an affinity for was the money. She had a loathing for Kyle, which he only tolerated for the love of their two daughters. It was time for good thoughts now, and he tipped back the champagne glass. Kyle watched the three men laughing and smoking big cigars. He sat with them and lit up a beautiful Payne-Mason Churchill as he enjoyed his friends' company.

With a sly smile, David's dark-haired wife Linda turned to the women and convinced them to join their husbands outside. They quickly changed into their bathing suits and headed out the door. Linda jumped into the hot tub, strategically splashing Kyle.

"I'm so sorry, Kyle," she said with a devilish smile, "but you're already wet." Kyle sat across from Suzette. It was larger than the average jacuzzi, and Suzette had an obstructed view of her husband though close. David preferred the dryness of the patio, sitting obliviously behind his wife, who gasped and moved closer to Kyle.

"Look how beautiful the bridge is from here," Linda whispered to Kyle as she attempted to slide her hand under his swim trunks. Her fingers were like a sea creature trying to creep up his leg.

Kyle quickly thwarted her, giving her a stern stare. She kept trying, gliding her hand up to his thigh. He finally had enough and turned to face her. "Linda, you have to stop. I know what you want, but you have to realize that you must behave."

Linda ignored him and moved her hand back to his thigh. "Come on, Kyle," she pouted. "My hand is under the water. Nobody will notice, and I promise you will like it." Nothing would deter her, not even her husband, just feet away on the patio.

Kyle turned to whisper in her ear. "Stop what you are doing, and I will share something with you that just happened to me."

Linda stopped and looked right into his eyes, "Okay, Kyle, I am stopping and listening. What is it you want to tell me?"

Kyle leaned in closer to her. "I had a dream last night that bothered me a lot. Are you sure you want to hear it?"

"Of course, please, please, tell me," she said as she smiled and reached under the water again. Kyle gave her a look, and she removed her hand, muttering apologies but not really meaning it.

"Okay, behave yourself, and I will continue. Got it?"

Linda raised both hands above the water and nodded yes.

"My dream seemed so real, Linda, but it was so out there that it confused me. It was about your husband but what was strange was this white candle kept appearing. I thought that was weird."

"What kind of candle was it?" Linda said.

"I don't know. I didn't pay that much attention to it. I do know that there was an argument between David and me, and he looked at me as if he wanted to kill me. He then jumped over my desk, trying to do what I suspected."

Linda looked stunned. "Kyle, that is horrible. David would never try to kill you. What happened next?"

"I'm not sure. That's where it gets confusing. I remember, like I said, David jumping over my desk and knocking me out of my chair. While I was rolling on the floor, he again jumped on me, trying to smash my head with my glass ashtray. I just know he wanted to kill me. Unbelievable huh? Well, here is where the candle comes in. As he jumped on me while I was on the floor, his foot kicked the end table, knocking the candle off. As he was trying to smash my head in, he stepped on the candle and slipped, hitting his head on my desk."

Linda asked, "Oh my God, what happened? Did he die?"

Kyle looked around at the others in the hot tub, and everyone seemed to be having their own conversations. He looked back at Linda with a confused stare and said,

"No, David did not die he is behind you. But that was where the dream ended. Confusing, isn't it, and your stupid comment did not help the conversation."

"Sorry, and yes, it certainly is," Linda replied. "Thank you for sharing that with me, Kyle."

"Let's keep this to ourselves, okay?"

"Not a problem." And with that, she dipped her hand below the water again and slid it under his bathing suit.

"Are you kidding me?" Kyle tried to move away from her.

"Please put your hand inside my bathing suit then, Kyle."

Kyle was losing his patience. "Okay, Linda, that's enough. Put your hand in your own lap, and as far as getting wet for me, you are sitting in a wet hot tub," he said, grabbing her hand and pulling it away from his growing crotch.

David's wife was relentless, thought Kyle. She whispered in his ear as she continued to try, "Kyle, come on, no one can see what I'm doing, and you are starting to want it. I want to touch it now."

Kyle pushed her hand away again.

"Your husband is sitting right behind you. What do you think he would say if he saw what you're trying to do?"

"He won't see. Just let me touch it."

Kyle, knowing he was not going to win this fight, raised his voice. "David, the water is great. Why don't you slip right down here with Linda and me and enjoy the tub?"

Just as Kyle was about to exit the Jacuzzi, Donna, the surgeon's wife, stood up and asked, "Who wants to meet me in the deep end?"

She took off her top and threw it at her husband. Linda accepted the challenge and ripped her top off, racing to the deep end. Everyone laughed and smiled, except Suzette, Kyle's wife. He watched as she got out of the jacuzzi and headed for the door of the house.

———◆———

Suzette was always insecure and jealous. Once Kyle had taken one of his sales agents out to lunch to discuss a large account she was working on. While he was at lunch, his wife came to the office and was told that Kyle was at lunch with Maryann, which was enough to set her off. She became irate. When Kyle returned, a large crowd was gathered in front of the sidewalk, his wife in the middle.

"Listen, I want you to get out and go straight into the office. I will see what this is all about," Kyle said to Maryann.

As soon as Maryann got out of the car, Suzette came after her like a lioness to a fawn. The crowd cheered her on. She grabbed at Maryann's ponytail and pulled her to the ground with a handful of dark shining hair. While on the ground, Maryann fought back and pulled her on top of herself. Suzette reached for Maryann's blouse and tried to rip it from her, exposing a white laced bra. Suzette took hold of it and, with a firm pull, exposed Maryann's naked breasts. The crowd was now in a flurry of excitement, watching Maryann trying to get her blouse and bra back.

Kyle ran through the crowd and grabbed Suzette's arm before she could do any more damage. He dragged her off and pushed her away, giving Maryann a chance to grab her blouse and bra and run for the office, tears running down her face. The crowd all started clapping. "Look at those crazy bitches!" some guy laughed.

Kyle held Suzette by the arms, "What the hell are you doing here, and why are you outside causing this spectacle?"

"I came to have lunch with you, and when I got here, they said you were out with Maryann, and that just ticked me off so bad," Suzette retorted.

"I was training her, and then we had a business lunch with two others. Nothing is going on. I cannot have you coming to my business and causing this kind of chaos—"

With that, Suzette swung her fists at Kyle's face. It was like she was trying to hurt him and show off to the crowd. He was caught by surprise, but instinct made him catch her fist, and then he had no choice but to take her down by pulling her hair until he could grab both of her arms. They were both on the asphalt; the crowd riled up for more. More people gathered for free entertainment, loving every bit of the altercation.

As Kyle tried to get Suzette on her feet, a young guy from the crowd pushed him over her, causing him to roll on the ground. Several others started to come toward them. Five dudes were staring at him, calling him names to provoke a fight. It could have gotten ugly fast. But a Cadillac drove up out of nowhere, and David appeared holding a shotgun and firing one time into the air. It scared the hell out of everybody. As fast as the crowd grew, it dispersed, thanks to Kyle's Vice President. The debacle was over.

Now that the show was over, Kyle went into his office after sending Suzette home, and to his surprise, she had cleared all the desks and thrown everything on the floor—pictures had been torn off the wall, coffee cups smashed, typewriters tipped upside down. It was a painful experience for all, especially Kyle and his staff. He felt hot with embarrassment. It was not as if he wasn't used to this behavior and never knew when she would go off the rails and cause trouble for the family and business.

Kyle had spent so many years supporting his family; financially, big houses, swimming pools, tennis courts, horse corrals, new cars, etc. They did not want for much. However, it was always on his mind that Suzette could try to destroy him and his business as she had constantly threatened. Her moving the threats to reality was the scariest part of it all, and she was doing it more often.

Speaking of reality, back at Doc's house, Kyle watched horrorstruck as Suzette took both of his girls by the hand and walked them right through the screen door, to the amazement of everyone in the pool.

"Girls, I want you to see your father, look at him with those women!" She roared with a deadpan expression. "I am taking the girls and going home," she announced to the party.

Kyle, still in the hot tub, looked around at the others and only shook his head. *Here is another get-together with our friends and she spoils it like usual.*

As he got ready to go out of the gate, Kyle said, "David, I will meet you tomorrow morning at the bank. Don't forget we have a meeting with Bill at 9:30."

"Don't worry, Boss. I will be there at eight. Bill and I are having breakfast before our meeting."

As he started to walk home, the surgeon stopped him.

"Hey Kyle,' he said, smiling. "Don't forget you owe me a new screen door."

CHAPTER 2

CONNIE IS ALWAYS RIGHT

Kyle was excited to start the expansion of his company with his franchisees. Howard, one of the businessmen who purchased a franchise, was being trained in the office early Tuesday morning. He was about fifty-five years old, gray-haired, and liked talking about spirits and séances. He seemed a bit obsessed with it and talked to anyone who would listen. Kyle and Howard sometimes had late-night drinks, and Howard would always talk about his beliefs in the supernatural. He said he would have séances at his home in Chicago, gathering around his large dining table, candles lit throughout the dining room, drapes drawn, and those eager to reach out and see if anyone was there.

One night they were wanting to contact family members who had left, leaving questions unanswered. Howard shared that after the participants all focused hard, mentally reaching out to the one chosen, they were right on the edge of enlightenment when they all felt warm air blowing on their necks. It brought chills to those sitting around the table. Howard went on to say that with the chills running down their arms, a picture near the end of the table came off the wall and started to float over the table, causing one older woman to faint.

Kyle did not know what to think, so he poured himself another tequila and tonic, admitting he found it remarkably interesting but hard to believe.

One night later, Howard had trouble sleeping and wanted to speak to Peter, his business partner in Chicago. He had been in the Bay Area close to a month now, staying in an apartment that the company was paying for. Even though he had been away from home for a while, Kyle made him feel comfortable at his house. That was easy to do with a large, beautiful home on the hills of San Francisco, overlooking the Bay. The manicured backyard, pool, and lit tennis courts only added to the ambiance. Kyle was immensely proud of his home, as it was an exceptional place he had built to enjoy with his family. They did not want for anything, even though Suzette seemed to complain about everything. Kyle spent so much time trying to make her happy. He wanted so badly to have happiness abound in his home. His childhood was vacant of any elated emotions.

Howard was there at Kyle's home so much; he wondered if the company should pay for an apartment. Kyle and Howard loved playing tennis, and with Kyle having his lit tennis court, they were smashing the ball back and forth nearly every day. Playing tennis was not the reason why Howard was there, however. With Kyle's colossal success with Stone Financial Corporation, several businessmen had already bought in; $85,000 was the initial payment, and Howard was the first to train. Once the payment was made, the franchisee was flown to San Francisco for a month-long training and given all the details of setting up their franchise.

Howard was the only franchisee in town, so he got a lot of attention, which was acceptable for everyone except Connie, Kyle's loyal assistant. She had already told Kyle that she was not comfortable with Howard for some reason. She could not put her finger on it, but something about him bothered her. It also bothered her that Kyle seemed to like Howard, and he was not heeding her warnings. She felt there was no good in this man.

Kyle was throwing a party at his home a week or so later, which he frequently did. Everyone in his company and their spouses always loved spending time eating and drinking, enjoying the views of the city.

Howard had too much to drink and was starting to get loud later that evening. When it got time to say good night, Howard was too drunk to drive home. Not liking him at all, Suzette reluctantly made up the guest room anyway and put a candle in his room to add to the ambiance. They all repeated good night, and Howard found his way to his room, where he went right to sleep as the drinks hit him hard.

Fast asleep and snoring away, he woke to the smell of the smoke coming from the candle burning on the dresser. He watched in shock as the smoke grew into a bubble, with the smoke so thick. Looking hard at the smoke wiping his eyes, he could not believe what he was seeing.

A faint, scary face was looking back at him, and as he looked harder to make sure it wasn't his imagination, the face spoke up and told Howard, "You will have an opportunity to ruin Kyle Stone financially. You have been warned. Do not do it, or you will face dire consequences. I repeat you have been warned."

With that spinning in his head, the smoke coiled back into the candle flame, and he fell back asleep.

Howard woke with the sun shining brightly in his room. He sat up and looked at the dresser and the lamp. Nothing seemed out of place or unusual. The candle was there, but it was not burning; it was as if nothing had happened the night before. He shook his head. It felt real and eerie to him. He was not sure if he should tell Kyle about the dream or leave it alone. Thinking about it as he got dressed, he decided he'd already shared too much of this weird part of his life with Kyle, and it would be best to say nothing.

The top floor of the company was where Kyle's office was based.

Connie worked right outside, and to her right was David's office.

"Kyle, Howard is on line three," Connie said.

"Thanks, Connie," Kyle sensed something in her voice, "Do you have something to say?

"No, I just…never mind, take the call, please."

Kyle picked up the phone to speak with Howard, not knowing what was bothering Connie. "Howard, how is your training going today?"

"Good. We are in the Embarcadero. It looks like a pretty large company."

"Sounds good. I hope you guys close the sale," Kyle said.

"Kyle, I wanted to speak to you about something that was bothering me, and I had a tough time sleeping. I walked by David's office yesterday afternoon, and he was on the phone with the financial company. It sounded like he was talking to Julie from corporate. It bothered me because I know you deal with her, being she oversees dispersing the money every week."

"I do appreciate your concern, Howard, but I am sure there is nothing to worry about. He probably wanted to go over some figures. You do know I like to stay close to my money though, so thanks and go close the big one," Kyle put the phone down. As he looked up, he saw Connie at the door.

"Do you have a minute?"

"Sure, come on in. Was there something bothering you earlier?"

"Yes," Connie said as she took a seat on the couch. "I can't figure it out yet, but something is going on with Howard and David. It seems like they are always sneaking around and, whenever I see them in their offices on the phone, they look away and whisper to whoever they are talking to. It's starting to bother me."

"Maybe something is going around. Howard told me to keep an eye on David. What are all the conspiracies about suddenly?" Kyle wondered out loud.

"I don't know. It's like I said," Connie repeated, "but I think there is something to it, and I am going to stay alert and will let you know if I hear of anything more."

"Thanks, Connie. You are always looking after me. What would I do without you?"

Connie smiled, "Go broke."

The next day, one of Kyle's female friends came by the office to say hello before going out. Kyle was not there, but David was, and he saw that she was in a playful mood and wanted to have a little fun in his executive bathroom.

David was in his office and heard Denise come in. He could tell she had already tipped the booze bottle, and he was ready to drop everything and go play with her. He left Kyle a note saying he would be taking the rest of the day off and would see him in the morning. It bothered Kyle that David cheated so much on his wife and never had any remorse over it. Kyle did not look forward to the morning. He knew that David would be there and would want to brag about his exploits, and he would have to sit there and listen and pretend to be interested. This activity was going to come to an end as soon as Kyle knew. As expected, David did just as Kyle knew he would. Kyle just sat back and let him rattle on.

"Kyle, what a night. I have to tell you all about it. It was crazy." David started with his story. "She stood there in front of the large mirror in a short red skirt, so short, I just wanted to slide my hand up those silky legs."

Kyle could tell the memory of it was getting David into a state of arousal.

"The black silk blouse was gorgeous, but I knew it would look better unbuttoned down to her navel, so I moved behind her and reached my arms around and started unbuttoning one at a time.

Denise, with a smile, said, 'Stop it,' but I knew she didn't mean it, so I kept on going. I had an ulterior motive, and that was to slide my tongue down from her belly button across her smooth stomach to the land of sweetness and pleasure. I pushed her skirt up and moved her now-wet panties to the side, gently licking and flicking my soft tongue, hitting the sweet spot. I knew she was there from the groans of lust and her rocking back and forth as her hands grabbed the back of my head, making sure I would not stop. After I stood up, we looked at each other and started laughing softly over what we had shared.

Denise, now satisfied for the short term, finally told me that she was going to a great party on a yacht in the bay and wanted me to go with her. Well, at this time, all I could think about was sexual pleasure after that, so I said I would clear my calendar and join her in what sounded like one of those sex parties you might have heard about. I was lost in the world of deprecation as I drove my Cadillac over the double-deck bridge with Denise's face in my lap. I yanked on her hair a couple of times as I was getting too close to launching, and I wanted to save myself for this party of socialites gone wild. As we found a parking place in the pier area and walked up to the ship, we noticed many beautiful women in long trench jackets.

I thought, 'This will be fun, but isn't it the men who are supposed to be in trench coats?' Denise agreed. The yacht, big and gorgeous, was all lit up and gleaming throughout its eighty-five-foot-long status. Topless waitresses immediately met us with flutes of champagne to help with the lustful mood. With the sound of the ship's horn blowing into the night and deck lines being thrown to the pier, she slowly made her way out to the harbor. With champagne in hand, Veuve Cloquet, Denise, dressed in that short red skirt and black thigh-high nylons without any panties, walked to the ship's stern where there was a large-breasted black woman in the hot tub, all alone. We stopped for a minute and conversed with her and got invited to join in.

Denise had never been with a black woman, and she was looking at all of her beauty as they spoke, and one could see in her eyes that she wanted to climb into that tub. I wasn't ready to mix up yet, so I just said they should go ahead, and I would just enjoy the show. She took off her black skirt and thigh-highs, leaving only her black blouse to take off before getting wet in the hot water. With her naked body in the tub, she went straight for the fullness of her companion's breasts, sticking right out, and her hands softly felt the firmness, and soon the sex was being felt, not only by the two participants in the tub but those who had gathered as well. I looked around. There was a small crowd now outside the hot tub, taking in a scorching show, and it was all free. They were both exhausted and now resting on the step of the tub. Denise moved against the tub and staring at her new friend in the wonder of what had just happened. I smiled at Denise as they moved away from the hot tub. I glanced across the bay water to the dock of the bay. It was like looking at a big mirror with the moonlight bouncing off the sea and the colorful lights of the city dancing on the horizon, as Denise also danced with her fired-up sexual emotions. In one of the larger rooms in the lower deck were fold-out deck-chair mattresses put in a circle, and there were so many hungry predators in different degrees of nakedness. Somebody told us that the room was for those who wanted to enjoy themselves in front of others, with the understanding that anyone can join in."

It was lunch by the time David had finished his story.

"That is way too much information. You have wasted most of my morning with your story of perversion. Let us get some work done," Kyle sighed. Again, he felt bad for David's wife and kids.

Kyle was at work as the morning dawned, but he was now concerned about a new problem that he had to take care of, a personal one that needed his immediate attention. David took up too much of his time with his private activities that usually included sex with someone besides his wife. Kyle was worried about their marriage. There seemed to be wanted distractions from both of them to the opposite sex. It would be impossible for any marriage to last with no trust between the partners. It was easy to punch holes in other marriages, being he was in one of those problematic marriages. Suzette was way too jealous to be married. She felt that only she should spend time with her spouse and anyone else who had inappropriate motives.

Kyle was up early in the morning, wanting the quiet of the house before everyone got up. With a hot pot of coffee on the kitchen counter smelling so good, he reached in the cupboard for his favorite coffee cup, filling it up and going outside to look at his great backyard with an incredible view of the bridge. He was proud of what he had built, starting from nothing, and now he had everything. As the morning progressed, he leisurely dressed for his meeting at the Bank with Bill. After a short drive into the city, he pulled into the bank parking lot and went to the 12th floor.

"Good morning, Kyle. Come on in and have a seat. David and I were just getting started," Bill said.

"Good morning, gentlemen. I am interested in what you came up with," Kyle stated.

The bank meeting went well, but it was not the only meeting he had that morning. Kyle was to meet with his attorney due to a pending lawsuit. They did not know why Kyle was being sued. It seemed to come with the territory. After the meeting with his attorney, Kyle decided to surprise his wife with a catered lunch. She was still a bit sore with him about the gathering at Ron's.

Kyle pulled his Ferrari into his driveway with the most delectable dishes, all of Suzette's favorites. To his surprise, Suzette did not appear to be home. He dashed into the house with the treats and thought maybe she went on a quick errand. He decided to ask the nanny.

"Good afternoon, Barbara. How are the kids?" Kyle asked.

"They are excellent, Mr. Stone. Just put them down for a nap," she replied.

"Great! Where is my wife?" Kyle asked the nanny.

"She just left, Mr. Stone, and she didn't tell me where she was going."

"Sit down, dear. Let us make this a little more interesting. I do know that Suzette would have told you where she was going. She would not leave and not care what happens to the kids. So one hundred dollars for you right now to tell me where she went," Kyle stated with a straight face.

She reached out her hand to take the money and told Kyle where he could find Suzette. As quickly as he strode into his driveway, he pulled out and sped down the street to a local bar and eatery where the nanny had told him he would find his wife. Kyle looked around upon entering the restaurant, and there was a dance floor off the bar area. Not wanting to be seen or cause a scene, he carefully peeked around the pillars to see if he could spot Suzette.

Sure enough, she was sitting at a table with a man Kyle had never met or seen before. Kyle could feel his muscles tighten up as his anger increased, watching them drinking and laughing. He wanted to jump right in there and let both of them know what he was feeling. He knew he could not do that. He would not be able to control himself once he opened up and let all the anger out. He could see they were asking the waitress for their bill, so they were ready to leave. He decided to get out of there and wait on the freeway on-ramp so he could see what she was up to. He was getting pissed off waiting and watching the cars go by.

It did not take long for Suzette and the mystery man to cruise past. The mystery man was driving the car Kyle had purchased for his wife. Kyle's blood was boiling now as he slowly moved onto the freeway, staying back from her car so he could follow and see what else they were up to. They took him off the freeway and onto the side streets, eventually pulling into an apartment parking lot. Kyle parked close enough to see her car but to be out of sight. He thought they would be getting out, but that was not the case as he watched them kissing and fogging up the windows. The fog was so thick on the windows that Kyle could not see in. He had seen enough. Walking up to the driver's door and looking in, he saw that they were lying down. This stranger was on top of his wife in the passenger seat.

In a murderous rage, Kyle knocked hard on the driver's window. It scared the hell out of them as they both looked up and saw Kyle staring in. As Kyle struggled to open the door to get at them, the stranger dashed out through the passenger door, running for the apartments. Hot in pursuit, Kyle ran after the man with anger, and when he got close enough, he jumped to reach the back of his shirt and pull him to the ground. Now on top of the son of a bitch, he was just about to smash his face in as he glanced back at the car and saw Suzette pulling away.

Kyle left the loser on the ground, wanting to get to his wife more. He ran to his car to chase her down. It did not take long for Kyle to go through the gears of the Ferrari and catch up, forcing her to pull over. Suzette had already gotten out of her car when Kyle walked up to her. She was leaning against her door, and when Kyle got in her face, she lost control of her bladder and pissed right there in the street.

"Go home, Suzette," he said. They could talk about it later. He did not want to go home, so he drove over to the park and turned off his car. Just staring out the window was all he could do; it was so much to deal with all at once.

Why now? He thought. Why does she have to start cheating on top of everything else I am dealing with. How much can one man handle? The thoughts kept rolling out of his hurting heart.

As he focused on the peaks on the horizon, he knew it takes two in any relationship to make it work, and if there were only one, it would be a challenging mountain to climb.

CHAPTER 3

YOU HAVE BEEN SERVED

With lunch getting closer, Howard was in the office while Kyle and David were away. He was on the phone with his partner, Peter.

"Listen, Peter. All is going as planned here. I think we have Kyle on the ropes," Howard said.

Peter looked out the window of his sixty-fifth-floor office, overlooking Navy Pier.

"Howard, you need to be careful. Kyle is smart. You must ensure he does not find out what we're doing, or else it would screw things up on this end."

"I know what you're saying. That is why I will be leaving here after this phone call. I do not want Kyle to see me here. As far as I know, he thinks we will wait the full sixty days as the court order stipulates. We will start taking people from him and secretly acquire his offices. I must admit, it is difficult to watch Kyle and his family and all who work here who were so nice to me, knowing I will financially ruin them all. Kyle has worked so hard in building this incredible company." Howard softly spoke so that Connie would not hear him.

"Yes, that's the plan. We must talk to all the managers before he does and do not go soft on us," Peter said. "This is huge, and the millions we can make will make up for destroying all of them. Do not leave out the possibility of having to take someone out. Remember, this is business. Only the strong survive."

"I got it and don't want to talk about that, but I have been watching David, the VP and Kyle's right-hand man. I think he's up to something."

"You keep an eye on him. I don't want to have any complications."

"I will. It is all good. I will take down Kyle, and it won't take much longer," Howard said. "You know the sad part of all this. I won't be able to play tennis with Kyle. I have really enjoyed it."

Peter scoffed. "You can buy your own tennis court; you don't need Kyle. Now get serious and let us get this done for all our sakes."

Connie had her antennas up, trying to catch anything Howard was supposed to report back to Kyle. After about an hour, Howard was off the phone and told Connie he would be out for the rest of the day.

Howard knew what he wanted the whole time he was in the corporate office and having dinner with Kyle and his family. He had a group of businessmen working with him to facilitate this takeover. He was as lovely as he could be with everyone, and soon, he fitted right in. Kyle had no idea that there was a thief amongst them, and his name was Howard. Howard would make his phone calls to his people after work, reporting all that he had found out during the day, putting a large file together for when he was ready to strike.

The time had come, and Howard had all his ducks in a row and proceeded to start the takeover of Kyle's company. Kyle and his VP and attorneys were working hard on this case and hoping to have it dismissed, being a fraud had taken place against them. Kyle never broke any laws. He was sure of that.

He had done his due diligence in packaging this franchise opportunity, sparing no cost of legal advice, knowing there was no crime there. The attorneys countered the lawsuit with one of their own, and this should have enough teeth to have all this dismissed once and for all, and then they could get rid of Howard. They were all anxious for the court date to come to put an end to the coup.

Kyle was aware that being the largest producer of financial plans had its difficulties. Once you are on top, many would want to take you out and steal what you have built. They felt they were entitled to take over Kyle's business. Howard was in Kyle's office for a month, learning the business to buy a franchise for his office in Chicago. Well, this was what Kyle and David thought was going on; however, they had been duped. Howard was gathering all the info he could to start a takeover of Kyle's company.

A lawsuit had been filed against Kyle for allegedly breaking state franchise laws. It was a bogus lawsuit from the beginning and part of the plan for Howard and his partner Peter, who seemed to have a long reach to take over the financial corporation and all the offices nationwide. So much was happening daily, and it was hard to keep up with it all. How many more players were involved in this plot?

Kyle was having a hard time wrestling with this and only wanted to talk to Connie; he knew this burned her so much. She was there from the beginning and knew how hard Kyle worked to build his company and how generous he was with Howard, thinking they were on the same page.

Howard and the Chicago bunch were busy contacting all the satellite offices, informing them that they would be taking over as managing partners and what all that entailed to them and their employees, all in violation of the court order. Kyle was busy contacting the same offices and seeing how many he could save under the new business climate. Kyle was counting on his past relationships with his managers in convincing them to stay with his company. He'd remind them how he had always been upfront and honest in all their business dealings and not to forget all the money they had made with him. Typically, this would be enough for a company to expend all their energy on, but not for Kyle. It was so much more complicated and seemingly complex.

The flag waved softly in the wind over the manicured lawn, rolling up to a very tall federal courthouse. Kyle and David went through the metal detectors before entering the courtroom.

"Just put your belongings in the bins, please," said the guard standing at the entrance. David and Kyle were feeling relatively good and especially because their attorneys were also confident about the case. They both emptied their pockets and put their briefcases on the scanner.

Kyle had worked long hours with Ron, his attorney, to be prepared for today, and they felt they had a strong case and should win easily. Howard and Peter were the two who wanted what Kyle had built; they were bound and determined to take it. Kyle could not fathom such action against another businessman just because you like what he has. An all-out assault of destruction until you get what you want and do not take any prisoners. It appeared to be the plan set in place to ouster him. What a shock to Kyle, not to Connie. She had tried to warn him when it all came out in the wash, and somebody discovered Howard was there under false pretense this whole time, gathering information he could use against Kyle.

Kyle's attorney kept saying, "Don't take this so personally. You will let it cloud your judgment." Well, easy for him to say, it was not his livelihood and family on the line. Kyle had to suck it up and prepare himself so that he could put down this coup.

"All rise." The judge entered the courtroom, a large man in his black robe approached the bench. "Be seated." It was time to begin. Ron started laying out their case and their opening arguments. Howard was being sued for corporate fraud and signing false documents, and Kyle was seeking damages of $4,000,000.

David smiled over at Kyle as if to say, "Not to worry, we have this." There was a bigger smile from Kyle as his attorney finished with the fraud and embezzlement charges and then took his seat. It was the plaintiff's turn to explain their actions of the last four months. This ought to be good, thought Kyle.

The plaintiff's attorney was no one other than Kyle's first lover, Allison Perry. Her maiden name was Parcens, and she lived up to the girl next door fantasy. She was older than Kyle and just turned seventeen. They created their own love game of Kick the Can. As soon as the game would get going, Allison and Kyle had their secret hiding place. It was a big shrub separating their driveways. He would usually run there first, in anticipation of that exciting feeling he had come to love so much. His excitement would grow as he heard her running to their love nest.

"Hurry, don't let anyone see you," Kyle whispered.

"I am so excited. Move over, Kyle," Allison said.

Soon, Kyle could feel her rubbing against him as the darkness fell upon them, and his lips searched for hers. He thought everybody could hear him because of their knees knocking against each other. Kyle kept pushing against her until she was standing against the branches, poking her in the back.

"I am sorry. Twigs are poking you," Kyle said.

"The only poking I want to feel is you, Kyle," Allison said, breathing hard.

Now, several years later, Kyle was staring at her as he entered the courtroom. She was still strikingly beautiful and gave Kyle a little wink as she stood. To the surprise of everyone on Kyle's side, she did not lay out a case. She just got up and said, "Your Honor, we were not given the 45 days required to produce exploratory documents before being summoned to court. Therefore, we ask that the charges against my client be dropped."

David nudged Kyle. "We got these bastards now." Kyle smiled back.

However, it was not time for smiles. "Counselor," the judge said, "upon my review, you are correct, and the said notice must be given before 45 days as stated. Therefore, I am dismissing the charges against your client. Court dismissed."

Two blank faces stared from the pews of the courtroom. Kyle was staring at the front of the room, motionless, then he looked at David. "What the hell just happened?"

"Well, I would say we just got royally screwed. The big one, right up the ass," David said, looking at Kyle, "How do you feel about that?"

Kyle hardly heard the question; he was off to another land where he thought he did not have to go. One of total dismay for justice and what is right. He knew what was wrong; this stupid, bogus decision.

Kyle responded after a bit of hesitation, "I feel like Rambo did in his movie when he took out an M-60 and lit up the courtroom. That is exactly what I want to do. David, I cannot believe what just happened. You cannot count on the court system to be fair. I really don't know what we should do now. The only good thing is they had sixty days before anything happens." As Allison passed by, Kyle gently stopped her.

"You fucked me in there," he said.

"It wouldn't be the first time," she smiled as she tossed her gorgeous red strands.

Kyle caught a glimpse of the massive rock on her finger. At that moment, he realized he might have married the wrong woman. This was another secret exchange between them, as Kyle had come up against Allison before in litigation; everyone assumed they were talking about court cases.

It was a noticeably quiet ride home. Kyle was deep in thought. "It is over. What do we do now?" Kyle asked.

David sat next to him in the car and said, "I have an idea. Let us talk at the office."

Kyle did not say anything. He drove through the tunnel straight to the office, still in a daze. As they sat in Kyle's office, Kyle got a couple of cigars and cut them with his cutter and grabbed two glasses with a bottle of fifteen-year-old scotch he had been saving for a better moment than this one. That was for sure. He poured one glass, gave it to David, and then poured his own as the bottle clinked on the crystal glass. The taste of smooth scotch on his lips, the only thing he thought he could still control.

"So, what is your idea, David?" Kyle asked, taking a big puff on his cigar.

"Well, you remember all the stuff about witches and shit that Howard always talked about?"

"Yes, what does that have to do with anything?" Kyle said.

"My idea is to hit him where he is the weakest, and we know now it is not doing it the legal way. So let us contact a witch. You remember I had once met one at the bar I told you about. I want to talk with her and tell her what happened, and that Howard is susceptible to witchcraft."

Kyle just stared out the window of his office, looking at nothing really, taking in what David was talking about and wondering what witchcraft was. David answered with his definition of witchcraft, and that was the practice of black magic and the summoning of spirits.

The summoning of spirits, Kyle thought. Are they going to be good spirits or evil spirits, and will they go away when the problem is solved? Is this like rent-a-spirit? He thought, smiling to himself.

"David," Kyle said, turning to him. "Let's think about it, and we can discuss it further tomorrow amongst ourselves. I am emotionally drained for one day."

"You got it," David said.

The following day, Kyle decided other matters required his attention, and one was the mess he had on his desk and in his life with the takeover of his company. He put several good hours into salvaging what he could of the morning and then having a gin and tonic for lunch. David came into his office just as he was deep into sales reports.

"Let's talk about my idea for revenge against Howard and all those involved in the fiasco in the courtroom," David said.

Kyle sat back and listened.

CHAPTER 4

AN APPOINTMENT WITH A WITCH

K yle looked up from the many files and papers spread out on his deskand said, "What is up? I am really in the middle of all this. Can it wait?"

"Well, it's imperative if you want to do something about Howard," David said.

Kyle was in the mood for anything at this point, so he told David to go ahead and tell him about his idea, well aware that David was not his friend anymore.

David continued, "You know about the witch I told you about? The one I met in the bar the other night?

Kyle looked blankly at David. "No, I don't remember. You've told me so many things after drinking all night. So now you met a witch?"

"Come on. We talked about it the other day. Anyway, I first met her after I got back from court. She was full of ideas on how to go after someone who has done you wrong and, more importantly, Kyle, susceptible to those things you cannot see. She also said there were different levels of revenge, depending on what you want the outcome to be or how bad you want to hurt someone."

"This all sounds crazy; you can't come up with any other way to get our revenge?"

"No, Kyle, this is going to work well. I just know it."

"A witch, are you kidding me, David? Is this really the best we can do to get at the bastard? How do we know what is going to happen if we swim in this questionable pond? What if it goes too crazy and a curse is put on you and me and our families? How do you know how this will end? I got to tell you, David, this is making me uneasy. I think we should go another way."

"Okay, okay, don't go crazy. What do you think we should do? What the hell is *your* idea? After what we just went through, doing it the right way, yeah, we got screwed badly. We can hire a hitman to take him out then."

"I think it is bad enough that we have had to take a huge financial hit, but we have not broken any laws yet, and I am not sure that I want to," Kyle said defensively.

"Well, if you change your mind, it will cost around $20,000. I still think that the witch is the best way to go, but if you want to go for the hit, then

I have people."

"Where in the hell did you get people who kill other people? You are starting to lose it, David." Kyle had a worried look on his face, "I am not on board yet. It scares the hell out of me. I want to sleep on it and will give you my answer in the morning. I am a little amazed that you have no hesitation in bringing a witch into our already existing problems. A witch, hell David, you have no idea what could happen, what could be released. I guess I was raised differently than you. I do not think I want anything to do with this."

That night, Kyle was uneasy, knowing he had to tell David yes or no about the witch in the morning. It would be nice to be able to talk about these difficult things with his wife. Isn't that why people get married, to share their lives? He thought. Well, Kyle knew better. Anything said to his wife would only accelerate into another disagreement and argument.

He knew it would be easier not to say anything and know he had to face this on his own.

After watching the late news, he called it a day and went to bed to hopefully fall into a deep sleep. With a glass of water on his nightstand, he reached over to turn off the light, bringing darkness to the room. After several hours of restless sleep, Kyle finally fell deep into a dream.

Nighttime had fallen in a bedroom in an apartment in Chicago. A queen-size bed with a blue bedspread on it was in the middle of the room, with dresser drawers in the corner. A light shone from a door to the bathroom, which was on the other side of a window covered with burgundy drapes. The bed had four posts and a marble nightstand next to it. On the nightstand were a white lit candle and a magazine. Kyle could see someone come out of the bathroom, and as the figure approached the bed, he realized it was Howard in a dark blue night robe, wearing a pair of dark blue slippers. Howard sat on the bed to take off his slippers, and as he reached over, the right sleeve of his robe caught the magazine, which hit the white lit candle and knocked it off the nightstand, rolling it under the window. Howard, now getting concerned as the white candle flame was touching the bottom of the burgundy drapes, stepped on the floor to go to the bathroom to get some water to put the fire out, but he slipped as he stepped forward on the magazine that had fallen, sending his head cracking into the doorknob of the bathroom door, knocking him out.

Kyle watched as if he was right there and could feel the fire burning hotter and brighter, quickly moving up the drapes and toward Howard's sleeve on his robe as he lay unconscious on the floor. As the fire burst in hotter yellow flames, taking over the bedroom, Howard woke up and was immersed in the burning red-and-yellow flame and smoke, screaming as he became engulfed in the smothering fire. The screaming was so loud and eerie, and the smell of burning flesh was prominent as it drifted down the corridor of the apartment. Howard burned to death on the floor with the white candle lying next to his charred skeleton of a body.

Waking up in a sweat, Kyle got out of bed and walked to the bathroom to splash water on his face, and then walked over to the window. As he looked across the yard to the neighbor's house, he could see a candle burning in the window. He wondered if he had ever seen that before. No, he did not think so.

Kyle was unsure why he saw so many candles now when he never saw them before David brought up a meeting with a witch. *What was up with seeing the white candle in my dreams and then next door?* He wondered, soaked in his sweat of fear, as he went back to the bathroom to clean his face. He went back to bed to get what sleep he could before the early-morning light.

Kyle stood by his office window with his hot coffee cup in his hand, watching the morning traffic down below moving as if they knew where they were going. He was still shaken up over the dream he had last night and knew that David was coming in to talk about the revenge plan again.

Kyle greeted David in his office, "Come on in. Did you get any coffee yet? Connie also brought in some great donuts."

"Yes, I did, and they were delicious. How are you this morning, Boss?"

Kyle turned around to face him. "I am having trouble with this plan. I had the craziest dream last night."

"Yeah, what was it?"

"Howard. I watched as he burned up in his apartment. How is that for a dream?"

"Well, that is what it was, a dream, so let it go."

"I will. It is still fresh, but you will not believe this. A white candle was on the floor where Howard was lying dead. Isn't that weird? Hey, that is not all," he said as he sat down behind his desk. "I got up after the dream and walked to the window, and there in the neighbor's window was a lit candle. The candle again."

"I think you are making too much of it. You saw two different candles, oh my goodness, how scary!"

Kyle replied, "Not amused, okay knock it off. This is all very uneasy."

"Whatever. Have you made a decision yet?"

"No, wait a minute. I just watched as a man working here for months burn up in a fire in his apartment. I heard the screaming, and David, I could smell the flesh burning. It was that real! Now you want me to see a witch who uses candles of which I have already had a dream about?"

"Okay, I'm sorry for not being sensitive to your witnessing someone burning to death in a dream. Now the present, please. We have to decide on what we are going to do," David persisted. "I want to move forward with the witch. This is starting to take up a lot of my time, and I want to get going."

"I heard you, but I am still not sure," Kyle said.

"It was a dream, Kyle. Come on, we all have them."

"Okay, I will agree, but I still have my doubts and, if anything goes wrong, I will hold you personally responsible. You know we are treading in waters we know nothing about. Does that not bother you?"

"Is that a yes?" David asked.

"Okay, okay, set it up. I am in for anything, I guess," Kyle said. "Let me make a phone call," David said. "And see what's up."

Kyle thought that this was out of the box even for him, but he remembered how Howard bragged about his life, how he and his family enjoyed sitting around the table for a good old séance. He had stated that they would go back in time and bring back Grandma Lucy or any other spirit. *So if that's what makes Howard click, then why not a witch to lead the way to revenge?* Kyle thought. If he could take out Howard and his people, he would only have David to deal with.

"Hey, she will see us now. I will drive," David said excitedly when he came off the phone.

Soon, both were off to a strange way to solve a problem, but Kyle knew he tried the legal way, and that was a disaster.

She lived in a first-floor apartment in a bad part of town, a subsidized development for welfare recipients. Inside the dark apartment was lit candles of different colors with black-and-red curtains on the windows, which were closed.

They sat down in the dining room around a small circular table covered with a red and yellow cloth with several crystals located around the small room and a large quartz in the middle of the table. David told her what had happened, bringing her up to speed since they had spoken to her. David reiterated who had done this to them and what they wanted from her, along with her suggestions. There was a long pause as she asked questions as to their expectations and desires, and then she went quiet, and her head was tilted down with her eyes closed.

It seemed like the longest time. Finally, with red-shot eyes, she got up from the table and walked behind her seat, looking down in thought as the incense burned and the smoke filtered in their noses as it rose from the burners. Then she spoke, "Okay, I now know what it is you are asking of me. I know who it is you want to expose. It has all come to me. This is what I have come up with."

She pulled out some small baggies from a leather pouch as she mumbled some incantations and hand motions and then put them on the table. She reached under the table and retrieved four black candles and a white candle.

"You are to take these candles to your office and write with a black Sharpie, thirteen bad things you want to happen to this person on the black candles. In this baggy are some grave parts. Sprinkle them on the black candles only and then wait until midnight, and you will light the black candles with a wooden match.

"Once you have done this, repeatedly say the thirteen things you want to happen to him. Take the white candle, and put that in your office, Kyle. It is there for the good spirits while the black candles will attract bad spirits."

She sat back down and asked if they were prepared for what would happen and asked for payment for this information and, most importantly, the curse. David said yes and proceeded to pay her what she had asked for. Kyle was still stuck on being prepared for what was going to happen.

"No need to piss off a witch," he said. They both looked at each other because they had never done anything like this, and it was starting to feel a little scary. David said to the witch, "Are there any guarantees this will work?"

"Well, no, but it is up to the spirits you contact as to what they want to do."

"So you are saying that we have no control over this, and we are contacting spirits to do our bidding? Gee, what is the worst that could happen?" Kyle asked in jest.

Both Kyle and David looked at each other and shrugged their shoulders as if to say, 'Okay, let the dice roll,' and with that, the two guys headed back to the office loaded with ammunition to get Howard in Chicago.

At the office, they went around to find the best place to put the black candle. They had enough candles to put in five offices with the one white candle to go into Kyle's office. With all that done, they waited until the dark of evening with wooden matches in hand and grave parts ready to be sprinkled at the stroke of midnight.

David said, "Okay, we want to light this right at midnight. Are you ready to do this, Kyle? I know that this kind of stuff is not your favorite." "Not my favorite, that is putting it mildly," Kyle said, looking a little scared. "You go ahead and light the candle. I'll watch."

They put the grave parts around the wick and struck the wooden match; the first black candle flared up. There was immediately dark, black smoke that came off the candle. They both stared at it and each other. An ominous feeling came over them both. Not knowing what they had done, they walked out of the office, locking the door behind them, and both headed to their homes, thinking that the fix was in for Howard.

Kyle looked at David. "Is it too late to stop what we have done, do you think?"

"It would be like putting the toothpaste back in the tube. It's not going to happen."

Heading down the elevator, David said, "Now remember, we must cuss at the candles when we walk by them, and we need to tell the employees to do the same thing."

"I hope they all don't just get up and walk out," Kyle said. "Don't worry, Boss. I will handle it all," David chimed in.

"You will handle it. You are the one who talked me into this. I am uneasy, David. After listening to the witch, I must admit that I fear what might happen. I have never gone after bad spirits to help me get someone. The thought of doing this is sickening to me."

David, acting in control, said, "You are letting this all get to you. We haven't even used the white candle yet. We only talked about it. I am sure it is something simple, and Howard will probably not even know we did this to get him."

"Well, if you think that this is all for nothing, then why the hell are we doing it? Maybe we should just put the candles in the trash and forget all about this crazy idea?"

"After all that we have already done, I think you are just overthinking this. We are doing the right thing, I promise," David said.

CHAPTER 5

DEATH TO VP

A s Kyle drove into the city from his home in the hills, he was thinking of what they had done with the candles the night before and wondered what was going to happen, if anything at all. When he reached his office, some of the employees who were Christians questioned both David and Kyle about the black candles in the office.

David had already explained to them what the Boss and he were doing and why. Immediately, several of the religious ones quit and said that they could not be around this type of activity. The rest of them watched in amusement as David and Kyle would both hiss at the candles and say bad things as they passed it.

A couple of days later, as the late afternoon started to creep into the day, Kyle was working in his office on an exceptionally large contract that he had to bid on in the hope of getting it. Kyle was thinking of how these large contracts were critical to his company's growth when Connie said that the gentleman who cleans his offices wanted to speak to him.

"Connie, not now. I have to get this contract bid in on time. Tell him that he will have to wait." Kyle pushed the button on the intercom.

It was not a minute after telling her not to bother him that Connie came back. "I am really sorry, boss, but he says it cannot wait."

"Alright, I am already mentally off of the figures I needed. Send him in."

Manuel Rodriquez was his name, and he seemed extremely upset and anxious to speak with him.

Kyle told him to have a seat. "Why is it so important to see me immediately? What could be so important, tell me?"

Manuel, with sweat on his brow, said, "What are you doing with the black candles in your different offices, Mr. Stone?"

Before he could answer his question, Manuel interrupted while being antsy in his seat. "Let me tell you, boss, what I see at night when I am cleaning your office, and I say your office because that is where all the activity takes place."

Kyle gave him a puzzled look. "What do you mean all the activity takes place in my office? What activity?" Kyle thought he would be protected if there were to be any so-called activity because he had the white candle in his office. That was what the witch told him. All should be good for me, he thought.

"It seems like you have invited a lot of bad spirits to your office, boss, even though you have a white candle in it." Manuel continued uneasily. "I have been cleaning here for a long time, and there was never a problem. I have always been here alone, or I thought I was. Ever since you put the black candle in the office and listed the bad things you want to happen to this man, and then you make it worse by spitting and cussing at it when you walk by it. Last night when I came in, I had a real bad feeling coming up the elevator. Something was telling me not to go here. Turn around, go back down the elevator, and never return was the message I was getting. I went up here anyway because you are paying me to clean. When I opened the door and went to the secretary's desk, I put a crucifix on it, leaning it up against her books, and went into your office. Oh my god, behind your desk, visible from the waist up, was a large spirit, and in slow motion, he opened his mouth and said, 'Come on in.' He made no sound, just mouthed the words slowly. Very freaky! As I looked around, there were two others on the couch with your cigars in their mouths. I am sorry,

Boss. I was so scared; I just about peed my pants."

Kyle stared at Manuel with his mouth open and then looked around his office, not wanting to believe him, but it was apparent that he was not making this up.

"Boss, I left quickly and went to the secretary's desk to get my crucifix and get the hell out of here. My crucifix had been turned upside down while I was in your office. I grabbed it with my shaking hands while making the Sign of the Cross with the other. I did not even bother with the elevator. I ran down the stairs to the first floor, and, Boss, I could not stop shaking. I came here to tell you that I will not be returning to clean, and I must tell you that you have done something terrible. I suggest that you contact someone from the church and have them do an exorcism in your office. I am sorry, Boss, but I promised my wife that I would not go back in. I have to quit."

Kyle, with a stunned look on his face, said, "I am sorry, Manuel. We've never done this before and didn't know what to expect. Good luck to you, and may God bless us all."

Kyle was not sure of all this. He had not seen any ghosts but went ahead with the recommendations from Manuel, being he was so adamant about what he had seen.

The next morning, when Kyle arrived after his usual long commute, he saw his office door open and wondered who had been in there.

"Connie, why is my door open? Who has been there? Did you put something in there?" he asked his secretary.

"Just go in," she replied. "You will see what is there, and the door was open when I got here."

He walked into his office, and on the far-right wall was written in what looked like blood, *DEATH TO DAVID*.

Kyle could not believe what he saw, especially after Manuel just told him his story of evil spirits. What the hell had he got himself into? He immediately remembered the dream he had the other night and how real it seemed, and now this message to kill on his office wall.

God help us all, Kyle prayed.

There was no reason to call the police; there was no crime yet. The office was all locked up all night, and there wasn't any cleaning going on. So how the hell did someone or something get into the office overnight to write this on the wall? The other possibility Kyle thought about was someone with a key had come in. How about David? He thought. He might have put this red liquid on the wall to look like blood. A sick joke.

Kyle told his assistant to have someone get some soap and water and get that off the office wall as soon as possible, and he then went to lunch to ponder on the strange activity.

Kyle had a few more than usual cocktails that day and went back to the office with a nice buzz going on.

His assistant could always tell when he had a buzz on, and she knew he would be playful if teased.

However, Kyle had too much on his mind to be playful that afternoon. The witch candles were not sitting right with him, and he was not sure what he had gotten into.

He went into his private bathroom, and as he was washing his hands, his secretary yelled at him, "Kyle, do not forget about David!"

Kyle was in front of the sink. "Yeah, I hear you. Oh my God, holy shit!" A loud crashing noise could be heard throughout the office.

Connie got up from her desk, "What are you yelling about?" "Come on in here. You won't believe what just happened."

Connie quickly walked to the private bathroom. "Oh my God, are you okay?" she said. Kyle was standing on a pile of glass from the mirror that shattered.

"You won't believe this, Connie. But as soon as you said 'David,' the glass shattered right in front of me. I was just washing my hands. I'm alright, none got on me or in me, but it scared the hell out of me."

Shaken, Kyle came out of his bathroom and headed for his desk to light up a cigar to calm down. Calming down did not last long when he heard from his secretary again.

"Kyle, have you seen this?" she yelled from her office.

Kyle, trying to calm down at his desk, said, "What did I not see, Connie?"

"You better come in here."

CHAPTER 6

THEY CONSPIRED TO TAKEOVER

It had been calculated that every office would bring in an additional $150,000 a month, so Kyle was excited every time an opportunity came up, and it was getting him closer to buying his own jet.

Kyle sat behind his desk, looking out the window at the main boulevard flowing quickly with so many cars and people on the street. He was thinking about inviting Julie from payroll. It was always a good idea to be with the one who produced the checks, and she had been talking a lot with David, another one to keep his eyes on, so he asked her to meet him at the airport so that he could finally put a face to someone so important in the everyday operation of the cash flow.

Kyle was going to have lunch with Julie before he and David were off to Dallas for a franchise meeting. She had been dropping a lot of hints about wanting to meet him and the massive crush she had on him even though she was married. Kyle had no intention of showing any affection to her. These situations usually did not turn out well and especially when the one you messed with was the one who wrote the checks. It would be absolutely the wrong move, and he was not looking for an affair. He had enough troubles on his plate already. Besides, she was not to become a lover when she was possibly part of a coup. Well, what were the next few days going to be about? David thought as he and

41

Kyle headed for the meeting in Dallas aboard a 757. Having Julie picking him up was exciting, especially with what he and Julie had discussed with plans to take over the business. He had not seen her before, but they both told each other what they looked like, and they seemed okay with the descriptions. She was in her late twenties, brunette with a medium build.

"Sir, here is your cocktail," said the stewardess. "We will be departing soon."

"With this weather, I am sure I will need more," Kyle said as he looked out the window after addressing the air stewardess.

The weather report was unbelievably bad in the Bay Area that morning, with winds at fifty miles per hour gusts. This made him uneasy; he did not like flying on a good day, and now this. He could not help himself start thinking about all the bad flights he had had and how much he hated turbulence as he looked out the plane window. He always felt that the worst part of flying was the shaking of the aircraft, not knowing when it would stop. With thoughts of a bad flight creeping into his head, he heard the passengers in front of him say that the Bay Bridge was being closed due to high winds.

As Kyle was pondering on this new development, the captain came on the intercom to welcome the passengers and warn them about the weather conditions and the rough ride they would experience until they hit their flying altitude. This was not what he wanted to hear as he looked out the window, watching a canvas blow across the tarmac with two workers chasing it.

"Maybe I should be one of them," he thought and not the one sitting on this plane. Soon, the engines roared, seat belts fastened and tightened. They headed down the runway; Kyle's mind went to where he did not want to go. He had a real fear that he would die in a plane crash, something he felt every time he got on a plane. Wheels up and hope and pray. Well, it did not take long before it seemed like they were in the thick of things. They had just reached ten thousand feet, and they hit their first bad air, and the plane started to shake and then took a sudden fall as the aircraft was making its right turn. It was so severe the pilot came on and said that he would talk them through this until they reached their cruising altitude, and hopefully, it would smooth out.

"Hold on to your seats," the pilot said. "We are coming upon a big cell, and we are not able to get around it but don't worry, we are flying an L-1011, and she is built to take this kind of weather."

Just as he finished speaking, the plane fell, as if one were leaping off the edge of a cliff, falling, screams, babies crying, adults swearing, luggage bins opening, and contents flying.

Then, the pilot said, "Well, that was a doozy. We just fell four thousand feet. Hold on!"

It was only seconds, and it did it again.

"Wow, that was another seven thousand feet, but we are still climbing."

One must ask oneself when one finds oneself in these kinds of situations, is it that damn important to get home? Why did I not wait? Kyle thought as he gripped the seat with all he had. This was not fun.

Everyone held their breath, just waiting and hoping for the plane to stop falling.

This is the worst flight ever, Kyle thought, the worst he had ever been on. He had been trying to read Harold Robbins's novel and wanting to get so deep into the book that he would not know he was on this damn plane.

Then, out the window, cruising altitude, blue sky, smooth air, bring on the cocktails, they all were going to live. It took a while for Kyle to get over the flight and have a smile on his face again. He could not shake the thoughts and fear of those sudden falls one after the other. The train sure was sounding like a much better way to travel. Kyle looked over across the aisle to David and held his drink up.

David knew what he meant and cheered him back. They were about to start their descent into Dallas airport, and Kyle had booked one room for him and one for David. Julie was presumed to be staying with David, and it was a good bet.

As they got off the plane from the worst flight ever, the limo was waiting to take them to the hotel.

Kyle had arranged for the limo driver to pick up Julie so that she could meet them at the plane. Coming down the stairs, Kyle could see a good-looking brunette wearing a dark-blue skirt with a white blouse and black high heels standing next to the limo. It put a smile on his face. As he walked to the limo, she started to walk toward him. She put her arms out as if to hug him but then walked past Kyle and went straight for David, grabbed his head, and laid a big kiss on his lips. This was not a good way to start the trip, Kyle thought. He did not get the respect he felt would come from her.

"I have been waiting a long time to do that to you, David."

Kyle, with a smug face, said, "You must be Julie. We have spoken so many times."

"Yes, I am Kyle, and I am glad to be here," she replied, smiling.

Kyle now stared at David, and it was not a good stare. David could see that his surprise at hooking up with Julie was not sitting right with Kyle. They walked to the limo, and Kyle opened the door for Julie.

David was next to get in. Kyle did not look happy. "You and I will talk at the hotel, got it?" Kyle said.

David nodded and then got into the limo, and they sped off to the hotel.

Kyle could not trust his VP David or anyone at this stage, and he now suspected him in the larger picture of collaborating with those who wanted to hurt his company. He did not want to believe it of David; they were too close, he thought. Kyle would have to hold on to his suspicions and keep a close eye on David. If David kept it up, he might not have a job when he got back.

The trip went great, and it was starting to get late in the day. The investor and franchisor both wanted in, and the visit to South Fork was successful, and the new offices would create another $150,000 a month for the business. For two guys who watched the show Dallas every week, it was a thrill being in South Fork and taking in all the sights they had seen in the show and being part of the fantasy.

However, closing another huge deal was an even more significant event.

Kyle walked to the car at the ranch. "I don't know about you, David, but I enjoyed going through the house and seeing what I saw during the show."

David, with a smile on his face, said, "I know what you mean. I especially enjoyed the balcony of the bedroom. It was bitchin'."

"That was special," Kyle mirrored.

Back at the hotel, David and Julie went up to their room, and Kyle stayed at the bar, finishing up his tequila and tonic while stressing over what to do about David.

Julie and David packed up the following day for their flight home. Kyle was to meet them in the lobby. David gave Julie the American Express card to check them out while he sat on the couch waiting for Kyle, reading the Dallas Times. When Julie was done checking out, she came over to David and kneeled next to him. He gave her a look and shrugged as she just smiled at him as if to say, "It feels comfortable."

Kyle came down and saw the two of them together. He walked over to them and said, "What the hell are you doing? She kneels when you are around?"

David smiled at him and said, "No one made her do it."

If Kyle thought he was stressed over this before, he now had new reasons to be overly concerned. Any time you witness a controller in charge of millions of dollars kneel on the floor next to your VP is a sign of weakness. You better believe you have something to worry about.

CHAPTER 7

A NEEDED HIRE

David looked at the young lady he had just met at the bar downstairs. "Come on in, my boss is at home, and we can use his office. Go ahead and put your glass of wine on the table, and I will put some music on."

He approached the woman on the couch and laid on top of her. As they laughed and fidgeted, his left knee accidentally knocked over the wine. Not knowing what he had done, the wine soaked into the expensive carpet Connie had picked out for Kyle's office.

When Connie came in the next morning and saw the carpet, she was upset that Kyle would do something like this. Kyle called to get his messages, and he was not expecting her impatient tone, "I'm sorry, boss, but I am upset. Why in the hell would you spill red wine on the new expensive carpet we just put in?"

"Hold on, Connie. I didn't spill any wine; I have not been back since I left yesterday afternoon."

The light went on in both their heads at the same time; it had to be David. Kyle agreed with Connie, got his things together, and headed to the office. As he drove by the Bay, he was disgusted at David, who was making it a habit of taking women to the office at night. He had told him not to use his office. He did not want anything to do with his cheating on his wife and kids. Kyle knew that this was a significant flaw

47

in David's character. The quiet afternoon went by, and it seemed strange that he had not seen or heard from David, which caused him to wonder what had happened to him. They were just at Ron's last night with their wives. Given the afternoon Kyle had yesterday, he decided to visit a different venue this afternoon for lunch.

Kyle, feeling hunger pains, thought it would now be a good time to go to his favorite restaurant, which was just around the corner from his office. He had his own table at the restaurant, which had been reserved for him and his party at any time. The sound of businesspeople taking time off to relax before enduring another four hours of work filled the bar. After ordering his favorite drink, he noticed David coming over to sit at the table.

"Hi, Kyle, how are you this sunny afternoon?"

Kyle looked up at him. "I'm doing fine. I was wondering what happened to you this morning. I did not get any message about you not being in."

"I'm sorry, my wife was in the mood this morning, and I wanted to take advantage of her loving, especially when she was so excited."

"Do I dare ask why she was so excited, or is it something you should keep between you both?"

"I can't put my finger on it. She just woke up in this sexy mood. She even said she wanted me to thank you for the good time she had at the party." David added that he had never seen Linda so thankful for being invited to Ron's and made it clear that she would love to go back there.

Kyle smiled and said that he had a good time and what an escape it was from all that was going on with the company. They had another drink and some lunch. Kyle always had the English muffin cheeseburger, and David always went with the pastrami.

Today's lunch was a little more special because they had a lingerie company come in for some sexy entertainment. This fox owned the company, Yvonne Lang, who went by the name YL. Kyle always loved to buy raffle tickets as they watched the pretty young girls with beautiful legs leading up to gorgeous lingerie. Yvonne seemed not to notice Kyle at the time; she was busy with the girls and putting on the fashion show. She seemed to be surrounded all the time by other guys trying to get to know her or get noticed. Kyle would be patient, knowing that she would come by and say hello when she had time.

Back in the office, Kyle returned from holding a training class for those he had just hired. He was expanding and franchising in other states and had to hire one more for the San Francisco office. He ran an ad he had called Opportunity Knocks, and an excellent opportunity for Kyle came a-knocking.

He spent the entire Monday interviewing prospective agents for the position, and to his surprise, when he said, "Send in the next applicant, Connie." Yvonne Lang walked in.

She was a gorgeous woman and former owner of the lingerie company. Oh my goodness, he said to himself as she walked in. She was wearing a white dress with blond hair to her shoulders, with earrings lighting up her beautiful face. 'Hot' was all he could say about her. If she were as bright as she was beautiful, she would be a winner.

Well, Kyle hired her, and it became one of his better decisions.

His sales manager took on the training of new agents. She enjoyed showing off to new employees and was always willing to take on anyone new.

David was there to console and make Kyle feel better. David had come over from a relative and friend of Kyle's that had worked at the company. He had said David was moving from New York and could use a job to take care of his family. Out of respect for this friendship, David was hired, and he seemed like a nice guy who worked hard and knew how to stay on Kyle's good side. It was not long before David had become a friend and respected part of Kyle's business. He needed someone he could trust and confide in. It was increasingly more difficult to make it in a world of deception.

Kyle was trying to get over seeing his wife with someone else. They had been together for a long time; he felt she deserved some slack. Besides, with everything going on, he needed a confidante at home, one away from the business with clear perception. But sometimes, he felt that Suzette just didn't get him. He wanted to ask her to accompany him to John and Karen's cocktail party tomorrow night.

Kyle was a newly commissioned officer when he met Suzette. She was four years younger than Kyle, who was swept away by her beauty. His family, especially his brother, was very much against this marriage. They knew it was ridiculous to meet someone and then, days later, get engaged.

His brother knew what Kyle had been through in his short life and wanted him badly to find the love he craved. Kyle not only wanted to look at her, but he wanted her gorgeous, naked body next to him so that he could make love to her all night long.

He decided to have food catered once again for his wife and kids. He was looking forward to sitting down and sharing his day and excitement about how well they were doing financially. Suzette knew it was a challenging climb to be where they were now. Kyle always wanted to make her parents proud of him in the absence of not having his own. He was poor as a kid and did not want his children to go through what he had to. After putting eleven hours in, making for a long day, he sat at his bar relaxing. It overlooked a bright blue pool with a seven-foot waterfall. Kyle continued to share with Suzette that he was at the state capital today again, as he told her yesterday, signing up state employees for the payroll program being offered by his company. He also shared with her that he was training new agents who were waiting for their test results so that they could actually sign-up employees as they were being trained.

Suzette was upset and wasted no time letting Kyle know about it. He thought she would be happy with all the good news he was telling her, but she was the opposite: upset that he was putting in too many hours, upset at him not being home with her, upset at the time he spent at the office. It seemed that she not only acted upset, but she also took action to make a point with Kyle so that he would spend more time with her. She was hesitant to tell him what she had done, and Kyle knew something was not right.

"I am getting bad vibes, Suzette. What is it you are not telling me?"

"Okay, I'll tell you; you made me mad, and I did not want you working so much."

"Come on, come out with it. What did you do?"

"Yesterday, you told me you were signing up state employees, and you were training new agents. All I did was write a letter to the Licensing Authorities telling them you were at the capital and unlicensed agents were signing up employees. I thought if you were to lose the state contract, you would not be gone all the time."

Kyle was in total shock hearing what she said and only hoped he heard it wrong. Kyle, in disbelief, asked, "I know that you are just messing with me. Why don't you give me the letter so that we can discuss it?

"I can't do that," Suzette said with a smirk on her face. "I put it in the mailbox."

"Are you kidding me?" Kyle said as he stood up. "Tell me you did not do that, tell me!"

"I really did. I only wanted more time for us." Suzette took her husband's information and twisted it so that she would accuse him of having agents unlicensed. They were only observing, but she bent the truth to punish her husband, but for what? She then wrote to the Oversight and Compliance department of the government and told them that her husband was operating illegally and there would be an investigation. Who in their right mind? he thought, as he went over what she did to their family, sharing information that was told to her in private over a cocktail and then lying to the authorities to make sure she did the most damage possible to her husband and children. It was unforgivable.

Kyle imagined the conversation of the previous morning between Suzette and the kids. "Good morning, Mom, what are you going to do today?"

"Oh, I thought I would initiate an all-out assault against your father. I am going to try and get your dad thrown in jail today so that we will not have any money." Kyle imaging her saying this, shook his head in total disbelief, knowing his wife could say such a thing to their kids.

His marriage was starting to be a farce as he thought back not on the great things she had done for their family, but what she had done against him: letting her husband be thrown out of her family home in the night and not checking on him; leaving their first apartment after two weeks and going back home; taking private information she received and using it to lose $70,000 a month from her husband, and unwittingly, affecting herself and the children. He could only justify her outrageous behavior by staying around for the children.

Kyle grew up in a divorced family, so he was determined to stay in the relationship for his kids, but it was getting harder and harder to do with all that had gone against him and his business. Kyle was seriously considering he should quit and get a divorce. Sometimes, Kyle thought he should not have gotten married at the young age of eighteen to someone he did not know for more than 8 days. Now he was paying the price for making this quick decision and paying for it big time. He knew that he had been a great provider, and he deserved better. How about a loving wife? What a concept. Being under so much pressure from all that was going on, Kyle gathered his composure and looked at his wife.

"I'm going to call it a night, Suzette. I am going to have cocktails with John tomorrow. I think I'll take David to the party with me."

Suzette sipped on her wine as tears streamed down her face. For once, she had nothing to say.

CHAPTER 8

THE UNFORGIVABLE

Kyle and David attended the cocktail party at John's. He was looking forward to spending some quiet time with his friends and getting away from the drama in his business. He introduced David to all his friends there, and it was indeed a congenial atmosphere as drinks were continuously poured. The rock and roll music and great conversation with friends was the excellent time Kyle needed.

"Who is this new guy you hired? Have you known him long?" John asked as they both sipped their cocktails.

"He came to me through a sales manager that had worked for me," Kyle replied, "I think he was part of their family. He came with great recommendations as being good at what he does."

John shook his head slightly. "I don't know, Kyle. I get a strange feeling about him, and we have known each other for a while now. I don't want to tell you how to run your company, but this guy, something's wrong with him."

"Well, John, I have never seen you jump into my business before. You seem bothered by him. I'll tell you what. I will have my office look deeper if that will make you feel better. I don't expect to find anything, but I will be happy to do it for you. We have been good friends, and I respect your opinion."

"Thanks, I am only mentioning it for your good. I am usually a rather good judge of character."

Kyle walked away from John to get another drink; he felt uneasy about what John had said. He especially felt terrible about bringing David over to this party now he had heard John's suspicions.

Maybe he should find David and get out of there. It was not feeling like the good time he thought he was going to have. Kyle was getting worried. He looked around and could not see David. He started walking around the house to try to find him.

Meanwhile, David was busy mingling. He zoomed in on a woman who seemed full of life. She was smiling and laughing. A good-looking lady as well. He knew exactly who she was - John's wife, Karen. She seemed a genuinely nice person. She always had a smile for everyone.

David slid up to her and introduced himself. "Yes, I came from New York when my cousin told me about an opportunity, he could get me into. I work for Kyle as a sales manager."

"Wow, that was a big move. Is your wife happy about moving? I presume you are married?"

"Yes, I am married, and she was not sure about moving to the west, being she left some of her family in New York, but she will get to like it. The weather is certainly better here."

"Much warmer, that's for sure. I hope your family will be happy with the move."

"Thank you, Karen. I have been looking at your house. It's real nice. Would you mind showing me your place? Give me a little tour?" David winked.

"Sure, not a problem. Let us start with the kitchen and then the backyard before it gets dark. We have spent a lot of money out there. You might like it," Karen replied.

They both went into the kitchen and then out the back door as Kyle entered the kitchen, still looking for David. Karen and David came back into the house through the hallway door then headed to the bedrooms. As David followed Karen into the master suite, he closed the door behind him and reached out to her.

Karen, with an overly concerned look on her face, asked, "What are you doing? I was just showing you the house as you suggested and as Kyle's guest."

David reached for her arm, and she freaked out. To her surprise, he blurted out, "Don't play me, girl. I know why you showed me your bedroom."

David had maneuvered himself, so they were by the edge of the bed.

He used his large body to block her way. His eyes pierced into her.

"Let me be. What are you doing? Get out of my room!" Karen tried to leave.

"I know what you want," he said as she tried to get to the door, but David moved in front of her and roughly pushed her onto the bed.

"Stop it! Stop it! Damn it! Get off me!" Karen yelled desperately. David was now lying on top of her, pushing her legs apart. "Come on. Spread those sexy legs. I know you want me."

"Get off me, you pig. I am going to scream," Karen warned him.

David reached over and grabbed a pillow. He shoved it over her face, reached down, and unbuttoned his pants. He grabbed his hardness and pulled it out. Hot now, he could not stop. He had to take her. He had to feel himself in her.

"You bitch! You want to play with me? Tease me," he said as he reached under her skirt to rip her panties away. She was trying to scream, but the pillow muffled the sound, making her gasp for breaths of air, crying as his heavy body still pressed her down. With her legs spread by his weight and his hardness smashing her panties as he tried to move them out of the way, he held the pillow on her face with his arm. She could now feel him, hard and wanting, as the fear ripped through her.

Kyle stood at the bedroom door. It was closed. Something made him wonder if David was in there. He knocked, and no answer. He hit harder and then listened, picking up some muffled noise like a struggle. Kyle threw the door open to find David on top of Karen, holding a pillow on her face. Anger and fear came over him as he leaped as far as he could, landing on top of David, knocking both of them off the bed onto the floor.

Rolling on the floor, Kyle raised his fist and struck David in the face as he laid on the floor. He pulled his arm back and swung again, slugging David in the face. "You fucking coward, trying to rape her and smother her, how could you do this?" Kyle hit him again and again. David had his arms up, trying to stop the beating. As Kyle readied another swing at David's face, which was now bleeding around his mouth, nose, and eyes, John burst in and tried to take in the scene. He jumped on Kyle, knocking him off David. David immediately jumped up and ran for the door.

Kyle, not sure what just happened, demanded, "Why did you do that?

I was beating the shit out of him?"

"That is why I stopped you. I was afraid you were going to kill him." "Well shit, he's got away."

John went to the bed where his wife was still sobbing. "Karen, you're safe now. He is gone," he soothed as he held her close. "I am going after him; you call the police."

Karen sobbed in her husband's arms, not wanting to let him go.

"Oh my god, are you alright, honey? If he hurt you, I'll kill him!" Donna, the doctor's wife who lived up the street, was now with Karen, taking care of her, smoothing back her hair, and trying to stop her sobs.

Without waiting for an answer, John opened the nightstand in front of him and grabbed his snub-nose Smith & Wesson, swung the bedroom door open, and ran out of the house wanting to catch up with Kyle, who was running after David in front of him up the street.

Outside, David was spotted in his car. "Stop, you son of a bitch! Stop now!"

David turned and saw the gun John was waving around and started running across the street to the park wall. As he jumped over the knee-high rock wall, John fired at David twice, hitting him with one bullet. It hit his foot as he rolled over to the other side. David looked down, thinking his foot had been shot, but as he looked closer, looking for blood, the bullet had hit the heel of his shoe and ripped it right off, but he was not hit. Lucky bastard! He looked up and saw both still running after him. He started down the grassy area to the parking lot, running as fast as he could.

Kyle and John kept coming, both jumping over the rock wall. They spotted him running down the hill toward a parking lot.

John was ready to take another shot when Kyle yelled, "No, don't, there are too many people around. You might hit someone."

"I want that bastard, damn it!"

"Let us get back to the house. The cops should be there," Kyle said as they both walked quickly back to the house. "I am so sorry, John. I had no idea David was capable of such a horrible act. I would have never invited him over."

"Don't beat yourself up. I know you wouldn't have brought him over," John said, starting to trot faster. The two men went straight into the bedroom back at the house to see how Karen was doing and find out what the hell happened.

The police had not arrived yet. "I am sick about this," Kyle said, "I know the cops are coming, but I think there has to be more punishment right now, not wait until after a long legal battle."

John replied, "You do what you think you have to do. I am staying here with Karen."

"Okay, I will talk to you later, after I figure out what to do with him. Again, my sincere apologies." Kyle felt so humiliated and ashamed that he brought this animal to the party and let him do this to his friends. Kyle promised Karen that he would get him and avenge this deplorable act.

"I am grateful that you will take care of this. What are you going to do to him, or do I not have to know?" John placed his gun back next to the bed.

"I have a couple of ideas. I need to sleep on it but believe me. I will get him where it hurts. Nothing close to what he just did, but it will hurt and hurt him deeply when I am done with him. I am going to talk to the police now. Then I will bring them into the room when Karen can talk to them. I will give them the information on David so they can go after him."

"Okay, but if he had stuck his nasty dick in my wife, he wouldn't be alive now," said John.

"Take it easy, John, and put that gun back in your nightstand before the police get in here. I know how you are both feeling, and you both know how sorry I am for this, but I promise you it will be handled. You can take that to the bank!" Kyle assured them.

It was difficult for him to keep going over what took place at the party. David was a cheater but never acted this way even when they were out of town, nothing like this.

Lying in his bed, the room dark with the silent night covering him and Suzette fast asleep, Kyle pondered how to get the revenge he promised. What could he do that would hurt him that bad? One idea kept coming to him: do something that involved David's wife, something that would stick the knife in deep, then turn it. How dare he do this to his friends was all he could think about as he fell asleep.

Back behind his desk, he was still thinking about the revenge and how he would get back at David for what he did to his friend, John's wife. It all went down unbelievably bad. You trust someone and introduce them into your inner circle. He felt the responsibility weigh heavy on him for everything *they* did wrong.

CHAPTER 9

THE SEDUCTION

Kyle was still fuming over the sexual assault and attempted rape accusations from his neighbor John and his wife, Karen. This all took place because Kyle invited David to a cocktail party at his neighbor's house. The better option would have been to take Suzette after all, he thought.

But now David must pay and must pay big for what he did was all Kyle could think about. What Kyle could not predict was how David would react to his punishment. Kyle had done so much for that man and his family. Not only did he give him a beautiful silver new Cadillac, but he also bought them their new home. How did he pay him back? By acting like an animal. It was deplorable.

The worse thing was that David acted like he was his best friend, but now, he was starting to act strange. What the hell was going on with him? It was obvious that he could no longer be trusted, and their relationship was done! Kyle only hoped that there would not be any other incidents against him or his family.

How dangerous was he was now the question?

Kyle knew that David's wife, Linda, was weak and could be controlled. How much control was the question if he was going to use her to get to David, knowing that he constantly cheated on her? Maybe the best way was to give him some of his own medicine, have sex with his wife, and then let him know. It shouldn't be too difficult. She was constantly coming on to him, even when her husband was sitting right behind them. He thought back to the hot tub and her nails sliding up his thigh. This might be the way to put an end to this dark nightmare he created Kyle thought. He would think about it and plot the best course for revenge.

Kyle was finding it difficult holding it all together. So much was going wrong at work when he had been all going so well. The growth of his company was impressive, and the profits were stacking up like gold bars. Kyle, known as the one with the golden touch—or was it the dynamite touch? —as it seemed like everything was blowing up around him. He continued to draw on his Churchill cigar, blow smoke rings, and ponder how he could use Linda. He wondered if he should make David aware of her sexual desires for his boss. Maybe he should sit on it, not knowing when he might need some ammunition against him. It was crazy that he had to think this way, but the present and past proved it was not the good old days.

While all that was going on at the office, Kyle had pushed the problems at home to the back of his mind. How unhappy and troubled his wife seemed to be. Worrying about his relationship with his wife and the happiness of his girls had taken his mind off what was happening all around him. It was not that he wasn't aware of corporate corruption and greed at its highest, coming from within the ranks of those he thought he could trust, the ones he had done the most for.

It was becoming difficult with his wife not wanting a divorce and only wanting to make his life a living hell. He often thought of being there at home for the children, his two beautiful girls. He loved them all so much, it hurt.

It was probably not the best environment for the kids, and he knew it. It just felt so complicated recently. Kyle tried to be patient in putting his life back together. There were so many different components. It was ironic that Kyle got married to feel the sweet emotion of love and have sex all the time. That is how you think when you are young and full of testosterone, and now after being married for a while, he was not feeling the love he hoped for, and he was not receiving the closeness that couples shared when they were in love. The other benefit was the children he had; they were everything to this young dad.

It was heavy on his head as he sat behind his desk, sipping on a hot cup of coffee. His secretary had laid the month's quarterly reports on his desk, and he decided to go over them to see what the profits were for the first quarter. It was quiet in the office with all others in the field selling financial packages.

The intercom buzzed, and he picked it up. "Boss, I got a call from—guess who? —David. He is out on bail and wants to come over and get some of his things," Connie said, sounding a little surprised.

Kyle, also surprised that he would even call the office, said, "What did you say? Is David out of jail? Who bailed him out? Does he want to come over? Is he coming by himself, or is someone coming with him?"

"He told me it would only be him. I am supposed to call him back and let him know if it is alright with you."

Kyle, with a hundred thoughts going through his head, replied, "Okay, go ahead, just let me know when he will be here. This could be a good time to get him for what he did. Out of jail, what bullshit!"

Kyle kept working but could not concentrate, knowing David was out of jail. Connie buzzed in again, "You won't believe this, but David's wife is on the phone for you."

"What the hell does she want? Does she sound mad?" "No, she sounded happy."

"Okay, put her through." "Okay, she is on line 3."

Kyle quickly struck on an idea; would this be the time to get David? He found Linda a pain in the ass but didn't want to hurt her for David's crime. Time was not on his side. Tired of David hurting everyone else, he felt compelled to exercise personal revenge for his friends John and Karen as he promised. David needed to learn a lesson once and for all.

It would only take a minute for Kyle to put his mind in a place he did not want to go. To start to talk about sex and making it real was not easy. Okay, he thought, I am ready.

"Linda, this is a surprise, knowing that your husband was arrested."

"Don't worry, Kyle, I am not mad at you. I understand what happened, and I am just as disgusted with him as everyone else. He is not taking it seriously even though he has been arrested. He's out on bail, but he just does not get it."

"He sure made a fool out of me when I introduced him to my friends. Linda, I want to hurt David. I feel that strongly about it. Every time I remember in my head what he did; it makes me sick."

Linda said with a soft voice, "I know how you feel, Kyle. That is why I was calling. I feel so close to you. I always have." Kyle looked up upon hearing her soft voice. Was it now time to get David, he thought?

"I was hoping you would be able to make me feel better. You know how I get when I am around you." Linda continued cooing down the phone at Kyle.

With David coming over soon, it was all coming together; destroy David where it hurt the most was the message he was getting.

Sitting back in his chair Kyle turned on the charm, "I have been thinking of you also. Are you at home?"

"Yes, I was just vacuuming the front room and could not stop thinking of you. Why couldn't I have found a husband like you to satisfy me?"

"Well, I am here now, and I want to get excited about you. Get the vacuum and turn it on."

"Really, the vacuum? I wanted to talk to you."

"I know," Kyle replied, "we are going to play with it, now put the handle between your legs, do as I ask."

"I have it there."

"Good, now feel the vibration on your clit. Are you feeling it?" "Oh, Kyle, I had no idea it could feel this good."

"That's the girl; rub it around and tell me how it feels again." Kyle clicked record on the tape machine while Linda panted down the phone.

"That is so hot. I want to see some juices on your panties. Do it. I want to hear you and the vibration."

Kyle imagined her standing there in her front room, naked with only her panties on, taking the handle and putting it on her pussy, letting the vibration take her off while she talked to him in his office.

"I can hear you breathing faster. Imagine that handle is my hard cock.

Rub it good."

"I am, oh God, I am getting so hot."

"I know you are. Don't you wish I was there?" "Oh, Kyle, this is so good. I am so hot."

"Is your sweet spot hurting? I heard you have a big dildo in your bedroom that you have named after me?"

"Yes, I do."

"I did not say to stop rubbing the handle." Kyle could tell from her voice that she was close. "That's it, now tell me how you feel."

"It is so good. I want you, Kyle."

"Okay, stop the vacuum. Go to your bedroom now, and I want you to get the dildo with my name on it, you understand?"

"Yes, I'll do as you say, Kyle."

"Good, because I am so hard," he told her while he checked the time. He was not hard at all. He was just doing this to get back at David and tried to stop himself from laughing.

"Take your panties off and spread your legs on your bed. Are you spreading your legs?" Linda went to the nightstand, where she grabbed her sex toy and took it to the bedside.

"I can't take it much longer. I am so hot. I am going to explode," she said as she lay back on the bed and spread her legs, doing everything Kyle told her to do, slipping her panties off, waiting for his next command. Sweat on her brow, one hand on her left breast, and her right hand working herself into a sexual frenzy.

Kyle felt guilty that he had to do this to Linda, knowing that she had no idea that Kyle only wanted to get her on tape so that her husband would pay the price his way. He knew that if or when Linda found out what Kyle did, pretending to be excited at Linda's sexual experience, she would be furious and embarrassed. Life was not fair. Kyle only hoped that she would never find out. With the recording now ready, Kyle would be patient. He just needed the right time to use it. It was not right, but it had to happen.

Revenge must be served hot.

CHAPTER 10

DO NOT MESS WITH A MAN'S FAMILY

David was about to arrive, and the recording of his wife was ready to go. Upon his arrival and after he cleaned out his office, his head popped round Kyle's office door.

Kyle looked up and said, "I don't want to see your face; I hate everything about you. I am astonished at what you have done. Just let me say this, you owe me that after all that I have done for you. You are a disgusting person David, and the sooner you are out of my life, the better. What you have done to my friends and family will be open scars on them for the rest of their lives. I could go on with my hate for you, but I will leave it to the police and courts. I do have one more thing to share with you before you leave, then I never want to see you again."

"What's that?" David asked.

"I thought you might get a kick out of it, and you probably need a good laugh after all that has taken place," Kyle said, knowing he was setting David up.

He had no idea what Kyle was going to do to him, but Kyle was good to his promise, and he promised to get revenge.

"You know how your wife always says she would love to go to bed with me, and we have joked about it? Well, I want you to listen to this, and believe me, it is good."

66

With that, Kyle proceeded to push the Play button on the recorder and sat back and watched David's face wondering when he would figure it out. He couldn't wait to see his smarmy face drop. Whatever he thought, it was intended to hit him where it hurt most. That was why Kyle was doing it.

Well, it was not long before David spoke up, "Is that Linda? Are you fucking kidding me?"

Kyle, not sure yet if it had hit home, kept playing it, thinking David was going to have to hear it all to get the maximum effect of hearing her come over another man. Kyle wanted him to have the picture in his mind of his wife stripped down to only her bra and panties and was playing with herself, doing as she was being told to do by him. Kyle looked over at David on the couch, wanting to see his heart with a knife in it.

"Shut it off, shut it off! Damn it."

"Oh no, you listen to it, and hear it all, let it sink in and feel the damn hurt, nothing like what you did to Karen."

"You—you son of a bitch, I'll kill you!"

Kyle wanted to see David hurt bad. He wanted to see him suffer but had no idea what David would do next. He sat in his chair that backed up to the window on the twelfth floor. David reached back then threw a massive punch at Kyle's face. Kyle instinctively moved his head back, hitting the window along with the back of the chair as David smashed his fists into it. The glass shattered, the chair fell on the floor, and Kyle was now being pushed out the window with glass cutting into his back. He yelled out as it sliced through his skin, David pushing him further out. Kyle was halfway out the window, glass scoring his back. He could feel the blood seeping through his shirt.

As Kyle looked down, he could see the people on the sidewalk who had heard screams and wondered what was going on twelve stories above. They could see two people hanging halfway out the window with blood dripping and falling on the cement. David had his hands around

Kyle's throat, muffling his screams for help. It was not looking good. He slipped farther out the window, sweat rolling down his face, and stared at the hard sidewalk, thinking it was unlikely he'd survive a fall that far. Fighting, hoping, and praying, Kyle mustered up strength from deep inside.

Fortunately for Kyle, he was strong, and his arms and legs were able to keep him from falling twelve stories to his death. Well, his prayers were answered. One of the guys he had just hired was in the office turning in his paperwork, and he had played professional football, a big guy.

Kyle screamed, "Get him off me!" as he struggled with David, who continued to push him out the window. There was a steady flow of blood now coming from Kyle's back. They were able to get their hands around David and pull him and Kyle back into the office. With force, they all fell on the floor in a heap.

David got up quickly and started to run for the door. He turned around and looked right at Kyle and said, "You better watch your back real good. I am coming for you and your family." With that, he picked up the white candle and threw it against the office wall setting it on fire. Connie scrambled to get a vase of water and threw it on the flame a couple of times, effectively putting it out, but not before it burned the carpet and wall.

With all this going on, the new agent, YL, came into the office with her trainer and found Kyle white as a sheet, bleeding and badly shaken.

"What happened to you? You look like you saw a ghost." YL looked most concerned.

Kyle told her what took place and how David had left, but not before trying to throw him out the window then threatening to kill him.

David was not done. As he left Kyle's office, he grabbed for one of the black candles right outside, grabbed it, and threw it at him like a lit missile on fire, and then started running for the stairs. The hot candle exploded, spewing hot wax and flame onto the carpet in the hallway, causing the baseboard and carpet to start to catch fire. There was a scramble for water to put it out. By the time the flames were extinguished, the fire had burnt up most of the office but hadn't gone inside the wall. The smell of smoke filled the air. However, it was evident that they would not be able to stay in the office due to the damage.

Kyle, very shaken, looked over at his secretary. "Go ahead and call the police. We will need a police report for the insurance company."

Yvonne said, "Oh my God, Kyle, I am scared for you."

Kyle looked into her eyes. "Don't worry. I can take care of myself. I must meet with the police, and then I am going home, just in case David shows up there."

"What are you going to do?"

"Yvonne, one does not mess with another man's family! That is when all boundaries become blurred, and you will do anything to make sure your family is safe, and that is what I intend to do."

Yvonne said, "Kyle, I can't believe all this is going on."

"I can hear your concern, Yvonne. I want you to know that this is not how things are done around here. We are God-fearing people who all have played by the rules and done the best we could in taking care of our families. Yvonne, you have come aboard at a difficult time for our company, but I promise you that there is so much opportunity for one to succeed with all that this company offers and without any more distractions from those who would like to do us harm. While I take care of eliminating the negatives, you go out and multiply the positives."

"Thank you for saying all that," Yvonne smiled. "I guess I needed a pep talk after all that has happened. I am with you, Kyle. I have seen the opportunity, and I plan to take advantage of it as long as you let me."

"I am here for you; any questions you might have, don't hesitate to ask, and in the meantime, concentrate on what we have taught you and go out there and get those sales. I will take care of things here. I promise, again."

Kyle thought about how well she was doing, even with all the distractions present at the office. She learned the business very quickly. Maybe it was his training that made her so good. He kept thinking of how good she smelled and how her lips were so soft against his—what a fox, so professional, a real class act.

Kyle had not met anyone like her and thought maybe it was time for some more training. He remembered when he had asked her if she had time to go out on a couple of appointments, and she said sure, and she would look forward to it. They went to the garage to get his car and then took off with Meatloaf playing on the radio. For the first time in a long while, he could smile and feel happy, and he knew it was because of the beautiful blonde sitting next to him.

YL had come from a middle-class family and was one of four siblings. There were twin brothers and an older sister. The two boys were incredibly talented in sports, especially football and baseball. The older sister was also exceptionally gifted, and she excelled in ballet and music. The music propelled her to success at a young age, taking her to college with an excellent scholarship. Her father traveled for his job and was not around much, leaving her mother to take care of the three older siblings and all the activities they were involved in. Yvonne felt alone. One could call her the 'forgotten child.'

This led her to seek attention in other places. She had one serious relationship, but it did not work out. Now, she was single and dating several other guys.

They had a good day, setting up two different corporations for enrollment during the next week, so they stopped at the bar for a drink and to talk over what they had done that day. Kyle had done nothing else but kiss YL and felt some strong vibes coming from her in the bar. It was getting him excited; however, he was her boss and did not want to do anything more inappropriate. After a nice late lunch and a few more drinks, the conversation turned to Kyle's relationship with his wife.

YL said, "I probably should not be so personal, but what is going on with your wife? I'm sorry if I shouldn't ask."

Kyle interrupted her, "Not a problem, you shouldn't hesitate to ask me anything. It should be discussed." He explained that his marriage was mostly window dressing; they were together for the children but were separated. He also explained that they had gone to an attorney, and they were filing for divorce.

This was interesting to YL. She had a big smile on her face as he ordered her a new drink. They talked more about it and then decided that they should head back. The music was great, and YL had drunk a few brandies, so she reached her arm over the back of Kyle's seat, rubbing the back of his neck.

Boy, did that feel good, he thought and even had some tingly feelings going down his spine. They laughed and sang as YL said she liked rubbing his neck and would love to give him a massage. Kyle told her how much he would look forward to that someday.

"Well, maybe we can accommodate you when we get to the office. I give a good massage," Yvonne said.

"I am a little surprised but also excited," Kyle said

She just smiled at him again and then said, "I don't know if I should admit this to you, but I have been checking you out. Those suit pants you wear, and the eel skin boots are so sexy."

"I am flattered to be the object of your observations," Kyle replied.

By the time they got back to the office, it was late. All others had gone home. Kyle had gone to the bathroom to clean himself up, and as he stood by the sink washing his hands, he thought about Yvonne, who was waiting in his office. He thought about the sexual vibes he was getting from her. She was different from other women. Maybe there was something special about this girl. When he went into his office, he saw YL on his couch holding her stockings which she had just taken off.

Sitting there in her short navy-blue skirt with smooth tan legs capped off by red high heels was a very sexy woman.

Kyle immediately thought, *Okay, she is different, so let's slow down with all the emotions.* He did not know if she had taken her nylons off because it was the end of the day, they were bothering her, or if this was a signal that she was getting ready for any advances he might be thinking of, but it was not the right time. He was tired and unsure that he wanted to start something with someone who was becoming so valuable in his company. It was time for action and not memories, even though they made him feel good. He laughed and thought, *I don't deserve to feel good; someone was making a point of that.*

CHAPTER 11

PROTECT YOUR VALUABLES

Kyle had so much on his mind on the way home that evening. On the one hand, he was still selling the positives of his business, and on the other, he was going home to protect his family from being shot by a disgruntled employee. He was not at all sure what was going to happen with David's threat. He was concerned enough about it and his family's safety that he called the police as soon as he arrived home. He explained to the desk sergeant what had happened and the threats he'd received, and to his surprise, he was told that there was nothing that the police could do without a crime taking place.

Great, Kyle thought, it's ok for a man to be pushed out of a window, but shots must be fired for the cops to get involved. It became clear that it was up to him to protect his family. He went to the gun cabinet out into the garage that he kept locked away from his kids. He pulled out two shotguns, loaded them with his shells, and took out a Glock 19 pistol for good measure as he checked the magazine and then loaded it into the Glock. He told his family to go over to Sharon's house, a friend of the family who lived down by the creek, and he would tell them when they could come home.

His wife did not want to leave their house and started to argue with him.

"I am not going anywhere until you tell me what is going on. You are not going to force me to leave my house," Suzette said.

Kyle was annoyed but understood. He had told her already, but okay, she needed more, only he did not have much time.

"Listen, this is not the time for attitude, Suzette. I want you guys to be safe if something happens. I am hoping that nothing happens, and you and the kids come right back. Remember, I already told you that there were some problems at work and David has made some threats. I am favoring the cautious side, so please, please take the kids and go to Sharon's house and do it quickly before David gets here," Kyle pleaded with her.

Suzette just stared back at him and then went to get her stuff and the children.

With the family finally gone and out of the line of fire, Kyle waited by the front door where he could see if anyone was coming up the street. It did not take long until he saw David's Cadillac turn the corner and approach his house before making the turn into his driveway. Kyle opened the door a crack and aimed at the front bumper of David's car with his shotgun. As he looked carefully, he could see a rifle barrel sticking out through David's car window. Kyle was shocked to see that David still wanted to hurt him and his family, and that just made it very real. He thought that he would be over his anger and come to his senses. They had shared a lot together. When one man threatens another man's family, there is a real pain to pay while the boundaries become blurred.

Kyle, with his shotgun cold in his hands, took aim and squeezed off two rounds. David seemed to heed this warning and put the car into reverse and backed onto the street to the sound of spinning wheels. The scent of burnt rubber hung in the air above the street. Kyle still kept a sharp eye on David. He could see the shiny barrel again coming into sight. He closed the door just in time as a bullet exploded at the top of the door frame, ripping the wood apart. Kyle grabbed his Glock as David drove back into his driveway so that he could get a better shot.

With David now on his property, Kyle fired four rounds into the fender and the door of David's car. It sounded like the start of duck season.

The smell of gunfire was now in the air. He heard a yell from the car, thinking that he must have shot him in the leg. That seemed enough for David as Kyle watched him back up and speed down the street. With his rifle still smoking, he wondered why David had come back. Oh well, he should not have threatened me, Kyle thought.

The loss of a friendship is painful for those who have had to feel the despair and emptiness left in one's heart, especially when a friend tries to kill you. It felt overwhelming and raw. You only want to sit down and cry your eyes out. However, with the sound of firing bullets in the neighborhood, it did not leave much time to dwell on the pain but to make sure everyone he loved was safe.

It was a low day for Kyle—trouble with his business being taken over, and worse of all, his good friend had tried to kill him and even threatened his family. Could it get any worse? Kyle thought as he drove through the tunnel heading to the city. The city he had lived in or around for the last twenty-five years had given him so much excitement. No wonder it was growing so fast. Well, he had a lot more to think about than how the city had treated him, he thought. What was he going to do now, he pondered?

Kyle was not sure what to do or how to handle the events of yesterday. He had contacted the police after the gunfight in his front yard. They were looking for David but had not found him yet. They started a police investigation on two fronts for attempted murder, including trying to kill Kyle by throwing him out the window. Tomorrow would be a new day and, hopefully, one with no drama.

"Well, what's up today?" he asked his secretary as he walked into the office wearing a three-piece suit and a smile on his face.

Connie looked up at him and said in a low voice, "Hate to ruin your day, boss, but there are two gentlemen in your office from the banking commission."

"Are you shitting me?" Kyle said. "What the hell now?" Kyle could not believe that there could be more drama and problems than he was already going through.

"Hold my calls," Kyle told his secretary as he entered his office. "Well, gentlemen, what did I do to deserve your attention this beautiful morning?" Kyle said sarcastically.

The tall one in a blue three-piece suit sitting on the couch said, "Mr.

Stone, we need to ask you some questions about your relationship with Alamo Bank and those who worked there."

"Go ahead," Kyle said. "They were my business bank that my CFO did most of the business transactions with. I would have him come in, but he is not here now."

"We know that he is not here. His whereabouts are of concern to us." "Why?" Kyle asked.

"Did he do something I don't know about?" "Well, that is what we're asking."

Kyle, getting a little annoyed, said, "Well, why don't you stop beating around the bush and tell me why you're here?"

The gentlemen sitting in the chair spoke up and said, "The VP of the bank has not been in for several days now, and your bank account has been hit for over $1,550,000—missing, gone."

"What the hell are you talking about? I did not have that much in there. I was talking to David about getting us some money, but he never did."

"Well, that is where your information is wrong. He did, and he put that money in there the other day." Kyle was worried now.

"Why would he do that just for someone to steal it? That does not make sense."

"Same question we had. Do you have any information that could help us figure out why?"

"No, but if I do, I will let you know. We will be in touch," Kyle said as the two investigators walked out.

"This is all unbelievable," he said to Connie as he walked out to her office. "Who in the hell did I piss off anyway? You will not believe this. Those two men were from the Banking Commission, as you know. They informed me that David made a deposit of $1,000,000 into our bank the day before yesterday, and I did not even know about it.

"What? Where did he get a million dollars from?" Connie asked.

"No shit, I don't know the answer to that question," Kyle said. "And here is the kicker: someone has taken that million and an additional

$500,000 from the same bank account." Connie looked perplexed.

"You are telling me that David put one million dollars in the bank the day before yesterday, and now the account has been emptied of

$1,500,000?"

"That is just what I am telling you, and nobody knows who took it."
"Do you have any guesses who took it?"

"Yes. You know I do. Nobody else but David had access to the funds, and I have not seen him since he tried to kill me." Kyle felt sorry for himself. "Who did I piss off?"

Connie, being a smart ass, said, "Well, inviting bad spirits in was not your brightest idea."

"That was David's idea, not mine."

"Well, you have to deal with the consequences now, don't you?"
"You know, I would rather take an early lunch than listen to you

remind me of the mess things are in. Call me at the bar if I win the lotto. If not, don't call."

And with that, Kyle headed to the glass of gin and tonic waiting for him; he needed it. He turned his thoughts to when his vice president, David, was there to help him build his company, not to tear it down or try to kill its president and principal stockholder. Everyone in the company wondered how he would take charge or not, lead, or give up? Kyle decided there was only one way to go, to lead and be positive. What else could happen to him and his company anyway? He had spent many hours going over the events and how they all came to this realization that someone wanted him out the way.

CHAPTER 12

HELLO FAMILY

Kyle sat at his favorite corner in the bar; he could not believe all that had taken place in only a few months. What the hell came over, David? When did he decide to be this type of person?

Depressed with it all, Kyle wanted to know what he had done to make his life so difficult. David was out there somewhere; he had jumped bail and hid from the cops, who had a warrant for his arrest. Things had gone very wrong, and he felt a surge of anger in his belly. Where was David? Kyle thought. He wanted to kick his ass so bad and screw him up the way his life had been turned upside down.

He had witnessed it right in front of his eyes while they were in Dallas. David and Julie did not care that Kyle saw them together. They had already come up with a plan to take Kyle down, so it did not matter what Kyle thought. Now Kyle had a lot of time to think about it. He realized how blatant they were. He sat there looking at his drink, moving the ice cubes with his finger, contemplating how difficult his life seemed to be. His wife was not happy, nor was he pleased with her. His best friend turned on him, collaborated with the controller, and he was now missing after he tried to kill him. An arrest warrant was issued for him, and he made a quick disappearing act going on the run.

Kyle could not spend any more time worrying about that bastard. He would continue to take care of his family, making sure they had what they needed. A business partner had tried to take over his business but ended up dying in a suspicious fire in his apartment. The bank that financed him had backed out. What a miserable mess. Hopefully, he thought the worst must be over.

Kyle had gone from making a quarter of a million a week to just enough to pay his staff and keep the offices open. He was down to just his office and a few brokers working for him. He had to give Yvonne credit for keeping everything running and even creating some new opportunities. God, help me, he thought. Kyle reached for his third gin. Two guys in suits showed up at the bar and then walked over to where Kyle was sitting.

"Kyle Stone?" "Who's asking?"

"Not important. What matters is that you are coming with us. We have a car waiting outside for you."

"If you don't tell me who you are, I am not going anywhere with you, got it?" Kyle said as he turned around to face the bar. He was definitely not in the mood for more drama.

The Suit reached out and grabbed Kyle's shoulder. Kyle reacted quickly and laid a hard punch to the man's stomach, bending him over as he stepped back to catch his breath. That was enough for his partner to see, who took his beretta from the holster and put it in Kyle's side. "Don't try anything stupid like you just did. Get up, and let's all walk out of here nice and gently."

Kyle had no alternative at this point but to do as he was told, as he was ushered out the bar to a limousine. The suit with the gun opened the door and said, "Get in." The limousine pulled away from the bar, heading to a destination Kyle had no clue of. It was noticeably quiet in the limo. No one said anything, and Kyle was in a daze thinking more shit was coming at him and not knowing why. He was taken to the other side of the city. The limo turned into a parking garage he was unfamiliar with, and he was bundled out toward the elevators.

"Are you going to tell me what this is about?" Kyle asked.

"You will hear soon enough," said the one poking the gun in his side. Kyle was ushered into a big office with windows looking over the bay of the city and told to sit down. A well-groomed, gray-haired gentleman came into the office and sat behind the large wooden desk.

"I am sure you are wondering why you have been summoned by two guys with guns?"

Kyle just sat there, staring at him. His question did not require a response, Kyle thought.

"Well, let us get to it then," said the grey-haired man. "You are friends with David, who works for you, correct?"

"Not sure you can call us friends," Kyle said. "What has he to do with this meeting you insisted on?"

"It seems that your friend and CFO had borrowed $750,000 from us, and we can't find him. Does this help your memory in any way?"

"The only thing I know is that he was talking to his family about taking out a loan for the business, but I told him to wait, and I would tell him when he should do it."

"Guess what, we are 'The Family,' and you are now part of it," said the one behind the desk.

Kyle, with a puzzled look on his face, said, "I think you got it wrong.

That amount of money is not in my bank."

"We are aware of that, and we also know you got a visit this morning from the banking commission looking for the VP of the bank and David."

"So then, you know I did not take the money that is missing," Kyle added.

"That might be the truth, but you are the only one still around and the only one we believe who can pay it back."

"That is crazy. I have nothing to do with your missing money, and you should be looking at the two who are most probably involved,"

Kyle said. "And I have my plate full of other problems I need to put my attention to, so sorry, I can't help you."

With laughter coming from behind the desk, the old guy continued, "You don't get it. We are now family, and we are now your number one priority."

Kyle was now getting menacing stares from the other two in the room.

The one sitting on the couch said, "You will now work for us and when we tell you. You will start working on one of our ships that are coming into the harbor. We will give you the time and what pier you are to show up at, and I will warn you now, you do exactly as we say, and you will tell no one about our arrangement. You will drop whatever you are doing when we contact you and show up at the pier. You will get instructions as to what you will be doing, and of course, the job will remain a secret until you have sufficiently paid back what you owe to the family."

"This is bullshit. I will not have anything to do with this. You got the wrong guy," Kyle said.

Kyle started to get up to walk out. "Sit down, or we can take care of this right now. You will do as we say, or you and your family in the hills will be deeply sorry that you did not do as you were told. Do you want them to pay the price of your fuckup?"

"All right," Kyle said. "Don't even mess with my family. You want something, then come to me."

"We won't have to as long as we have this understanding," he said. "They will take you back to your office. You will wait to hear from us. Do you understand, Kyle?"

"Yes, I understand. Just leave my wife and kids out of this. I mean it."

"Well, that will be up to you, Kyle," the one behind the desk said as he stood up and the meeting was over.

After being dropped off at the bar, Kyle decided that he needed to be at home around his family. While driving to the suburbs, he thought about his dad and how he had killed himself to get away from whatever was eating him alive. He could, for once, understand why one would end their own life.

The problems got bigger and bigger until one could not see any way out of it. While feeling so sorry for himself and having these thoughts of suicide, he woke up and remembered what his father's suicide had done to him and his brothers, pain that would last the rest of their lives. Not knowing why a father would leave his children after a divorce, Kyle kept trying to reconcile the immense pain and questions of what I did to my dad that would make him leave me forever? As Kyle went through the tunnel, he thought about how much he missed his dad and wished he were here to help him figure out his life now and how to fix the mess he had got himself and his family into.

CHAPTER 13

THIS CHILD IS NOT ALLOWED HAPPINESS

The realization of what the future was going to bring all started to develop in front of Kyle one Saturday morning many years ago. He was excited this morning to get to his girlfriend's house.

He was about forty-five minutes into his journey when he passed the house, he had spent his high school years in. What memories were in that house, the memories of a young family trying to make it in this crazy world. It would become a shame that the new memories that would fill this country home would be memories of a family self-destructing.

His family had vacated the home a few months earlier due to his parents not getting along, to put it lightly. It was a mother of three who wanted her freedom after twenty years of raising the boys and now felt the need to spread her wings and taste the elusive freedom. A father who was buried in depression going back to his childhood. A man who was blessed with the talents of an artist but could not pursue them due to having to make a living, a situation, so many other people found themselves in. Kyle could remember seeing his father sitting in front of an aisle with his oil paints before him and the beginning of a colorful picture emerging. His dad's ability to create something beautiful started with a blank canvas. What talent to possess. Kyle was highly impressed.

84

The boys knew that something was wrong between their parents as they continued to hear the fighting escalate. It became obvious that a train wreck was going to happen between a depressed father and a mother demanding her freedom with the kids caught in the middle.

Kyle walked past the side yard facing the road, his thumb out, hoping to get lucky since there was never a car on this dirt country road, and he did not want to miss one, nor did he want to walk all the way there.

When he reached the driveway of the empty, cold house, an eerie feeling came over him, drawing him to the haunted house. It was like a powerful energy force, making Kyle look behind him, not wanting to leave the road. He decided to go with the feeling.

It seemed as if he was being pulled or called to the garage attached to the house. As he approached the dwelling and looked through the windows, nothing looked suspicious until he glanced over to the kitchen where the garage door was. The door swung open and then closed, open, and then closed. Kyle looked harder to see if something he was missing, a draught somewhere that would move the door back and forth like that, but the house was all locked up, making what he saw impossible. He tried the front door, shaking it to see if he could open it and find out what the hell was going on inside the house. This was the house he grew up in.

He heard a car approaching, and a familiar voice called out.

"Hey, Kyle, Kyle!" Steve yelled out of his car window, trying to get his attention.

"Steve, what's up? What brings you out this way?"

"Get in. I'm heading to the beach for the surfing competition." "Man, that is what I wanted to do, but listen, there is something weird

going on inside my old house. Come on over here and help me find out what's happening in there."

Steve parked his car in the driveway and walked over to the front porch, where Kyle was still messing with the door.

"Kyle, can you hear that noise coming out of the garage? I noticed it after turning off my engine and getting out of the car. I am not sure what it is, but we should see if we can get in."

Kyle and Steve started to walk around the front porch to where Steve parked his car. They both stood still, trying to make sense of what they were hearing. It was coming from the garage, as Steve had said. The oversized garage door was locked as they tried to pull it open, and they both saw the side window and decided to try it, hoping it would not have been locked. As they reached the side of the garage, they moved the boards with long rusty nails to the ground out of the way so that they could get to the window. As Steve reached for the last panel, a rat ran out from under it and scared the hell out of the both of them. After they regained their composure, Kyle tried to slide the window open, but it was also locked.

"Damn it," Steve said. "I was hoping it would be open."

"This is crazy. Can you smell something strange, or is it just me?" Kyle moved his face closer toward the window.

"Now that you mention it, I am picking up something. It smells rotten to me, and I mean that in the literal sense of the word."

They both crushed their faces to the window as their eyes went back and forth, trying to see something.

"Okay, Steve, before you got here, I could swear I saw the door from the kitchen to the garage swinging open and then closed over and over again, and now you say you can smell something rotten. This is getting pretty weird."

Steve looked at Kyle. "Can you get a hold of your mom to let us in?"

Kyle, still looking in the garage through the window, said, "No, she's sleeping after working late last night, and I don't dare wake her. Plus, we are selling the house, and I don't know if she still has a key." Kyle stepped away from the window and stared out toward the mountains.

"Okay, let us break the glass to get in. I can't take it any longer." Reaching down where the lumber was, Kyle picked up a rock and smashed it into the glass. It was louder than he anticipated as the glass shattered to the ground. As soon as he did, they were both overwhelmed with the smell emanating from inside, and the sound of a car running became much louder.

Kyle picked up one of the boards and used it to clean the glass away from the sides of the window and had Steve lift him so that he could crawl through to the inside of the garage. He could see the reason for the foul smell. A dead black cat lay on the cement in a frozen pose. Kyle helped Steve get in as they plugged their noses and ran to unlock the garage door to open it and let the fresh air in. Kyle looked over at the truck that was running. With a weird look on his face, he went to open the truck door to turn off the engine. As he grabbed the handle and pulled the driver's side door open, he gasped with horror.

"What's the matter? What are you seeing?" Steve was at his side.

Kyle said, "My dad's wallet and money clip are on the seat, but no sign of him."

They looked in the back seat of the truck, but it was also empty. The boys looked at each other in bewilderment, not knowing what was going on. Meanwhile, a car pulled up in the driveway, and the realtor got out and walked to the back of the truck.

"Hey, guys, what is going on? I saw the garage door open and wondered if there was a break-in."

Steve said, "Yes, there was a break-in. It was us."

Kyle explained what had taken place and why they broke the window to get in. The realtor said that he would get the window fixed and remove the cat. They closed the garage door and then went on with their day.

Kyle was now on his way back to his girlfriend's, leaving those eerie feelings behind. What they did not know was that in that vacant family house, a man lay dying underneath the truck-bed cover, one place they did not look on that overcast cold Saturday morning.

"Miss you, Dad, so much," Kyle said with tears in his eyes. He wiped them away, now realizing he was a dad, and he better get tough because the going was getting tougher, and he had to do all he could do to protect his wife and children.

He pulled into his driveway as the rain came down hard, parked the car, and sat there with his head on the steering wheel. Kyle had buried most of what had happened with his dad years ago, and now all that stuff had opened old wounds as if it were yesterday. Two emotions came to the surface, two memories that he had put in the safe. And now they were out.

CHAPTER 14

WE WILL GIVE IT ONE MORE TRY

Young Kyle was just done with another day at school, and his father was there to pick him up, but that did not happen very often. They had not seen much of each other ever since he had left the house after his mom asked his dad to leave. He had heard his parents argue over who he could take. His dad wanted to take Kyle, but his mom would not let him, and the older brother was the one who was sent packing. When he left, his dad chose Kyle's older brother to live with him.

As they walked to the truck, Kyle asked his dad, "Are you taking me home, or do I have to get a ride from one of my friends?"

"No, I will run you up there. Will your mother be home?"

Kyle, sitting on the passenger side, said, "Yes, she will, Dad. I want you to come in and see her."

"No, I will just drop you off. I don't want any arguments or anything."

"Dad, I want you to come in and talk to Mom. I think she will let you come back."

"I wish that were the case, son. No, I will just drop you off."

"Come on, Dad. I'm serious. She has been talking, and she misses you.

You can get back in with us," Kyle pleaded.

His dad was now getting interested in this idea. "Do you honestly think she will take me back?"

"Yes, Dad, I do. That is why you have to come in."

His dad said with a serious face, "You know, Kyle, I have missed you so much. I love you forever, son, and I don't know if you knew, but I tried to take you with me, but your mother wouldn't let me."

"I know. I heard the two of you arguing."

"Okay, if you think she will, I will come in and talk to her and, Kyle, I am doing this for you, and of course, the others, but you know I love you so much."

"I love you too, Dad. You won't be sorry; I know she loves you."

The two of them drove through the hills to the outskirts where their home was. His dad drove into the driveway and parked by the garage.

"Kyle, do you have an extra garage opener? I was thinking of getting in there and getting some of my tools."

"No, I don't, but you can come over any time and get them. But what are you talking about? You are going to come home. You don't need to take any tools."

They both got out of the truck and headed for the front door. As they came into the house, Kyle walked to where his mother was standing in front of the kitchen sink doing some dishes.

Kyle said, showing a little excitement, "Mom, I brought Dad in. He picked me from school and brought me home."

Kyle's dad walked past him and toward his mother. "Hello, Elizabeth. It's good to see you."

Kyle's mother looked straight ahead out the kitchen window while she stood over the sink.

"Why are you here, Bob?"

"It is like Kyle said. I brought him home, and he suggested that I come in and say hello to you."

"Well, you have done that. You can go now."

"Liz, I want to come home. Can you let me back in? I miss all of you so much. You don't know how many nights I have cried myself to sleep, and that is not easy to say."

Still looking straight out the window, his mom said, "No, it is not that simple. I am sorry Kyle gave you the wrong message. You can leave now."

Kyle was now terribly upset. "Mom, don't do this. Let him come home.

We all want him home."

"Kyle, stay out of it," she said as his dad headed for the door.

"Come on, Mom, let him talk to you. Please, just five minutes, you and him. He needs us so much, and we need our father."

"Kyle, I told you to stay out of it."

Kyle looked to the door, and his dad left. He went out to the Datsun truck where his dad was sitting, opened the passenger door, and got in.

"I am so sorry, Dad. I didn't know she was going to be that mean to you."

"You know, she would not even look at me. That is what really gets me. After twenty-three years, and she will not even look at me," he said as tears rolled down his face.

Kyle looked over at his dad as he started to cry. "Dad, it hurts me to see you like this. I feel bad that I had you come in."

Wiping his eyes, his dad said, "It is over, Kyle. Your mother and I are finished. I am going to leave."

"Dad, I am really sorry. I love you so much." "It's okay. I will call you soon."

With that, his dad left, a defeated man, and Kyle had no idea how far into the darkness his father was going to go. If he only knew, he could have stopped the inevitable.

Kyle walked back into the house where his mom was sitting in her chair, watching her soap opera.

"Mom, what was that? I cannot believe how you treated Dad. You should have seen him crying in the truck. Do you know that this is a man who has hit bottom, you have taken everything from him, doesn't that bother you? Mother?"

"I can't help that, Kyle. You must let it go. Your dad and I are over, and he should know that, and you shouldn't get your hopes up. It's too late."

Kyle always remembered his mother saying, "It's too late." However, his father remembered it more.

It was a Thursday afternoon, and his father asked him to meet him at the old house so they could load up the washer and dryer because they were selling the house now that mom and dad had broken up. The same old place where Kyle and his friend Steve had been when his father was dying in his truck. His dad had asked him to help move the washer and dryer out of the old house they were selling.

As they were unscrewing the hoses from the back of the washer, his dad said, "I am not doing well with you boys and your mother not around, and I don't like this divorce, and to tell you the truth. I have been thinking of killing myself."

Kyle was shocked and looked to his father, "What the hell did you just say? Excuse my language, but did you say you wanted to kill yourself? Do not talk that way. You have so much to live for, and do not forget about your three sons, Dad. We will not be able to continue without you, and I am seriously bothered that you would say something like that. Am I supposed to take this seriously? Let us talk to Mom. I am sure she won't continue to break up our family."

"Well, Kyle, it sounds good, but the train has already left the station." "Don't worry, Dad. Everything will get better, I promise," Kyle said. He continued to remember the conversation with his dad.

"When we sat down at the house and shared a Coke, Dad, you told me about our heritage. You said we are fighters, and we do not give up, and neither will you, okay? As soon as I know more about our family, I want to sit down with you, so stop that talk of killing yourself. Our family members are fighters, Dad, and that is what you need to do."

Kyle shook his head as the lightning cracked around him, bringing him back to the present, which was a dark, cloudy morning. Sitting at his kitchen table with a cup of hot coffee with a shot of Jameson in it, looking over his backyard, swimming pool, tennis courts, hot tub, horse corrals, and all the things he had provided for his family. How was he going to keep all these secrets? These were the questions going through his young mind. He was now going into existence that he never dreamed of, one of secrecy and so far from anything he had ever experienced before.

CHAPTER 15

THE NOTE

The phone rang at home, and he answered, "Hello, oh, hi, Connie. I am on my way in. What's up?"

"I called you because I am sitting here, and I see a note coming under the door, and it has your name on it. I didn't know if you needed to read it right away?"

"Thanks, just put it on my desk. I will be there shortly." Kyle had a good idea of what it was, probably the new instructions they said he would receive. *Great, this nightmare just continues to get better,* he thought sarcastically.

Pier 36 was at the far end of the harbor, kind of far away from the others, and from what Kyle knew, it seemed appropriate, being the note said to arrive at ten-thirty. As he stood at the side of the pier, looking up at the ship docked there, someone aboard the ship yelled at him to come on up, so Kyle walked up the plank to the boat to be greeted by a tall man with a beard who said, "Follow me."

They entered a cabin on the officer's deck, and he was offered a seat. "Kyle, I am called Bossman, and you will call me that also. You will be helping unload the cargo hauls, and you will not speak to anyone as to what you see or hear when you are aboard the ship. Do you understand?"

"I got it. You will not have to worry about me. How long do I have to do this, Bossman?"

Bossman replied, "That is not up to me. I am sure they will let you know. All I know is that you are to be here until this ship is unloaded and probably working on the next ship that comes in. Now, go ahead and get started. Tom will show you the cargo haul and where to unload the merchandise. Kyle, as long as you show up and do your job, there won't be any problems with me."

"Thanks, Bossman." And with that, he was off to his new adventure in one completely messed-up life.

Kyle felt so alone in this dark hole and wished he could talk to his wife about all this, but he knew he could not trust her. She would try and find some way to use it against him as she had done before, causing him so much emotional hurt and financial ruin. He still could not believe that she had turned him in after sharing his tough nine hours at the office with her over a cocktail. He had done nothing wrong. It was unconscionable what she had done, and not only to him but to the kids. Why would a mother want to hurt her children just to get back at her husband for something he did not do? She was so stupid. Having an investigation of her husband's company by the government meant the end to most companies.

Kyle worried about his kids, as he was not around as much anymore and was never home at night to put them to bed and show them the love they deserved from their father. His wife did not seem to mind so much. Kyle thought that he wanted to have a wife who would be concerned about his whereabouts.

After several months of working on the docks and keeping everything he had seen and heard a secret, he had made the Bossman happy with his performance, and the Bossman knew that Kyle wanted to get this over and get back to his life he had seemed to have easily left behind. However, he was still working at his business during the day, even though he had to scale it way back from where it was. He was now down to just his office and a few brokers working for him. Kyle had gone from making a quarter of a million a week to just enough to pay his staff and keep the offices open. He had to give Yvonne credit for keeping everything running and even creating some new opportunities.

This working for the Family was screwing everything up, and he was scared that he would never get out; he was starting to hear too much of what was going on, which was not a good thing. He had spoken to some of the other guys, and they were all sure that this was what they would be doing for the rest of their life. They were now permanent members of the Family.

Kyle could not stop thinking about the situation at the docks as he drove home. He remembered Suzette's mother would be there, hopefully, to cook a great French meal. As he pulled into his garage, he could smell the food being cooked. His mother-in-law was home and knowing the master chef was at work put a smile on his face.

He came into his house and put his jacket in the closet, heading to where the delicious smells were coming from.

"Good evening, ladies. I hope you are all doing well?"

Suzette just gave him a dirty look and went to fill up her wine glass. He gave a kiss to his mother-in-law and glanced over to the stove. "It sure smells great. When do we eat?"

"It is just about ready. Why don't you get a cocktail and tell me about your day?" Kyle was happy to do that. It was nice someone was nice to him as he looked over at his wife sitting at the kitchen bar. Kyle asked Suzette how her day was.

"I don't know why you bother to ask; you are never here anymore, and I have no idea what you do."

Kyle trying to be patient, replied, "Come on, Suzette, that is not fair. I have explained my situation to you and how I am handling it. Believe me. I am doing the best I can considering the circumstances."

"You explain that you are now working for the Mafia. What the hell am I supposed to do with that? You are just full of lies; it sickens me."

"Give me a damn break Suzette, now is not the time with your mother here."

"Why, don't you want her to hear the crap you tell me, working for the Mafia?"

"Suzette, you know I love you and only want you to be happy."

She put her glass of wine down and walked to the garage door located off the kitchen, then turned around and said, "Let me show you what I think of your bullshit." With that, she proceeded to open the garage door and disappeared to the back of the garage, where his red Ferrari was parked.

Kyle looked at her mother, "What the hell is she talking about? Do you know what she's up to?"

As soon as Kyle asked that question, there was a huge crashing sound coming from the garage. Both Kyle and her mother bolted for the garage to see what was going on and see if Suzette was okay. To their utter amazement and horror, they saw her standing in front of his Ferrari with a long ax over her shoulder. She had already taken the ax to the headlights and up the hood, ready to strike that beautiful red metallic hood again. Kyle was scared about what might happen.

"What the hell do you think you are doing?" Kyle said as he ran to her, watching her strike the Ferrari repeatedly. She started with the hood, then smashed the windshield up to the convertible top before he could grab her and take the ax away. Kyle, now with the ax in his hands, stared at his damaged car in shock. He could not help it, but he thought about putting the blade of the ax right through her head, what a sight that would be—she who would be known forever as the Ax Lady.

Her mother, who was still standing at the door in shock started crying, as Kyle approached. "Don't worry. We will work this out. It's just another obstacle to our happiness, making it harder and harder to find."

Her mother wiped her face full of tears and went to talk to her daughter, who had gone too far with her unmanaged anger. This time she had crossed the line. Crazy bitch, ax lady! Now that it was all axed and done, the crazy woman had damaged the Ferrari for a tune of $16,000. Now that was not going to make a peaceful, loving home this car-crashing night.

Kyle would go to work again, disappointed by the lack of love in his marriage and the outcome of his wife's insane acts. The other part of this was the charities that Kyle was donating to and how they would not receive any more money until he could figure this out. Too much disappointment all around. If it were not for his kids, there would be no reason to stay in this bipolar, dysfunctional relationship. It was becoming obvious that Kyle would be a failure in his first marriage; however, the gold was in the children he had and all the love they gave him.

CHAPTER 16

SENATOR IN LAS VEGAS

It did not take long to be sent back to the present as he was summoned to the docks again. He had not been there for a while, hoping that they had forgotten about him, but no, he was in demand.

Kyle knew that his problems being over was a joke as he drove to the bay to take care of a problem David had dropped in his lap. A smile did come to his face as he thought about Yvonne and what they had just shared. It was nice that a woman could make him feel excited again, even with all his problems.

Once upon the ship, he saw Gary. "Hey there, Kyle, I thought maybe you made it off the ship, you know, one of the lucky ones?"

"I wish. However, I have been summoned. Have you seen Bossman?"

"I saw him in the wheelhouse a few minutes ago."

"Thanks, let me go see what this is all about."

He met with Bossman, who was the one who asked for him to show up. "What's up, Bossman? Been a while since I have seen or heard from you," Kyle said.

"Yeah, I bet you thought we forgot about you. Well, that is not the case. We have a job for you."

"Another job?" Kyle asked. "I thought I was done on the docks?"

"You are," replied Bossman. "The job is in Vegas."

"Las Vegas? Why in the hell do I have to go there?" Kyle said, irritated at the news.

"Well, we are not done with you, and you will meet with my boss in Vegas, and he will give you the details of what we want you to do."

"Okay, when do I have to leave?" Kyle did not want to go. His feelings for Yvonne were getting stronger, and he wanted to spend more time with her, not less.

Bossman said, "You are expected to arrive on Friday night, and you will be going to Caesar's Palace. You have a reservation. Check in, and you will be contacted. Listen, Kyle, if you do well, there is the possibility you could be released from the Family. I said possibility, and I have given you a good word to my boss. Do not make me regret it. Here, this is for you, a little something for the good work you have been doing." Kyle took the envelope.

"How much is in here?"

"$15,000. It is not all work here. We do reward those who do as we say and do it well."

"Well, I guess thanks. I want out of this mess. Sorry, but I am tired of not being in control of my life, even though it seems I screwed that up also. Thanks, Bossman. I will catch you later or never if I am lucky."

With that, the two men shook hands, and Kyle was on his way again to another adventure.

Sitting by the large pool in Vegas, watching all the beautiful people enjoying themselves, it seemed like he was on a different planet. This one was full of laughter and fun and every sort of bathing suit. Some looked like they had nothing on as they surrounded the pool enjoying the cool water on such a hot day. Kyle wondered what they would want from him this time. He hoped it was not as dull as the job on the docks, loading, and unloading. God knows what. Just then, a hand fell on his shoulder.

"Are you Stone?" a man in a striped suit said.

Kyle turned around to look at the voice but could not make out his face with the sun shining so brightly, assuming it was the boss. "Yes, I heard you would be looking for me."

"Well, it is not me you are meeting with. Come on. He is waiting."

Kyle followed along to the elevators, up to the sixty-fifth floor, and into a huge suite. Kyle thought why these guys always had the best. He thought of this because Bossman had offered him to stay in the Family, be one of the lieutenants, live large just like he had seen these guys do. That thought was always in the back of his mind. The business he spent so many years building now a shambles. Why not chuck it all in and start over as a member of the Family?

"My name is Ralph. They call me Ralphie, Kyle, and I have heard good things about you from Bossman."

"Thanks," said Kyle, eager to hear what he had to say.

"We have a special assignment for you, one that may provide freedom for you if you should desire. All this is based on how you complete this assignment so that we can call your debt paid or take the promotion you have been offered."

It all sounded good to Kyle but all so scary with all the marbles on this one.

"Here is what you are going to do, and this type of assignment would normally be given to one of our seasoned members, but we want to see what you can do, and we believe you can accomplish the task. We have a senior senator coming into town who will be staying at this hotel. He has made a lot of enemies, and those enemies want him out of power, and we need to take him out."

"Take him out?" Kyle said, a little surprised.

"No, not what you are thinking. Take him out of the Senate. Shame him. How do we do that? Here is the plan. Listen up," Ralphie said. "You will plant cameras in his room before he gets there, cameras that will show everything he does in the room. Once he is there, you will have a prostitute come to his room for his pleasure. You will have instructed the prostitute to ask certain questions that we will record, and she will hold out on the sex until the questions have been answered to our satisfaction."

"How will we know, and how will we communicate with her?" Kyle asked.

"She will be wired, and you will be in a truck parked on the strip where you will be able to see and hear everything. Once we have the audio, she will continue with the kinky sex he requested, and we have been told he likes being dominated."

Kyle shook his head. *What is with these influential people? Kyle thought. They act all mighty in public, but when they get a chance to do what they desire in private, it is usually something that makes them feel weak, and then throw in some nasty, and they will be coming back for more. The public puts these elected baboons on a pedestal, and really, they are so full of flaws, they must keep most of their lives secret from the public eye. The facade is so much better than the real thing.*

"So we will have her get a full can of the film on him being whipped and humiliated. When we have all that, she will expose herself to him, making him suck a cock with tits until she comes into his face. Once we have all the film we need, we will edit it in the van, and then it will be given to the CIA, and they will take it from there. Any questions?"

"Wow, that seems pretty risky, and a lot of things could go wrong," Kyle said.

"That is where your freedom comes in, and your debt is paid. Do a good job, get all we are expecting, and we will then have another conversation about your future."

"When will this go down?" Kyle asked.

"Saturday night. Put it all in the can as they say, and I will meet with you on Sunday morning."

Kyle had never done anything like this before. However, his freedom was on the line, so he knew he better kill it, maybe the wrong word.

He set up a meeting with the prostitute for Saturday morning, a 5'9" tall redhead, the Senator's favorite, who will be called Suzy, making sure she knew what to do and to do it so well that the Senator would not understand what was going on. Kyle had her go over the plan thoroughly with him again. Suzy said she had it all down and working with powerful men who like to be told what to do was something she was exceptionally good at, and Kyle was counting on that.

As the night drew closer, Kyle was in the van with all the electronics he had seen in the movies and excited that this could be the last thing he would have to do. He checked all the cameras and their angles, and then he rechecked them. He had to get this right.

Three hours later, the pictures started coming into the van, and it was not pretty but great footage for Kyle. The drunk, naked senator was ripe for the picking, and Suzy was a pro and knew how to play him. She had said she was good, but this was awesome. She had the senator begging for more in no time. After a couple of hours of fun, it was time for the finale, as he was on all fours. She put herself on his head, and when he lifted it to see what was there, a picture was taken of his face one inch from the hard cock.

"We have him!" were the yells from the van. "Close the deal, Kyle." Kyle waited outside and entered the room.

"Well, you can get off the floor now. Throw on some clothes. Senator, I am going to tell you how this is going to go down. You will immediately resign from any committee seats you sit on, and you will inform your re- election committee that you will not be running for re-election."

The senator, sitting on the chair, trying to put some clothes on with an expression of one getting caught with their hand in the cookie jar, just looked up at Kyle with sad eyes and had nothing to say. It was over! The edited copy was delivered as instructed, leaving Kyle pondering if the CIA worked together with the Family. Things one would not know unless they fell into the pit of defamation.

Kyle was early for his meeting with Ralphie, anxious to hear what he had to say. Kyle felt confident that he had completed his mission, and everyone should be happy. Ralphie showed up and ordered a cup of coffee with whiskey in it from the waitress and asked Kyle if he wanted one.

Kyle eagerly said, "Sure. What did you think about last night? Did we all deliver you a successful package?"

"You did, Kyle, and it was done with such excellence in detail. We talked it over last night, and we agreed that we would like you to stay with us. We will make you a very nice offer."

About that time, one of the guys with the pinstripe suits came in and said, "Can I speak to you, Ralphie, alone?"

"Sure," he said, and they walked over to the window where the suit was telling Ralphie something that made Ralphie go from someone happy to someone overly concerned about what he had just heard.

Kyle, being concerned himself, said, "What the hell is up? You don't look happy like you were."

"No, I am not, Kyle. It seems we have a complication to the mission you were given."

"What the hell would that be?" he said, thinking that he was being played after being promised his freedom if he did as they said.

"Here is the deal," Ralphie started to say after a sigh. "It seems that there is a pigeon on this mission, and it knows too much for some reason. Kyle, you are now directed to eliminate the pigeon before it flies away with all the secrets of this weekend."

"This was not the deal," Kyle said. "You promised me."

"The hell I did. You were told if you do a good job, there is the possibility of your debt being paid."

"If I were to do this, I'll let you know I have never killed anyone outside of Vietnam. Not sure I can do this."

Ralphie ignored Kyle, "There is a limo waiting for you, and you will pick up the pigeon and do as the driver instructs you. Kyle, we are done here. Good luck!"

Kyle could hardly feel anything as he left the meeting. His life had changed so much; he had gone through fraud, business corruption, infidelity, ghosts, and now, this. *Dad, I might be coming soon. You might have had the right idea,* Kyle thought as he took the elevator to the garage to his waiting limo. *Killing someone you do not even know is so cold. Could I do it?* It was for all the marbles again; the thoughts spun through his head. In the garage, the limo was waiting for him. The door in the back was opened, and Kyle took a seat. The driver named Stan reached back and gave Kyle a 9mm with a silencer on it.

"We are to pick up our target, and I told him that they would pick up the pigeon and take him to the back of the garage behind the hotel, and then Kyle would take him out of the car." Shaken, Kyle took the gun and sat back as the limo drove off.

The pistol felt so heavy and cold in his hands, and there was a pit in his stomach, as it seemed like a lifetime before the limo pulled up, and an older man with a white beard and blue suit got in and took a seat. Kyle told him that they had to go to his car for some papers, and it would just take a minute. As the driver drove to the back of the garage and parked,

Kyle got out of the car with the gun and silencer hidden under his jacket. As he walked over to a gray Cadillac, he motioned to the guy to get out and see something.

Walking around the car, he said, "What is it you want me to see?" Located now in the back of the garage, Kyle turned around to face the gentleman. As he was reaching for the gun in his jacket's inner pocket, two shots rang out. Immediately, Kyle hit the ground, a reaction from Vietnam. As he lay there, dark-red blood started trickling into a puddle by the body of the man he was supposed to shoot. Kyle looked up to see who had shot him, and to his surprise, it was Bossman.

"Bossman, what the hell are you doing?" Kyle asked. "Get up and get in the car. They will get rid of the body."

Kyle got into the back of the limousine, not sure what had just happened.

"Bossman, what did you do that for? I thought I had to do that for my freedom," Kyle said.

"Don't worry. It's okay," said Bossman. "We investigated your past and found that your family comes from royalty in our world. The real Bossman is a Freemason, and he wanted me to take care of the pigeon and not have this on you. And he wants to meet with you tomorrow. I will take you back to the hotel, and we will meet in the morning."

Kyle was not sure what just happened. He remembered what his dad told him that Thursday afternoon before he killed himself on Friday the thirteenth. He said that someday this information would help him in a big way, and it sure did today. Thanks, Dad.

CHAPTER 17

KNIGHTS TEMPLAR

Waking up, Kyle had a smile on his face. For the first time in a long time, he felt good about himself, and maybe his life could get back together. It had been a steep, fast slide to the bottom, and really, he was not quite sure if he was out of the woods or leaping from the frying pan to the fire.

I guess the meeting this morning might shed some light on it, he thought. He had heard of the big boss but never thought he would meet him or had any reason to do so. He was in Las Vegas, so that was convenient, being as Kyle was already there.

"Mr. Stone, Mr. Jacobs will see you now," said the good-looking blonde secretary sitting behind a French desk with a fresh bouquet in the corner.

"Thanks," said Kyle as he walked past her through the double doors into a gorgeous office suite with a captivating view of all Las Vegas, including the famous Las Vegas Strip. The building, the suite, was all so beautiful and did not look like the mob's offices; they all seemed normal.

"Kyle Stone, come on in. I have been anxious to meet you," said Mr. Jacobs.

Kyle was taken aback. *Anxious to meet me? Why?* he thought. "Thanks, Mr. Jacobs."

"Let's stop there," he said. "Call me Woody. My friends do."

Kyle looked at the leg he was pointing to; it looked like and sounded like wood.

"Thank you, I will," Kyle said, taking a seat in one of the chairs in front of the large mahogany desk.

"It is not very often we get individuals like you in our Family," said Woody. "I think Bossman told you a little about me, that I am of the order of the Freemasons, which is the reason you were brought here to see me. You have been given several tasks to complete for us, and my reports say that you have done a great job completing them, which is very impressive. However, that is not enough for you to be here in front of my desk. We have looked at your history, Kyle, and found that you are a direct descendant of Hugh de Stone, the founder of the Knights Templar. Were you aware of that?"

"Yes, my father told me about my family history and the Knights Templar before he died. He made it sound as if it was a family secret," Kyle said.

Woody asked, "You do know the relationship then between the Freemasons and the Templars?"

"Yes, I do. I have spent some time researching my linkage and how the Freemasons came into existence after the Knights Templar were executed, well, those they captured, which is about 25 percent of the total Knights," Kyle continued. "I believe many of our Founding Fathers—George Washington, Thomas Edison, Benjamin Franklin, Thomas Jefferson, Paul Revere, and several others were Freemasons. Also, if you look at the dollar bill, you will see the pyramid with the eye. This eye would be prevalent in the government."

"You have done your homework, and I assume you know quite a bit more."

"I do, and what really interests me is what happened to all the Templars, and the treasure that disappeared after the King of France ordered the Templars to be gathered up and tortured, burned at the stake on Friday the thirteenth, October 1307, which incidentally is the date I was born on, October 13, a Friday.

"They say that most of them escaped on a fleet of twenty-three ships with the treasures they had acquired over the years. Treasures of the Ark of the Covenant, the Holy Grail, and many more important artifacts of the time. They said that the fleet went to Scotland, where they helped King Robert the Bruce fight for Scotland's freedom from Europe. From there, the treasure might have been taken across the seas to Nova Scotia, then buried on an island. Treasure hunters have been searching for it for over 200 years. They had found an old map in one of the researcher's books which seems to be an original. It shows the ship routes to Nova Scotia and to Oak Island, which would have been taken after the roundup and deaths of the Templars. For the most part, they were young, strong men and known for their engineering abilities. If they took the treasure, as some are suggesting, then they would have put together an elaborate system of booby traps to stop all others from finding this most valuable treasure."

"You do know a lot. I probably could learn more about them from you.

What about the buried treasure?"

"Well, on this island, Woody, three boys playing in the area, came across a large tree with grass covering up a hole. The boys removed the leaves and dug down, and there they found short logs. Upon removing the logs and digging further, they came across another set of logs. Again they removed the logs and dug some more. This time there were not any more logs, just a treasure chest. The boys got rich off what was in the chest. There was also a map showing a hundred times as much treasure further down. That treasure has not been found to this day. They also found carvings of the Knights Templar cross with the crooked X symbol, so they may have been there before Christopher Columbus came to America. The history is so interesting to me, going back to 1126 after my great-great-grandfather founded the Knights Templar.

The pope wrote an order establishing them as a military unit entrusted with keeping safe all the Christians who wanted to come to Jerusalem and worship and come to the Holy Mount to see the covenant if they were holy enough to be allowed in. The Muslims were fierce in their efforts to kill Christians in the day," said Kyle.

"Well, some would say that that has not changed," Woody responded. "We have a good order of Freemasons here in Las Vegas, and I would like to offer you an invitation to join us as a Freemason. I have told some of the leaders about you and the history you bring to us. As you know, Kyle, one must be invited in, and I am extending that invitation to you."

Kyle knew he had no other answer but yes to give to Woody.

"I would be honored to accept your invitation, Woody," Kyle said. "Great, I will have my secretary get you the next date and details,"

Woody said. "Tell me again about the treasure on this island. What do you know?"

As Kyle looked out the window to gather his thoughts, Woody called his secretary and told her to hold his calls.

"The story I know, which is the most accurate one, is like I said, three boys back in the 1870s were playing on the island and came across a shallow hole next to a fallen tree. They dug down to find three boards lying together, so they dug them out and kept on digging. They hit another three boards and dug some more until they uncovered a chest. It was full of gold trinkets and jewelry, and they took it back to their house. They dug again and hit three more boards about fifteen feet down. The story goes that every fifteen feet are three more boards to two hundred feet."

"How do you know this?" Woody asked.

Kyle continued, "In 1886, several men started a dig to get to the bottom to see what treasure was buried there, but they ran into booby traps of water from the ocean that came into the hole from a series of trenches. When this happened, two of the men working the project were father and son, and when the father, who was in the hole, started to have problems staying afloat because of the water coming in, his son jumped in to help him, both ended up drowning. Not long after that, other men tried to go after the treasure, and the same thing happened to them, and this time, they had three men in the hole at depths of ninety-eight feet when they too were overtaken by the water booby traps and died. Now they are saying that there is a curse and that until one more person dies at the site, the treasure will not be found."

"That is incredible. I am impressed that you are so well informed. What kind of treasure are they talking about down there, and how far down it is?"

"Well, Woody, what I have learned is that this is the treasure from the Templars, and they put it down two hundred feet into a large cavern. In 1945, the treasure hunters drilled down at that depth and hit a large box that they assumed the treasure was in. However, they put those booby traps that allow ocean water to flood the hole and have killed six men so far. The items they suspect are the Ark of the Covenant, a powerful golden box that holds the Ten Commandments, the chalice that Jesus drank from at the Last Supper, the Jewish menorah, and the original manuscripts written by William Shakespeare. I find it all very interesting. There are new treasure hunters now going at it and using the newest technology. They have located the treasure box but have not been able to get to it. That is about it, Woody. They are still looking for gold."

"Thank you for that. I was all in with every word but let us return to the present and talk about you. You have mentioned on many occasions that you want your freedom. Is that correct?"

Kyle said with a smile on his face, "Yes, I guess I have mentioned it several times or so. You know that I never intended to be here. It was my CFO who took the money."

"I am aware of that, but I want you to relax and wait for me to put together something I think you will like. In the meantime, I know that your family and business are in the Bay Area. I will let you use one of our jets to get you back and forth, and then we will meet again. Let me tell you, though. You have done an incredible job with all we asked of you.

The hard part is now behind you, Kyle. You have done well."

"Thanks, Woody. I will take you up on your offer. But I do need to get home and take care of some loose strings."

CHAPTER 18

DIVORCE

Kyle, now knowing that he would be tied up in Las Vegas until he could clear his name and reputation, was not sure what he should do about his wife. What should he tell her? She had already been told about his involvement with the Family, but she never believed him. Kyle had always cared for his kids and made sure there was money for them while trying to figure out what he would do.

Kyle was back at his hotel after a busy day meeting many influential people and being welcomed into the Family. As he lay in bed, unable to sleep with so much in his head, he decided that it was time to ask his wife for a divorce. All that was going on was not fair to her, and she should move on with her life. Kyle did not know how long it would take in Las Vegas to clean up his life and get out of there in one piece.

The next day, he decided to call his wife and set up a meeting that weekend to talk to her about their relationship. Kyle did not want to say too much on the phone, but the conversation soon took a wrong turn, and she was yelling at him about their life and calling him names. Kyle continued with the conversation and set the meeting for Saturday. It was time!

Kyle woke up Saturday morning feeling refreshed after a good week in Las Vegas, many great dinners, shows, and of course, gambling. The Family had offered one of their private planes to take him to Oakland.

Kyle said yes, of course, and again another perk was being put in front of him. It seemed that they were trying to make him not want to leave The Family by giving him bonuses that he could not get anywhere else. His thoughts turned to his meeting with his wife, but he sure liked what he had seen so far from his new employer, who did not have any money problems, as they paid him quite well.

After a great plane ride with beautiful stewardesses, champagne, and coffee with a warm breakfast, he felt relatively good on the drive from the airport. He remembered what his father had told him about his heritage and that he was royalty. He never believed his father, and that was bothering him that he did not go further with the story and embrace his father instead of disbelieving him. So, many years later, and he was indeed being treated like it. All these great thoughts kept his mind from what he was about to do.

He had been married for many years and never anticipated getting a divorce after seeing what the divorce had done to his parents. His father's suicide almost certainly because of it and the negative effect on the whole family. After the divorce, his mother had found someone else and lived with him for many years before it ended in a breakup. Who won from this experience? Nobody was the answer, and this always made Kyle mad. For these reasons, Kyle had been putting off the inevitable, but it was time now. He knew it.

As he pulled up into his driveway, he noticed large trash bags full of clothes on the front lawn. This is not a good sign, he thought. Kyle walked into his home and was immediately greeted by one angry woman, throwing insults and hate all over him.

There was only one question he had, and that was, "Where are my kids?"

"They are down the street with Patty, and they will stay there until you and I have it out," Suzette yelled.

"This is not about having it out. I only thought that with all the confusion in our lives and the indiscretions that have happened, it would be a good time for this conversation."

"Fine, all you want to do is leave me. You are such a bastard!"

"Let us not get into name-calling. I think we are past that, don't you?" "Go to hell!" She screamed at him.

"Nice talk. I have tried to explain my situation to you, but you will never believe what I am telling you, and that is a problem."

"What? I don't give a damn about the Mafia. Why don't you also bring in the CIA?"

"Well, that's good. I can see you are not taking this at all seriously. I have heard many guys have told their wives or girlfriends that they are working for the mafia so that they do not have to say where they have been. Well, I am here to tell you that this is the truth, and I am not making any of it up. You better smart up; this is the truth. Listen, we must protect our children and allow them to grow up without bad memories of their childhood or about the fighting their parents always did."

"You have no intention of trying to save our marriage?"

"Well, when I pull up and see bags of probably my stuff on the front lawn, I don't know what to think. What is in the trash bags?" Kyle asked.

"Why don't you go out there and see for yourself?" "Okay, I will," Kyle said as he headed to the front door.

Kyle, knowing that this was not going to be good, took his time walking out there. He grabbed the first of the seven bags and slowly opened it. He feared what he might find. Sure enough, it was his clothes, and as he inspected the other bags, he discovered that his wife had cut up all his suits and stuffed them in the trash bags.

Kyle was fuming and angry, looking down at all his suits in pieces. These were expensive suits that he would need in his new job. It was now more than evident that the marriage was over—time to put a fork in it.

Kyle walked back into his house and found his wife in the kitchen, looking out the back window at the beautiful yard with the magnificent pool and large boulders surrounding it, creating a gorgeous ambiance. The tennis courts with lights that he had loved so much and entertained so many guests on. Of course, the courts, the hot tub with luscious lawn flowing to back where the horse corrals housed two beautiful mares. Kyle thought how much he was going to miss this place. It could have been the most incredible home he ever owned if it were not for all the fighting and hate his wife threw at him. Kyle now approached Suzette.

"I guess you expect me to start yelling and screaming at you for cutting up my suits. Well, if I still cared about us, I would, but at this point, we only need to be concerned about the children. Why are you crying?"

"I don't want our marriage to end," Suzette said.

"Well, you have a weird way of showing it with that stunt out in the front yard. Did you think that it would make me want you more? Life is too short to be in a relationship guided by hateful deeds intended to hurt the one you claim to love. I wanted to love you so much, to have a happy family full of love. I did not have that when I was a kid, Suzette, and never felt the love. I chased with my heart to feel what everyone said was so warm, and I tried to embrace it like no other emotion, but I never got there with you. I knew we were taking a big gamble getting married so young. But I wanted to feel love and be loved so bad."

Turning around to look at Kyle, Suzette said quietly, "I want the same things. We can make it happen."

"I am sorry, but it is over. So listen, I have given this a lot of thought. I am going to give everything to you, the house, the furniture, and the cars. I will have my attorney draw up the papers, and we can make this as easy as possible."

"Do whatever you want. All I want now is for you to get out of here."

"I will, but first, I want to know where the kids are. I want to say goodbye."

Suzette's stare hardened. "Leave the children alone. I will tell them about our divorce."

"No," Kyle said. "Don't even think that I am going to let you spin this as you have with most things to make me look like some kind of monster who does not love them. Let me continue." Kyle felt the anger rise and stood right in her face. "Don't you even think of causing any trouble with my kids? I have no patience left with you, and I will come down so hard on you, Suzette. You better listen well. Do not mess with me. Do you get that? You will do well financially, so you do not have to worry about the money. You will be hearing from me."

Heading up the hill to Patty's house, Kyle had so many emotions going through him. But mostly, sadness seemed to fill him up as he approached the front door.

"Hi, Patty, can I see my kids?"

Patty said, "Does your wife know that you are here?"

Kyle looked stern, "I am their father. Tell me where they are, please." "They are playing in the back. I will get them for you."

Kyle was happy not to have another confrontation. "Thanks, I'll wait here."

The kids came running down the hall when they saw their father, and as Kyle kneeled, they ran right into his arms. Now there was some love.

"Hey, guys, let's go outside for a minute. I want to talk to you."

"Sure, Dad," they said, and the three of them went outside to the patio and sat down at the table. It was a beautiful day with the sun shining so bright and warm, a slight breeze moving the colorful red flowers lining the walkway, a picture that Kyle will have in his heart and memory as he tried to tell his kids that their mom and dad were getting a divorce. Right before Kyle got started with the kids, Patty came out with some lemonade.

Kyle said, "You know that I have not been around much, having to work to keep the money coming in for the family."

The kids had no idea what their father was going through. He knew that if he did not pay back the money David stole, they would come after his family. They had made that threat very clear, He had heard stories about individuals who did not make whatever was bad good, and it scared the hell out of him. He would never let that happen, even if he had to work 24 hours a day.

"Both of you have to know that when I was not here, you were with me in my heart, and I missed both of you so much. You know that I would have been here if I could have. There is no other place I would want to be than with you both." Kyle, now with tears in his eyes and running down his cheeks, said, "I love you both so much. You must always remember that."

With wide eyes looking at their dad, the children asked, "What's the matter, Daddy? Why are you telling us this? Is there something wrong?"

"There is something I have to tell you, and I want both of you to remember that your mother and I love you so much. Your mother and I have decided to get a divorce."

The kids now had tears in their eyes as they heard the word divorce. "Daddy, why are you doing this? We don't want you to break up."

Kyle's heart broke watching them cry.

"Listen, sometimes, moms and dads aren't happy together, and it is best not to be together. But you guys must know that it is not because of you and neither of you caused this. It just happens, and it is best to have separate houses."

The youngest said, "What are you going to do?"

"I will be leaving and will get my own place. I want you to remember that I am always available for both of you. I will give you my pager number to get a hold of me anytime you need me. You know that I will be seeing you all the time. We will have so much fun doing things you guys love to do."

"Daddy, we love you and don't want you to go."

They were now in their father's arms as they held each other, emotions running strong with tears all around. Kyle wiped the tears from his eyes.

"I am going to take you guys home now, so get your stuff."

<hr>

Kyle drove through the country roads to the airport, full of emotions after meeting with his wife. In one regard, he felt relieved to be on the other side of this destructive relationship but was hurting in his heart over his kids and seeing them cry. He was glad that he had been honest with his wife and relieved from the guilt that had been so heavy on his shoulders. Kyle did not want to spend the rest of his life feeling guilty, living the life he had been dealt. Life was hard enough without carrying around feelings that were not happy and not positive but destructive to anything he did.

Kyle made a pact with himself that he would not allow anyone to put that kind of guilt on him again. He was now free of it and could start his new adventure and his new job.

CHAPTER 19

THE FAMILY

Jill said, "Are you ready to head back to Las Vegas, Mr. Stone?"

"Yes, Jill, ready when you are, and send Yvonne Lang a beautiful bouquet with a note of admiration," Kyle said with a smile on his face.

"Of course, Mr. Stone."

Sitting back, watching the jet leave the runway, and sipping on his usual tequila and tonic with lime, his thoughts continued toward Yvonne. He was amazed at her ability to work so professionally and with such responsibility, even with everything going on around her. There was something about her that made him want to explore more deeply where her satisfaction lay. When it came to YL, there was certainly more to explore.

After a short flight and limo ride back to the Casino Hotel, Kyle was looking forward to meeting with Woody again and discussing his new responsibilities.

"Good morning, Mr. Stone," Ms. Black said with a smile on her face. "Woody requested that you go into his office. He will be in shortly. Would you like your usual coffee?"

"That would be nice. Thank you," Kyle answered.

"Good morning, Woody. How have you been doing?" Kyle said as Woody walked into the office.

"Excellent, Kyle. It is good to have you back in town. Did you get all your business taken care of?"

"Yes, it was hard to do, but necessary in all accounts. It was time to end the marriage."

"That is always tough. I wish you and your ex the best," Woody said as he sat behind his desk on the sixty-first floor with a panoramic view of Las Vegas and the Strip.

"Thanks, Woody. I appreciate your kind words. I am excited to talk about what it is you want me to do for the Family."

Woody lit a Maduro Cigar. "We have had several meetings while you were gone, and I think we have a handle on how we can use your talents to help us out with some problems we have been dealing with. Oh, I'm sorry. Would you like a cigar?"

"Thanks for asking. I sure would. Do you have anything besides Maduro, maybe something a little milder?"

"I sure do. Here, try this, Churchill. It has tobacco that has been in the humidors for eight years, and it has a nice, aged Connecticut wrapper."

Kyle reached for the cigar. "That sounds like a perfect smoke. Thanks."

Woody handed Kyle the smoke with a cutter and lighter. "We think that you can help us in the most high-profile situations where we have to change the thinking of a high-profile person. What we want to do would be something like what you did for us with the Senator. We were so impressed with you and how you handled that situation. Our New York office was also briefed on the events and how you tied them up for delivery. They were pleased, and that makes me pleased."

"Thanks, that sounds exciting and something I know I can do," Kyle said, now drawing on the cigar Woody gave him.

"I would hope that what I do would always be a good thing for the Family but also stop someone who is using their office or position to break the law and hurt those around them. That way, I would know that I am doing something good for all."

"Perfect, then we need to get started. Let us meet in the morning. I will need some time to identify the next situation we will need you to remedy for us," Woody said.

"That works for me. I need a good night's sleep so I will be fresh and rested and ready to go." Kyle headed up to the Sky Bar for a couple of drinks before he cashed it in. Kyle, unsure of what the future was going to bring, could only have faith in himself that he would make the right decisions and not get deep in some serious trouble. It was still his goal to get out of the Family, and he would have to keep his nose clean if that had any chance of happening.

The sun came up over the Las Vegas mountains to shine brightly on all the gleaming buildings reaching for the sky. It was the beginning of another day of another life.

CHAPTER 20

MR. S

Woody's secretary smiled, "Good morning, Mr. Stone. Woody is waiting for you."

"Thanks, and a good morning to you also," Kyle said.

Woody was on the phone, looking out toward the mountains when he glanced back at Kyle with a smile and a nod. Kyle took a seat on the couch and picked up the morning paper to glance at the newest crime figures in the city. The secretary came in and brought Kyle a hot cup of coffee and placed it on the table.

Kyle looked up and smiled at her.

"Kyle, how are you this morning? Sorry for the abrupt phone call." "I am doing fine, Woody. Had a good night's sleep and was anxious to greet the day."

"I had a plan for us today, but that phone call was from New York, and they have some business they want us to take care of first before we get into our discussion," Woody continued.

"Not a problem, my time is yours. What do they have in mind?" Kyle asked.

"It seems that Mr. S is coming into Los Angeles with a couple of his buddies. He is on his seventy-two-foot sailboat, and the others are flying in. We know from past experiences that they can get into some trouble with the populace, so they want you to be in the Los Angeles area to provide some guidance as needed."

"I assume when you say Mr. S, you are talking about the Mr. S? The one and only?" Woody said.

"Why are you looking so blank?"

"Well, let us get this right. You, they, want me to tell him what to do," Kyle said, perplexed and smiling.

Woody laughed. "You will find out that the way the Family wants things is the way things will be. No exceptions. So do not worry because when you are representing the Family, you have all the power."

"Good to know. When do you want me to leave?" Kyle asked.

Woody leaned over and handed an itinerary to him. "The plane will be ready for you at five this afternoon. The rest of the details are in the folder. We will be in touch with you with the latest ETA. I will be waiting for you when you get back, and we will go to lunch and continue our discussion."

Kyle took the folder. "I look forward to lunch when I get back. I will go pack for LA. We will be in touch."

Kyle left the office and headed down the hallway, smiling, thinking about his first mission on behalf of the Family and how it was with Mr.

S. *How great is that he thought, and they say I have all the power. He felt giddy, like a kid.*

It was a short flight into LAX out of Las Vegas. Kyle was getting used to this first-class treatment. They knew his name and welcomed him most politely and with a lot of respect. He was onboard the private jet with its white leather captain chairs and couches, all surrounded by beautiful burl wood. As it was most other times, he was the only passenger who flew in one of the Family's fleet of jets. Becky, the stewardess, welcomed him on board.

Becky said, "Nice to see you this beautiful afternoon, Mr. Stone.

Would you like your usual tequila and tonic or TNT as you say it?" "I sure would, Becky, and how are you today?"

"Just wonderful and excited about our trip. When we leave LA, after dropping you off, we are heading to New York. I will be able to catch a show on Broadway tomorrow, and I am stoked."

"Fantastic. I wish I could go, but I am busy in LA for a few days. You have fun."

"I will, and here is your drink, Mr. Stone."

"Call me Kyle. I think I know you well enough. Been on a few flights with you now."

"Thanks, but we are instructed to address all the Family members by their last name."

"Not a problem. Don't want to break any rules while I am still learning them," Kyle raised the glass to her and smiled.

The captain, Ron Goodman, spoke up, "Good afternoon, Mr. Stone." Becky looked over at Kyle and smiled as if to say, you see?

The captain continued, "We are ready to start our taxi. Get yourself situated, and we will climb the mountains of LV and head west to the sunset. A quick flight, so sit back and enjoy."

With that, Kyle buckled up, sat back in his chair, and tipped his crystal cocktail glass, and enjoyed the taste of cold TNT. Kyle had been drinking gin and tonic for so many years and thought it was time for a change. He had always liked tequila with lime. Add some tonic, and there it was—you have a refreshing cocktail.

Upon his arrival to LAX, Kyle walked out to the street side and waited where he was told to stay, and instantly, a limo pulled up and greeted him as a VIP. He had chosen a hotel in Santa Monica overlooking the ocean. He enjoyed the restaurants and bars that were prevalent in the area, all with an ocean view. After checking into a gorgeous suite with a wet bar and hot tub in the corner overlooking the very blue Pacific Ocean, it was time to get some dinner. The bar seemed the likely place to start his evening and dining pleasure. Kyle was sitting at the bar and enjoying his TNT and looking over the menu when a gentleman approached him.

"Mr. Stone, my name is Jared, and we were informed that you would be in town for a couple of days and wanted to let you know that anything you need or anywhere you want to go, just let me know. Here is my card."

Kyle looked at the card and then at Jared, wondering how he knew he would be here.

"Well, thank you. My schedule is pretty busy, but I will keep your card and let you know if you can be of any assistance."

"Thank you, and please enjoy your stay, and by the way, I am with the Family."

Kyle smiled at him as he turned and left the restaurant, thinking what a well-run organization this was. Kyle could not help but be impressed with the Family. He had never been treated better. He felt that as long as one was scoring high on completing missions, it was all gravy. He did not even want to know what it would be like if he failed. He tucked the card in his pocket. He already knew. It was those guys at the dock unloading ships. He decided to do his best to stay on top.

The morning arrived with the sun shining through his window. Kyle was just finishing up shaving but still had shave cream on his face when there was a knock at the door, and his pot of coffee and breakfast was served. He did not have a lot of time. He needed to get down to the Los Angeles Yacht Club. There was a very special visitor arriving soon. After coffee and breakfast in his room and a beautiful new suit pressed and waiting for him in his closet, he soon was dressed and ready to head downstairs and out to the new day.

As he walked through the glass doors outside the hotel, a limousine was waiting for him amid the hustle of cars and people. Kyle had to smile to himself. He did not think that anyone besides movie stars got the sort of treatment he was getting. With his limo waiting for him, he was soon on his way to be the greeter.

The driver gave Kyle an envelope with a letter to him with instructions on how to handle the special visitor. It seemed that a large yacht was coming up the coast and should be arriving around ten. The letter explained that the visitor was Mr. S, and the yacht club members did not want his vessel to dock there. It was Kyle's job to intervene and explain why the yacht would not be able to stop there.

After reading the letter, he looked out the window of the limo and shook his head, knowing he was the one who had to break the bad news and tell them not to dock where they intended. He kept pondering on how he should handle it. He couldn't just say they were not welcome. He had to use diplomacy so that no feelings got hurt, and more importantly, he wanted to please Woody and the boys in New York.

With the waves rising and falling on the dock, seagulls flying low, and the sun making the docks feel alive. A large yacht went by. Kyle looked down the coast to see if he could see the boat he was to greet. With binoculars in hand, he could see a ship approaching, but it seemed too small.

As he waited and looked again, it grew larger, much larger, and was headed right for him. Kyle began to feel anxious about this, so he positioned himself at the very end where they would be going to dock. About fifty yards away, he could see what a beautiful yacht it was, and he started to motion for the vessel to come alongside the outside of the docks and not enter the berths. As the ship pulled alongside, the captain could be seen leaving the bridge, and Kyle waited for him to appear on the aft side.

"Who the hell are you, and why did you stop us from entering the yacht club?" the captain called out.

"My name is Kyle." But he was immediately interrupted.

"I don't give a damn what your name is. What the hell are you doing out here, and who are you?"

"Well, Captain, I was going to explain."

"Explain shit! Do you know who is on board?" The captain was getting quite upset as he looked down at Kyle.

"Hold on, Captain. I told you that my name is Kyle Stone. I am here representing the Family."

The captain now looked like he just got whacked in the face. "Did you say, 'The Family'?"

"Yes, I did. I was hoping to talk to Mr. S?"

"Yes, please come aboard. I will let him know, and please accept my apologies for my misspoken words," the captain said quickly.

With a smile as he started to board, Kyle thought what a change in the captain as soon as he found out he was with the Family. *I am going to enjoy all this power and instant respect.*

As Kyle approached the railings, the captain came out to meet him. "Mr. Stone, permission granted to board, and with my apologies, sir. I had no idea."

"Not a problem. I am glad we cleared that up. I need to talk to you about the situation here at the yacht club."

"Please, please come aboard. We can talk in the main cabin. Follow me." As they made their way downstairs to the cabin area, the captain turned around and said, "Don't tell my boss what an asshole I was. I don't need him being mad at me."

"Don't worry. All is good with me," Kyle laughed.

As they went downstairs, upon the deck were two beauties, lying on lounge chairs, taking in the late-morning sun while sipping on champagne and orange juice. They were both blondes, and Kyle always had a thing for blondes, especially ones looking as good as these two.

Getting his mind back on business, he entered the cabin and sat at the table. In the middle was Mr. S.

The captain started the introductions, "As I told you, this is Mr. Kyle Stone, from the Family, and he has something to tell us." With that introduction, Kyle did not want to wait any longer to tell them the news if they might get upset.

"Have a seat, Kyle. Can we get you something to drink?" "No thanks, Mr. S. I am fine."

"To what do we deserve the honor of your presence this morning?"

"You are way too kind. As you know, the Family sent me to greet you and welcome you to LA and to talk to you before you docked. It seems that there is some kind of problem with the yacht club board. I am not aware of what it is. However, the directive came from the New York office." It seemed like everyone's ears popped up when they heard New York.

"However, I have been instructed to tell you and the captain that you are not able to dock here and that you should dock somewhere else. Now, remember, I am only the messenger, so if—"

Mr. S interrupted, "Kyle, nothing for you to worry about. You are only doing your job. Cap, find another place we can dock and take on some fuel."

"Yes, sir, I will get right on it." The captain headed back upstairs, leaving Kyle and Mr. S at the table.

"I am sorry this happened to you," Kyle said. "I feel bad about the fuel situation."

"Don't worry about it. Cap will take care of it. He will find some way to get us some fuel. I am curious. It seems that someone on the board must have gotten the Family involved. You don't know who that would be?"

"Sorry, none of that was shared with me."

"It's okay. This will be handled outside of you and the Family. Just keep that our little secret." Kyle now felt a part of the club.

"That's fine. You do not have to worry about me. I am only glad you are not mad at me."

"You are new to the Family, aren't you?" Mr. S said. "I do not think you know how much power you have. Nobody will cross you and be stupid enough to argue with you, Kyle. How did you get into the Family if you can tell me?"

"Well, it is a long story, but I can tell you that when Woody found that my heritage went back to the Knights Templar, my stock went through the roof."

"Interesting. Are you going back to the 1100s, and how are you related?"

Kyle was now happy to talk about his past. "My dad, before he died, shared with me our heritage and how it went back to the founder of the Templars, who was my great-grandfather many times over. I wear this medallion," Kyle showed him the silver image that hung around his neck, "and you see that there are two men on a horse. The one in the front is my great-grandfather."

"Well, I can see why you have been given such reverence."

Kyle, feeling pretty proud at this time, asked if he could get a cocktail, as he wanted to share one with Mr. S. With the boat slowly rocking in the shiny bay waters, Kyle looked out the portal and was in amazement at how his life had changed. He thought about this while he waited to have a drink with Mr. S, who treated him with total respect. The captain joined them in the cabin.

"Don't worry, boss. I found a fuel barge about a mile up the coast.

They think they should be able to accommodate us."

"What do you mean?" Mr. S asked, "You *think* they can help us?"

"Well, we take on a lot of fuel, and sometimes, the barge has obligations to other boats."

"Let's do this then. How about Kyle comes with us as our insurance?" Kyle smiled at being mentioned.

"What can I do that you can't do?"

Mr. S smiled at him and said, "You still don't get it. You are one powerful son of a bitch, Kyle."

"In that case, I would be happy to float on for a mile and see what we can do to make sure you get the fuel you need."

On this bright, beautiful, sunshiny day with the gulls singing as they flew over the boat as if they were going to land, Kyle was above deck sitting with Mr. S and the captain, finally feeling his luck had changed for the better.

"Come on, Kyle. Sail with us up the coast to San Francisco. I think you know the city well. If my information is correct, you have a sweetie up there," Mr. S said, tipping a cold one back.

"First, I would love to spend more time with the both of you. It has been fun, and I have really enjoyed meeting you and hearing all the stories. I am not sure what my next assignment is, and I better check-in." Kyle replied. "Secondly, how did you know that I had a sweetheart in the Bay Area?"

"Well, you are not the only one who knows people. I hear she is beautiful, and I would love to meet her and, of course, see you again."

"Thanks. When our paths cross again, I would love to introduce her to you. I know she would love to meet you. Hey, I better get out of here. I think my job is done. I will tell Woody you said hello."

"Thanks, Kyle, for all your help with the fuel. It has been a real pleasure."

They started to motor over to a dock north of the fuel barge where the limo was waiting for Kyle. The deckhands were securing the anchor with the lovely young ladies watching them when Mr. S came over to help. He must have wanted to show off because this was not something he usually did. Kyle was watching from the bridge when a deckhand threw the line to the other, and it hit Mr. S and knocked him right over the sow railing into the cold bay water.

"Man overboard, man overboard!" Shouts could be heard, as well as, "Where are the safety rings?"

Kyle could not wait any longer. He watched Mr. S slip down and down into the dark, cold water, disappearing into the darkness. Kyle jumped in to grab him. He could feel a hand grab his shoulder and start to pull him under. This was getting a lot scarier than he anticipated it would be. He had to stop him from taking him deeper and deeper as he tried to get them both to the surface.

Kyle, unable to see much, reached back and grabbed some clothing and pulled Mr. S closer to him. They looked into each other's eyes, and for a moment, they seemed to know what to do to get to the surface. That moment was enough for Kyle to push Mr. S up into the light, but his foot stepped on Kyle's belt, and as Mr. S pushed off, Kyle was sent deeper into the cold water.

Kyle looked up to see if he could see the surface and could only vaguely see the bottom of the boat, a place he did not want to be at. He then looked down, and out of the corner of his eye, he thought he saw the light. He was now confused and looked up and down. Why was there light under the boat? Kyle tried hard to make sense of things as he was now desperately in need of air. The light had to be the surface, he thought. Now believing that he figured it out, he swam to the light, but it only took him deeper with no chance for air.

Kyle was now desperate for air. He could not keep his mouth closed for much longer. His mind was saying, gasp for air, gasp for air. He knew he had gotten himself into a horrible situation and started to feel that he would not be able to get out of this one. As total desperation took him over and the end so near, out of nowhere, a strong flow of air grabbed him and took him as a baby and delivered him to the surface. Once his head emerged, he took a big gasp for air and several more. Hands grabbed at him and pulled him aboard. Lying on the deck, coughing salty water through his nose and mouth, he looked up, and there was Mr. S with a big smile on his face.

"We are so glad to see you. We thought we lost you to the depths of the ocean."

Kyle, weak from the near drowning, smiled back at Mr. S. "I hope your fans appreciate me risking my life for you?"

Mr. S, being smart, said, "Check with my manager, and he will give you a free ticket to my next concert." He reached down to help pull Kyle to his feet.

"Kyle, get the hell over here and warm up," said the captain, throwing a towel at him. Mr. S was sitting at the back of the boat with a towel over his shoulders, his pants and shoes drying over the side. Kyle took a seat next to him, feeling the warmth of the sun again.

The captain came over after a deckhand relieved him on the bridge. "What the hell happened, Mr. S? You are not new to sailing?

"All I can say is I am damn lucky Kyle was there, and thank you for jumping in. I was sinking fast."

"I'm just glad that I could help."

"Help! Shit, you saved my life! I was going down fast. I don't know if you were looking for a new best friend, but you now have one. I do not take this kind of bravery lightly, but I must ask a question. When I fell in the water, I went down fast as if the current was taking me under. How did you get to the top with that same current?"

Kyle dried off his face. "I know what you are talking about. I felt the current also, and it was scary. When I looked up, I saw the bottom of the boat, an eerie sight. I must tell you, Mr. S, I saw a flash of light underneath me when I was going down, and then it was as if the current changed itself and jettisoned me to the top. I can't explain it, but I'm very thankful for whatever happened."

"Kim, go downstairs into my cabin and pull out a pair of my finest slacks and white shirt. I think you and I are about the same size."

"You don't have to do that," Kyle said, still with a towel over his shoulders.

"I don't, but the clothes you had on are just a little wet?" Kyle smiled. "Well, thanks, it is appreciated."

"Speaking of appreciation," Mr. S. continued, "I want you to know, Kyle, that I am indebted to you, and I will say this one time. Anything you want or need, I owe you big time. You just ask me, and I will make it happen." With that, the two men hugged each other in a true sense of bonding. Mr. S then took the medallion in his hand that was around Kyle's neck.

"What is this? It is shiny silver and feels a little powerful in my hand."

"This is an incredibly special piece that I always wear. It shows the founder of the Knights Templar. As you know, my great-grandfather is the one depicted on the horse. I am impressed you could feel the power, and the more you believe, the more powerful it gets."

"It is special, Kyle. I felt it as soon as I touched it."

The two men spent the rest of the morning talking about their ordeal and getting to know each other. Kyle could not believe how this turned out. Not even was anyone mad at him, but he now had a new best friend who was famous and wealthy.

Soon, the boat was full of fuel, and goodbyes were said, and his new friend was on his way up the coast to San Francisco.

CHAPTER 21

NO CAR INSURANCE

eading for the airport, Kyle was on the phone with Woody. "Mission accomplished, boss. All went well."

"I know," Woody said, "I already got a report. It seems that you have made a new friend. He could only say good things about you, and that is what I like to hear. I don't have anything for you right now. Take the Gulfstream up to the Bay Area and check in with your kids and, of course, all the women you like to play with."

"No, not all the women. There is only one that is pulling on my heartstrings," Kyle replied.

"Well, give her a call then, and by the way, if you want to stay on our ship, Camellia, in the estuary, let me know, and I will give them a heads-up that you will be their guest. Anyway, have a good time. We will be in contact."

"Sounds good. Why don't you go ahead and let them know? I think I will take advantage of your offer."

"For the future, Kyle, you won't have to go through me. You can let them know yourself and check on availability. We have a couple of guys on the East Coast who always stay there when they can. They love the bay breeze on a warm California day."

On his way to the Bay Area in the Gulfstream G650, Kyle asked the captain if he could fly over the Bay Area after picking up YL. She would love to see her city from the air. The captain gave him the thumbs up, so he called YL and told her to meet him at the airport, gate C7, where he would surprise her.

Yvonne watched the jet taxi, and the steps lowered, and she saw her boyfriend smiling like he just won the lottery. Yvonne shared a hug with Kyle.

"So good to see you. I like the way you travel these days," she laughed.

"That is why I asked you to meet me here. How would you like a personal tour of the city from three thousand feet?"

"Are you kidding me, a tour in this jet?" she asked with a big smile.

"You got it. Come on aboard and let us have a glass of champs while they get us ready."

Yvonne entered and gasped at the interior decked out with burl wood and white leather as pretty as a picture. Just gorgeous, she thought. In a few moments, they were back in the sky in the beautiful jet flying over the Bay Area, viewing it as she had never seen it before.

"What's up, girl? You've been staying busy?"

"I have, ever since you talked me into running this business while you jet around."

"I have been keeping a watch on your progress, and I must compliment you on being such a fast learner and able to handle all those grumpy men," Kyle said. "The reason I called you, besides this incredible tour, I wanted to let you know that I would be in the area for a couple of days and was wondering if we could spend some time together tomorrow? I have notified the crew of the Camellia, a 150-footer my new employer owns, and it's docked in Alameda. They have it set up for guests to enjoy. I am going to stay there for a couple of days to check out the services. I was hoping that you would join me. I took the initiative to order up some large and juicy lobsters. I remember how much you love them."

"Who doesn't love lobster? That sounds great. I would love to."
"Super, I will pick you up at your apartment around eleven. That will

give us time to head down to the wharf and have some brunch at the Buena Vista. I know how you enjoy an Irish whiskey with your eggs benedict."

"You have my mouth watering already."

"Boy, you are easy, but that's okay. You can swoon over me."

"Funny, I was talking about the eggs benedict, but you are pretty yummy, too."

"I'm excited as I also have a surprise for you. I think you'll get a kick out of it. See you tomorrow at eleven."

Kyle had the driver take him to his kids' house so that he could pick them up and surprise them with a Giants' game at Candlestick. He had already gotten the tickets through Woody's secretary, and they could use the owner's box. Not only great seats but then the opportunity to go to the dugout and meet their favorite player. This was going to be a great afternoon, and the weather was beautiful to play ball. The limo pulled up outside the house, and soon, both of his daughters came running out before Kyle could even get out of the car. The two young girls got so excited to be traveling in a limousine, and this one was full of their favorite drinks. Hugs and kisses with so much excitement are all followed by his ex-wife coming out the front door, heading straight for the limo with that familiar 'I hate you' look. The passenger door was open, and the children crawled around inside, barely containing their excitement.

"Kyle, what are you doing with this limo? Did you steal it? Who does it belong to?" Suzette started.

Kyle was not happy they were going to have this negative conversation in front of the kids again. This was supposed to be a happy day. Driver turned around to face Kyle, with the window down.

"Do you want me to handle this, boss?"

"No, that's okay. I don't think she would want that to happen to her."

"The limousine belongs to my company, Suzette, and I haven't seen the kids for a while, so I wanted to take them to a Giants' game this afternoon. I already cleared it."

"Aren't you the fancy one? I am with the kids all the time, cooking, cleaning, school, and you show up here like some kind of big shot."

"Well, call it what you want. I just wanted to show the girls a good time. They deserve it."

"Well, show me your insurance then. They aren't going in any car without insurance." Suzette folded her arms and glared at Kyle.

The driver was getting annoyed again and looked at Kyle and shrugged.

Kyle told him to wait, and he would handle it.

"This type of vehicle does not carry insurance papers in the vehicle, but it is insured through the fleet, and if anything happened, they would be covered and, of course, taken care of. Good?"

"No, it is not good. I want to see insurance papers, or these kids are not going anywhere."

The driver was antsy in his seat and said, "Can I explain, boss?" "Sure, go ahead. It couldn't hurt."

"Ma'am, the way we do it with all our limousines is if there was an accident, the driver gives his business card to law enforcement, and it is all taken care of."

"What a bunch of bullshit! You can take that card and shove it up your ass. Come on, girls. You're not going anywhere."

The driver started to open his door when Kyle told him to stay seated, feeling a little embarrassed that this nastiness was taking place. The poor girls were pleading with their mother with tears to let them go, but they knew there was no changing her mind when she got like this. Kyle did not want to take this any further.

"I am sorry, girls. I had a great afternoon planned for us. I will come back in my car with insurance papers, and we can spend some happy time together."

The girls followed their mother into the house with tears and hugs, letting her know how upset they were. Kyle hated to see them like this; he only wanted to see happy faces and happy children.

CHAPTER 22

A ROLEX

Returning to the city, Driver spoke up, "What the hell was that boss?" Kyle sighed in the backseat. "That was the ex. Lovely person, isn't she?" "I don't think anyone will blame you for divorcing her, maybe marrying

her, though," he laughed.

"That's enough. Your point is well taken."

"Sorry, boss, I got a little carried away. Where do you want me to take you?"

"Let us head for Camellia. I want to see the accommodations for tomorrow when I bring Yvonne aboard," said Kyle, reaching for a soda pop.

As they made their way out of the suburbs, Driver made his way through some tight curves while Kyle made some phone calls. As he hung up the phone and looked out the window, he noticed Driver was slowing down.

"What's up," he asked. "Why are we pulling over?"

"I think I saw something," Driver said, "looks like a car in the creek down the ravine. Should we check it out, boss?"

"I don't have any appointments to get to. Sure, let's go ahead and see if everything is alright," Kyle ordered. Both got out of the limousine and started to walk down to the creek. Kyle looked around the trees, "There it is. Let's check it out. I hope nobody is in it."

As they approached the car, a black Cadillac had the two front tires in the water and the back tires wedged on a rock. Driver looked in the front window and saw nobody, he looked in the back seat and nobody there either, "I think nobody is in the car, maybe they left and walked to get help." Kyle walked to the back of the Cadillac and stared at the trunk. For a moment, all he could think of was his father's truck in the garage.

"Driver, look here. There is a piece of clothing sticking out. Come on and help me. We must open the trunk to be sure nobody is hurt or in there."

Driver looked around to see what he could use to snap the trunk open. Not seeing anything, he started running back to the limo to get a tire iron. Kyle kept knocking on the trunk, trying to listen to see if he could hear anyone answering.

Driver returned to the car. "Okay, boss, we can pop it open."

"Good, I have a feeling about this, and I hope I am wrong, but go ahead and pop it, then we can stop guessing."

With that, Driver stuck the tire iron under the trunk and pushed hard.

The trunk popped opened.

"Holy shit," Kyle said, as they both saw a naked woman lying in the trunk, her clothes torn off. She was either dead or knocked out. They reached in to see if she was alive.

"Okay, I have a pulse," Kyle breathed a sigh of release, "Let's get her out of here and get her breathing again." They lifted her out of the trunk and laid her flat on the backseat. Kyle got in with her, putting his jacket over her naked breasts, and slapped her gently on the cheeks trying to get her to wake up.

Driver was again back at the limo, fetching some water for her. When Driver returned and handed Kyle the water, he watched as Kyle tried to get her to open her eyes. "She is opening her eyes. Way to go, boss."

"I got her; she is coming around."

"Hey, you okay?" Kyle noticed now that the woman was beaten around her face, chest, and stomach.

The young lady opened her eyes up wide. "Please–please don't hurt me anymore," she cried.

Kyle sat next to her and said, "It is okay, we just found you in the trunk of this car that went into this creek. We are not going to hurt you, okay? We want to help you, got it?"

She looked at him warily and then at Driver as Kyle poured some water on the cloth and started to wipe the blood off of her face.

He turned to Driver, "Take off your pants. I want to give them to– what is your name? Don't worry. We are here to help."

In a soft voice, she replied, "Sheri–Sheri is my name."

"Okay, Sheri, you have my jacket, now take these pants and put them on."

Driver kept watching as he stood there in his boxers. "Who did this to you, Sheri, and do you know why?"

Kyle interrupted, "Hold up on those questions. Are you hurt anywhere, Sheri? I can see a lot of bruising, any ribs broken or anything?"

"I don't think I have any broken bones," she said as she started to cry, sipping some water. "They beat me in the face and stomach and my chest." She cried harder as Kyle pulled her to him to hug her.

"They took their turns raping me," she gasped, sobbing hard.

"Okay, Driver, let's get her to the limo, and then we can get her some help."

"You got it, boss, come on, Sheri, let's get you out of here." The two guys gently helped her up the hill to the limo, and then they were back on the road.

"Driver, let's take her to the hospital and get her checked out."

"I don't want to do that. I am alright, please don't take me there!" Sheri said with tears in her eyes.

"I am not sure about that. You should get looked at, not knowing what they did to you."

Sheri looked down at the floor of the limo, "They slapped me around for their enjoyment, and then they took their turns abusing me. If I had a wish, it would be that they get what is coming to them, let them feel the pain of total helplessness."

Driver looked back at Kyle. "Should we involve ourselves in granting her wish, boss?"

Looking over at Sheri. "Do you know who did this to you?" "That was what I was asking her earlier," Driver said.

"Driver, now it is relevant. Sheri, do you know who did this to you?" Sheri replied, "I do not know their names, but I know where they are." "How do you know that?" Driver asked.

"I heard them talking about where they were going when they were done with me. I think they were going to an apartment behind a small business. They said they were going to party after raping me."

"It sounds like you totally want to get revenge," Kyle said, holding her hand.

"Yes, I do. It is the only thing that will make me feel better about what I just went through. But I don't want you guys to get any more involved, you have been great, and I am grateful you came and found me and took care of me. You both probably have a nice job to get to."

"Well, let's say that our type of job lends us to help you get your revenge. It tears me up to see this kind of injustice put on anyone. Maybe we should get the justice you deserve, and Sheri, I think it will make you feel better, and I know it will make me and Driver feel better," said Kyle looking at Driver, who gave the thumbs up.

Driver said, "Well, that settles it, tell me where their apartment is, and we will take care of some business."

"They said it was in Oakland on 7th street, next to Togo's restaurant," Sheri explained.

"I know where you are talking about, be there in no time."

Driver drove to the street she talked about and parked a couple of spaces away from the apartment. The guys got out and started to walk towards the apartment, turned around, and saw Sheri following them.

In hushed tones, Kyle turned to her and said, "Sheri, you cannot come with us. I want you to wait in the car. You should not be moving around. As soon as we take care of this matter, we will take you to the hospital, so please stay in the car?"

"Okay, but you guys, be careful. They are animals. I hate those bastards."

Driver went in first without knocking. He was the only one who was carrying. As they entered, the three hoodlums were sitting around a table laughing and knocking back some whiskey. Kyle came at them quickly and kicked the table over on them as Driver pointed his pistol at all three of them.

"I hear you guys are pretty bad, bad boys. Is that right?"

"You are so tough it takes three of you to bodily attack a woman," Kyle added.

Driver held the gun toward their faces. "They not only sexually abused her boss, but they also beat her up. What low lives do that?"

Kyle jumped in. "Driver, the low lives are standing right in front of us, and I know what we should do to them, you know, let's have a rape party but just with the animals."

"Sounds good to me," Driver said. "Well then, let's party. You three stand over by the doorway. I want you to take your pants off and stand under the doorway with your arms up, got it?"

The three did as they were told, looking scared. Driver got them tied up with their arms over their heads, standing with only their underwear on and not being able to get loose.

Good timing as Sheri entered the apartment. "Oh my goodness, you got the bastards," she said, looking right at the three men who had attacked her.

Kyle reached over in the corner with a smile on his face, picked up a baseball bat, and handed it to Sheri. "There is your revenge sweetheart, do what makes you feel good."

With that, she took the bat, walked up to the first one that raped her, looked him right in the eye, and with a big swing, landed the bat right between his legs, knocking his balls to his throat. The screaming was unbelievable as Sheri looked at Kyle and smiled after her first swing of the bat. Kyle looked over at Driver and motioned that it was time for them to leave, revenge was being served, and one angry woman was at the right end of the bat, getting her anger out and making her feel a whole lot better. Driver smiled at Kyle, knowing what they took the time to do would make a big difference in her life, and for that, they both were happy.

Kyle looked at Driver and said, "Let's head for Camellia. Our job is done here."

"You got it, boss, but can we stop and get me some pants first?" Kyle laughed and nodded, and they both exited the apartment.

Camellia was docked in the San Francisco Bay estuary on Alameda Island, where the docks were. They drove from the suburbs to the city and then across the Oakland Bay Bridge to the tunnel that connected the island to Oakland. The limousine pulled up to the ship, three hundred feet long used for a troop carrier during WWII.

"She has eight decks going down to the engine room, and she does not sail anymore, just floats here for parties," Driver explained to Kyle.

They walked up the stairs on the outside of the ship and then on to the main deck. She sure is a massive ship, thought Kyle, as the crew chief greeted them.

"We are honored to have you aboard, Mr. Stone, and we would like to welcome you to the Family," the chief said and, with that, handed Kyle a diamond-encrusted Rolex watch. Kyle was astonished at how beautiful and expensive the watch was.

"I thank you very much. She is gorgeous. You caught me by surprise."

"On behalf of all the Family, you are welcome. I understand that besides you, there is also a special guest joining us?"

Kyle, still looking at the Rolex, said, "Yes, Miss Lang will be joining us. Did you get my request for lobster for dinner and then eggs Benedict for brunch?"

"Sure did boss. I also have a few other surprises for you to enhance your dining experience."

Kyle went up to the bridge to the office's quarters where he would be staying. It was like a small apartment with couches, tables, dining tables, and the bunk area. They had all the tables covered with white linens, and everything else was spit and polish, ready for a king.

The next morning, Kyle worked out at the hotel gym, looking forward to seeing Yvonne for brunch at the Buena Vista.

They had met under the worst circumstances with the witches' candles, the takeover, and of course, David turning evil on them. If any couple could find love where it was not supposed to exist, there was certainly reason to explore something good. He knew this was the reason he was anxious to see her again, even though he was not looking for a serious relationship after just divorcing his wife and starting his new career. He did not need a full-time distraction.

He headed down the stairs to the limo, and he could not help looking at his new watch. They did not know how much he loved jewelry, especially watches. There was one exception: the medallion he wore around his neck showing his ancestor, the founder of the Knights Templar. He did not know why, but he felt more secure when he wore it. He would take all the protection he could get. Kyle only wished that his dad would have told him about his forefathers earlier. It might have protected him from some of the bad decisions he made and would like to take back.

It was now time to start to head over to Yvonne's apartment in Pacific

Heights, and there might be a lot of traffic going back across the Oakland Bay Bridge into the city. She lived in a nice place with a view of the bay and Alcatraz. If there ever was a lover of the city, it was Yvonne, and, with the perspective she had, you could see why.

Kyle dressed in Dockers, a casual shirt, and deck shoes. He felt a little giddy as he walked up to her door, like going on a first date. That had not happened in twenty years. As he waited for her to come to the door, he looked at the view. It was like a magnet to the eyes. Just like Yvonne when she opened the door, as beautiful as he remembered, even though he had just seen her a week or so ago.

Yvonne said, "Come on in. I want you to see my apartment. I love it here."

Kyle looked out the window. "I guess you would love it, Yvonne. It's fabulous."

"Would you like a beer? I have Heineken and Sierra Nevada."

"A Heineken would be great, thanks." Sitting back on the couch, Kyle asked, "How long have you lived here?"

"It's been about three years now, and I don't ever want to move," she said, smiling.

"I can see why. These kinds of apartments are in big demand," Kyle said, finishing his beer. "I am anxious to take you to the ship and see what you think. We have a fabulous dinner planned for us tonight, but first, let us have some champagne at the Buena Vista. No, I think I want one of their Irish whiskeys with some linguini and eggs. I woke up hungry, I think!"

"That sounds great. I want to talk to you about the financial business and what your plans are with it."

"Not a problem. Why don't we start over at the Buena Vista, and we can discuss it in the limo."

It was a beautiful day in the Bay Area, with soft, fluffy clouds floating by against a bright blue sky. It will be a great day, thought Kyle, as they sat at the restaurant and enjoyed each other's company very much.

Yvonne was easy to get along with, always with a smile on her face, and when he was with her, she made him feel like the most crucial person in the room. Kyle had never been around anyone like this, and he was starting to like it. They were just coming out of the Alameda Tunnel that went under the bay when he looked at Yvonne, enjoying the ride with a fresh glass of champagne in her hand, and her other hand reached out to hold his. Kyle was finding out that she liked to touch and show affection, and he liked that. How great to be on the way to a fabulous ship with a crew that was there just to make sure she and Kyle had everything they wanted. Could it be time for Kyle to find that happiness he had been looking for? And if he were fortunate, he could find love again. The limo pulled up to one of the largest ships docked in the estuary.

"Wow, Kyle, is this it? It's huge."

"Huge it is. It belongs to the Family, and it used to be a troop carrier during WWII, and now it is used by the Family as a getaway for members. Let us go aboard."

The crew chief was waiting for them on the main deck with two crystal glasses of bubbling champagne.

"Welcome, Mr. Stone, and a special welcome to your guest, Miss Lang."

Kyle reached for the glass. "Thanks, chief. We are looking forward to enjoying our stay."

"We are excited to have you aboard. Let me show you to your accommodations." The driver had brought their bags aboard and followed them to the officers' deck and quarters. Kyle and Yvonne walked out to the ship's bow to see the great view of the waterway and boats going by. They sat in the deck chairs to take it all in with drinks in hand.

Yvonne said, "I appreciate you taking the time to discuss the financial business with me. I know that you have been quite busy."

"You are quite the sweetheart. It is I who appreciate you for taking over for me. I do not know what I would have done without someone jumping in when I had to leave so suddenly. You are a lifesaver."

"I wouldn't go that far, but I am glad that I could help you, and of course, it has been good for me. The lingerie business was getting to become a downer with a lot of problems. The biggest one is the models not showing up when they were supposed to be there."

"What do you do when they don't show up? That would really piss me off."

"There was only one thing I could do beyond canceling the show. I had to do the modeling."

Kyle smiled. "As far as I am concerned, that would be a good thing coming from someone who enjoys your beauty."

"You are too kind, Kyle, but I wanted to get away from it. That is why I started my company. Well, it sounded like a good thing at the time, but now, you have me doing something different."

"Yes, and I am impressed. Not too many models have the business savvy to take over an existing financial company, especially one that has gone through so much. You are a special lady, Yvonne, and I am happy to be sitting here with you, soaking in your beauty, long blond hair, and that angel face that I can't stop absorbing myself in."

"Kyle, you have always been quite the talker. Can I ask you about what you are doing now, or is that off-limits?"

"No, it is not off-limits, but I need another drink. It is warm out here." Kyle motioned for one of the crew members who were standing near, waiting to be of service. It was not long until he returned with two drinks and a large shrimp cocktail with crab and lobster in it. It looked so good.

Yvonne took a bite out of the seafood cocktail. "You sure know how to live it up, Kyle. This is wonderful."

"I am glad you are enjoying yourself, and I guess you are wondering about this situation, being you were there to see how it all developed. I was not sure myself what I had gotten into after David took the money and left me carrying the bag."

"Well, I was worried about you and what they were putting you through," Yvonne said as she took another bite of the lobster.

"I have to admit, Yvonne, I was a little scared in the beginning, not knowing what they would make me do to pay back the money that was stolen."

"Something good must have happened because look around, and you will see there are people here just to make you happy."

"It is amazing. When they found out about my family, the Knights Templar, they looked at me totally differently. It was like night and day. My father told me that the story he was about to tell me before he died would change my life significantly, and he was right. I only wish he could be here to see all this and to see that he was right."

"I am sure he would be impressed. They are treating you like royalty. I'm sure that cannot be hard to get used to. I know that I am blown away to see all this and who you are now."

"I haven't changed any, Yvonne, just taking it in as it comes and thankful for all that's happening. That is why I told Woody. You remember me talking about him, don't you?"

Yvonne nodded as Kyle continued talking.

"Well, I wanted him to know that the only work I wanted to do for the Family would be work that is helping people, getting rid of bad guys who take advantage of those less fortunate than them, and they make them the victims. Now I could only say that to him after he acknowledged my heritage and how the Family felt about my royalty, as they called it."

"That is great. How long is this going to continue? Is this a permanent situation?"

"At this point, I do not know. I am kind of taking it one day at a time, but it has never been my desire to stay in the Family, but we all know it is nearly impossible to leave after knowing where all the bodies are buried, sort of speaking."

"Sounds good to me. I have no problem enjoying being treated like a princess."

"I am glad you are here. I now implore you to share with me this beautiful sight. Watch as the madam of this evening tips her hat to us as her golden globe says good night for now, and those clouds of earlier that came floating into our lives, no longer to carry rain or usher storms, but add their color of magnificence to our sunset sky."

CHAPTER 23

PERMISSION GRANTED

It was getting late, and dinner would be served soon. They both were relaxing in the luxurious captain's suite, listening to some Huey Lewis and the News, a Bay Area band that was doing well with a couple of albums already out.

Yvonne was the one who told Kyle about them, and she was really into their music. She once told Kyle that of all the men she knew, it would be Huey Lewis that she would choose to marry. So I guess she really liked him, Kyle acknowledged. He also thought that he would like to impress her, and maybe, with his new power, he could set up a meet and greet with him.

The Chief walked into the suite and said, "Dinner will be served in about an hour in the main cabin. Do you want your drinks freshened up? We will be serving a crisp Kendall-Jackson chardonnay with dinner."

Kyle said, "Sounds great, Chief. No hurry, we are enjoying this fabulous caviar and scallops."

At that time, one of the crew members entered the cabin. "Chief, there is a gentleman out by the limo requesting permission to board."

Chief said, "Thanks, we will handle it."

Kyle looked concerned. "Chief, I will check it out and take care of it." "Is there anything you want, Mr. Stone? Are you expecting anybody?"

"No, I am not. That's why I will see who it is." Kyle walked out to the main deck and looked over the railing down at the dock to see who it could be asking for permission to board.

"Holy shit," said Kyle as he looked down the dock, there was the sailboat tied off the bow of the ship... "Permission granted, come on up." Kyle smiled. "Welcome, my friend. Good to see you. I did not know you would be around the estuary."

"I am happy to see you," Mr. S said with a big smile on his face. "I was not sure if I would meet you or not. I wasn't sure you would be here."

"Well, we are here now. Let us celebrate. I have someone special to me who would love to meet you. She is not aware of your visit. She is in the cabin."

"Fantastic, if she is a sweetie of yours, then you know I want to meet her. What is her name?" Both men walked to the cabin.

"Her name is Yvonne, smart and beautiful." Kyle opened the door. "Yvonne, I have someone for you to meet. Come on over here."

Yvonne turned around and started walking to the other end of the cabin.

"Oh my God! No, no, I cannot believe this. Kyle, you should've told me," she said, just about crying. Kyle had a big smile on his face.

"My goodness, Yvonne. Get a hold of yourself, and come here," Kyle said, smiling. "I want to introduce you to Mr. S. I guess she must be one of your biggest fans, with all that?"

"Don't listen to him, darling. I am just as excited to meet you." Mr. S opened his arms to give her a big hug.

"That's great. I am happy this happened. Come and let's have some champagne." They all went over to the couch.

"Now, Kyle, you be quiet, and let me tell her about our experience on my boat."

Kyle looked over at him and smiled. "Go ahead," he said. "Did Kyle tell you about how he saved my life?"

Yvonne had a curious expression on her face. "No, he didn't mention that to me. What happened? You guys got me all concerned."

"Sit right there, gorgeous, and let me tell you a story. We had just left the fuel dock and were heading north to another dock to let Kyle off. The crew was bringing in the lines over the anchor, and I happened to be right there, and one of the lines hit me and knocked me overboard. I was shocked how deep I went in and got scared for my life, not being a good swimmer and all, but there was a current that grabbed me and started to take me down. The guys on deck were looking for the safety rings to throw at me, but Kyle, seeing that I was struggling and could not see me, was so deep below the surface. Kyle, let me tell you, without hesitation, after seeing that I was not surfacing, jumped over the railings with all his clothes on to rescue me."

Yvonne now looked overly concerned about what she was hearing. "Oh my God, are you both all right? Kyle, why did you not tell me?" Mr. S continued, "No, wait, let me tell you what happened next. So,

Kyle is now in the water also, and he is trying to feel for me. I reached for his shoulders to pull myself up, and our eyes locked on like they were talking to each other. I put my shoe into his belt, and with my hand on his shoulder, I pushed as hard as I could to get to the surface. But by stepping into his belt and pushing off, I drove Kyle deeper while I went to the light at the top."

Yvonne said, "You guys are scaring me. Kyle, what happened?"

"Well, pretty much as Mr. S has told you, but while I was looking at Mr. S and being pushed toward the bottom, I was in desperate need of air. I looked down at the darkness to see how deep I was, and for a second, I saw a light, like a candle, in the darkness of the ocean, and suddenly, a gush of air came up, and I rode it to the surface, gasping for air at the top." Both men looked at each other and shook their heads in disbelief at what they had experienced.

Yvonne reached over to hug Kyle. "I can't believe you guys went through this, and Kyle didn't mention it to me."

"I hear you, Yvonne. I love this guy. It was crazy nuts," Mr. S said.

"I'm telling you; we shared something huge out there, and we are both alive to tell the story," Kyle said.

Yvonne gave Kyle a big hug.

"Come on, how about me?" Mr. S held out his arms. "Don't I get a hug? I just about drowned too."

Yvonne reached over to him and gave him a friendly hug, in disbelief that she was hugging and hanging out with Mr. S.

"You know, guys, we should celebrate our good fortune of still being alive. Let us take my sailboat and go over to Tiburon for dinner. There is a great restaurant that we can sail to, and they have a dock right there."

Yvonne smiled, looked over at Kyle for an answer. Kyle said, "I know Yvonne would love to go there. My hesitation is the work these guys have put into a special dinner for us. Do you know what we will do? Let's give this great dinner to the crew. I am sure they would appreciate it." Kyle smiled because he saw the faces of a couple of the crew light up when they heard that they would get the glorious meal prepared for him and his guests.

CHAPTER 24

DISABLED DRIVER

With the afternoon sun starting to hug the towers on Twin Peaks and the gentle breeze touching the bay, the three of them boarded Mr. S's sailboat. It was about seventy-two feet long and gorgeous inside, including a fireplace next to the galley.

Mr. S had invited Linda, one of his sailing companions, for this dinner trip. He gave his crew the night off except for two who would serve the guests. He felt it would be nice if they captained the boat for the evening cruise.

Kyle and Yvonne were busy checking out the boat and the great hors d'oeuvres. The large shrimp were plentiful, along with the best tasting caviar. They both just wanted to eat all the goodies and forget about dinner. Kyle continued to tour the boat with YL, being it was new to her, but she enjoyed it so much. Kyle had been on the boat before in LA, as Mr. S took the helm and motored them out to the bay.

Yvonne asked how long he had been sailing, being he looked so good holding on to the wheel. He told her that he grew up on the water. His parents had sailboats as they grew up in the Pacific Northwest. "Come over here, Yvonne. I want you to take the wheel and help us get out of this side of the bay."

"Okay, I would love to, but don't let me run into anything," she said. With a big smile on her face and the wind blowing her blonde hair, she looked great.

"Hey, Mr. S," said Kyle, "now that you relieved the crew for the night, who is going to get me my TNT?"

Yvonne looked right at Kyle. "I can't believe you spoke to Mr. S that way, Kyle."

"I was just kidding. He knows it. Relax, what do you want? I am heading that way."

"Yvonne, please drop the 'mister' you make me feel so old."

"I am so sorry; it is a habit and out of my respect for you. I will try to remember to do so," YL said, smiling.

With smiles on their faces and the late afternoon upon them, they decided not to put up the sails and just enjoy a leisurely ride enjoying their favorite alcohol. Yvonne was in seventh heaven any time she was cruising on the bay and enjoying all the incredible sights of the city and Alcatraz, and not forgetting all the other boats out enjoying an afternoon of winds, sun, and sailing. It took them about an hour and a half to get to the restaurant next to the dock. They all gathered their things and walked over to the restaurant.

The patrons were all breaking their necks to see Mr. S walking into a private dining room with large windows overlooking the docks and the gorgeous boats. Kyle was pleased because they were serving petrale sole; it was Yvonne's favorite dish. Kyle would have swordfish, the closest thing to a good steak.

The conversation went on for hours, with Yvonne asking most of the questions and Mr. S being so cordial. The conversation turned to the white candle when Yvonne brought it up in explaining how they met. It was an intriguing conversation the two of them were having. Kyle decided to stay out of it and let Yvonne explain how the white candle exploded at the sound of a name and exploded hot wax to cover the blood-written message on the wall, and after the explosion, the candle was still lit. Nobody could explain what had happened, and all were in awe of the story. Kyle just listened again to a story that was so far out there, but he lived it with her.

Kyle looked out the window. "Yvonne, can we change the story? It makes me uneasy. I don't know why but it does. So, if you don't mind, can we move on?"

"You know, Kyle," Yvonne said, "when you talked about the light you saw under the water and then the jet of water that saved you, it kind of made me think about the candle, just saying."

Kyle quickly changed the conversation, thinking of all that had been said and wanting Mr. S to explain more of the workings of the Family to help Yvonne understand. He went ahead and explained his understanding of the Family and how women of lieutenants and captains exist in this man's world. Mr. S explained that most women were thrilled being a part of something so inclusive, and they were given most of what they wanted for themselves and their families. They did this so that the women would be happy and not pressure the men to tell them where they were going and when they would be home. The men in the Family answered to the Family and not their wives or lovers. They were also to respect their wives, and any harassment or abuse was not tolerated. Any guy who disrespected them would have to answer to their immediate supervisor or Woody in Las Vegas.

Yvonne was interested in what he was saying but did not want to seem too anxious, being she and Kyle had just started seeing each other. What she heard, though, was that if she and Kyle got serious with each other, she could not ask him about where he was going or what he had been up to.

She wondered if she could do that in a relationship. It seemed so different from everything she had learned about being with someone and sharing everything they did with each other. She would have to give it a lot of thought if this was going to be their future. Those women who could wrap their heads around this type of relationship would enjoy a want-for- nothing existence as they were treated like princesses. The only bad part of it all was when their man wanted anything, including sex, and it was to be given immediately, and one better act like one loved it and that he was the best lover one ever had. If they could do that, then they were golden.

As the day turned to dark and the diners had eaten their fill, it was time to make the trip back to the mothership, Camellia.

With Mr. S at the helm, they motored out into the bay; the others enjoyed the view of the Berkeley Hills to the left of them and the Oakland Bay Bridge in front of them. It was hard to see because there were no lights on it for some reason, but the beautiful city was gleaming on the hill. Now into the deep waters, Mr. S yelled at Kyle to come to the bridge.

"Hey, I am in the mood for love. Why don't you take the wheel and take us home? I will be downstairs in my cabin." With that, he took off, and Kyle grabbed the wheel, knowing he didn't have enough experience to do what Mr. S wanted him to. It would have been nice if he had asked Kyle first if he could do it safely. Darkness was now upon them, and Kyle was feeling stressed about his new responsibility of getting them all safely to the dock at the estuary.

"Hey Yvonne," he called, "come on over here and take the wheel. I think you should take us home tonight."

Knowing it was a joke, YL laughed and kept smiling, but she felt his stress because Kyle was not shy of sharing it. With tequila and tonic in his left hand, he tried very hard to see whom he was sharing the bay with. It was dark now. There was no moon or stars to light the way. Clouds had come over the Golden Gate Bridge, bringing rougher seas to navigate through.

Mr. S seemed to have no stress about the situation that was about to get even worse with the weather changing the way it was. Alcatraz, now on their port side, was even getting hard to see, and Yvonne was holding on to Kyle's arm, helping him see what was in front of them as they moved swiftly through the darkness.

Yvonne said, "This is getting a little scary, Kyle. Should we get Mr. S to come up and take over?"

"No, not yet just help me pick out the boats that are in our way. I am contending with the currents and rough water."

A huge wave hit their starboard side about that time, pushing the vessel hard as Kyle grabbed the wheel to steady her. They were now approaching the Oakland Bay Bridge, at least that was what Kyle thought it was, considering there were no lights on it. As he looked hard at the bridge, a huge barge, the size of an aircraft carrier, passed right in front of them, causing Kyle to take a hard right on the wheel. Kyle was genuinely concerned.

"Holy shit, Yvonne, did you see that come out of nowhere? We just about hit her straight on."

"You better believe it. I saw it but was so scared. I couldn't say anything.

My words froze in my mouth."

Kyle said, "Well, you are a lot of help. Don't worry, we are just about to go under the bridge, and then it is an easy sail to Camellia."

About that time, Mr. S came up from below decks and asked how things were going with a smile on his face.

"Well, things are simply fine now," Kyle said. "Where were you a few minutes ago when I just about put your boat into the middle of an enormous barge that only had one light in the stern? Things are good now. We are just about to put this baby to bed. I imagine you were consumed in lust down there, being you never checked in with the bridge."

Mr. S laughed, "I had all the confidence in you so that I could enjoy this beautiful woman who shared my cabin and a few other things."

"I am glad you enjoyed yourself while Yvonne and I risked our lives sailing back to Camellia."

"Look at it this way, Kyle. You are now more experienced in sailing.

You can use all that new talent on your next excursion," said Mr. S.

"Thank you so much for your undivided attention while you were mastering my skills."

The joking continued as they put the sailboat to bed and walked over to the limousine.

"Yvonne and I are going to call it a night. I am going to take her to her apartment."

"Sounds good. I enjoyed our time tonight." Mr. S said and turned to Yvonne. "You are such a lovely lady, Yvonne, and I look forward to seeing you again. I am going to camp out on Camellia tonight. Kyle, I will catch up with you later."

They gave each other hugs, and the limo drove away, headed back to San Francisco and that beautiful apartment overlooking the bay.

CHAPTER 25

COMMISSIONER

Kyle woke up overlooking the bay. As he read the San Francisco Chronicle, he sipped a hot cup of coffee laced with some Baileys. It was the time of Mayor Diane Feinstein's administration during a development boom referred to as *'Manhattanizing.'* Skyscrapers sprung up primarily in the Financial District. Along with the skyscrapers, bulky residential high- rise condominiums. A fight was going on about who would get the best view when they finished building these buildings that filled the skyline.

Kyle read about the City, which was getting ready for the 1984 Democratic National Convention, during a particularly uneasy populist. The growth of homelessness was causing a massive problem as they decided how they could hide this large group of down-and-out people. There was no way they wanted the cameras showing them during a time of electing the next best leader.

It was a breezy morning as Kyle watched the boats taking the wind into their sails. Yvonne came out to the patio where Kyle was sitting and brought him a warm-up for his coffee. What a beautiful woman to wake up to, he thought. Driver, who was down below in the parking area, came up to tell Kyle that Woody was on the phone and wanted to talk to him. They both walked back down to the car, and Kyle got into the backseat where the phone was.

"Woody, how are you this beautiful morning, and how can I help you?"

"I am doing fine, thanks, but I can't see the ocean. Listen, I have another mission for you."

"I have the time. Where do I need to go?"

"It is right there in San Francisco. We have a county commissioner who is also a land developer and has been in the news lately because he developed inadequate housing. Because of that, he has had tenants hospitalized. So far, one resident has died due to his shoddy wiring, electrocuted the fellow. He is now sponsoring legislation that would allow him to develop in the earthquake zone, putting many more families at risk. We were hoping you could pay him a visit and convince him to drop the legislation and resign his position. My office will contact you with all the details as usual and what we have started to expect from you, do a professional, clean job. It is always appreciated."

"I am glad you have been happy with my work. This sounds like something right down my pike. I will let you know when I wrap it up and let you know the results."

"Thanks, Kyle. I look forward to hearing back from you."

It was time to wrap it up with Yvonne too. They both needed to get to work. It was a great weekend, and both left feeling a little closer, and the tug on the heart grew a little stronger.

The research had been done, and Kyle found that the commissioner had a place near Coit Tower, overlooking the piers. It was time to put a plan together, and how could he, with the power he had, change this man's mind? What would make him cave in totally? He decided to head over to the Cannery and have one of his favorites while pondering his next job.

Sitting outside the commissioner's house early Tuesday morning, Kyle waited for him to leave, enjoying a great cup of coffee and a pastry. The wait was not very long until he saw the commissioner backing out of his garage. One knew he was important. He had a garage, Kyle thought. With camera in hand, he crept up to the front window to spy on his wife, who was wearing pink slippers with white ears and a shmaltzy T-shirt with a picture of the family on it.

That makes it easy, thought Kyle. He headed outside to the side yard and in the flower patch to investigate the dining room window to see her daughter and a terrier dog playing together. She wore a baby-blue shirt with silver sequins on it. *That should be enough,* thought Kyle as he headed back to his limo.

Having all his ammunition in hand, he headed to the county courthouse where this gentleman had an office. Kyle waited outside of his office and watched as his secretary came out to make sure that there was no one else in there. It took a while for her to come out. Kyle was happy, though. It gave him a chance to catch up on his local news with the *San Francisco Chronicle* lying next to him on the coffee table.

When the secretary appeared, she asked Kyle, "Oh, I didn't know you were out here. How can I help you?"

"No problem," Kyle said, getting up out of his chair. "I have a meeting with the commissioner."

"Well, that must be a mistake. He doesn't have any meetings scheduled." Kyle headed to the office door.

"This meeting is. I guess he didn't tell you about it. Why don't you hold his calls and his coffee? Thank you." Kyle walked right past her and into the office, closing the doors behind him.

The commissioner saw Kyle approach his desk and quickly got out of his chair and stood with his hands on his hips.

"Who the hell are you, and why did you just walk in here?"

Kyle smiled. "Let's do the first question first. My name is of no concern to you, and the answer to the second question—I am here to convince you to cancel the vote on allowing new substandard developments in earthquake zones in the city."

"I am going to ask you one more time what your name is, and then I am calling security."

"Why don't you take a seat first and put the phone down, and I will explain my need to be here with you at this time."

The commissioner, a large man, looked Kyle directly in the eyes as he was putting the phone down. Kyle was always in control.

"You see, Commissioner, you have pushed some people the wrong way, and we have to fix that. The way we fix that is to have you stop the vote."

"…hang on a minute–"

"Quiet, I am talking. Perhaps my card will help." Kyle handed his card to him.

The commissioner looked at it and then threw it on his desk. "You think that this little card will make me change my mind?"

"No, well, yes, for some people, but that is a different story. In your situation, I think there needs to be more. I was fortunate to be able to have a cup of coffee outside your house this morning. Your view is to die for."

The commissioner shuffled in his seat, turning a shade paler than when Kyle entered his office.

"What the hell are you doing around my house? If you mess with my family—"

"You'll do what? Shut up and listen. I am trying to talk about your wife and how cute I thought her pink slippers were, especially those fluffy white ears, and you are taking all the fun out of it. Fun, now that is what your daughter was having with her terrier. We can do this the easy way or the way you and I don't want to, you see," Kyle said, now getting his mean look on. "You messed up and pissed off some nasty people. By showing you these pictures should make you realize this is a dire situation. Let me make it clearer. You do as I say from here on out, or you will not see your family again. Now you take my card and those pictures, and hopefully, you will see it my way. Now, what is more important? Your family or the silly vote? Commissioner, I forgot to give you one more picture. Here, these are the guys outside your house waiting for my call. So do I make the call, or do you? You are not looking so good, Commissioner."

With sweat on his brow, the big man stared at the card when Kyle took it from him.

"What will it be? Tear up this card, and your family disappears, or you pick up the phone now and cancel the vote. The clock is ticking."

The commissioner looked at Kyle, knowing he had lost this one, picked up the phone, and made the call that ended the vote. Then he picked up his briefcase and walked out of his office. He later resigned from his position. Kyle, now outside the office, called his guy at the house.

"This is Kyle. Go ahead and pay the two homeless guys, and thank them for helping us out," Kyle headed down the escalator with a big smile on his face. Mission accomplished. Kyle was happy to solve the commissioner problem and needed to check in with Woody and give him the information and results.

From back in the limo, Kyle dialed up Woody. "Hi, boss, the job with the commissioner has been handled. He has seen it our way and has canceled the vote."

"That is amazing. You impress me, Kyle," Woody said. "These jobs usually take weeks to close, and you have been doing it in a matter of days. You are going to have to hang there in the city. I didn't expect you to be available so soon. I will be back in touch. Have a good time. You have earned it."

CHAPTER 26

JOIN ME FOR DINNER

What a beautiful day in the city. Kyle lay in the grass by the Cannery, looking over the bay with a Payne Mason cigar and a shot of Don Julio 70 tequila from his flask. A great place to watch people, Kyle thought as he observed all the different nationalities walking by. It was like the United Nations.

There were several swimmers in the water. He heard that they came out early in the morning and had their daily swim in the freezing bay water. They must be nuts, he thought.

He had put in a call to Yvonne, wanting to know if she could meet him for dinner, as he would be around for a few days. His driver was reading a book and was going to let him know if she called, and sure enough, he motioned to Kyle that there was a phone call for him. Kyle went over to the limousine and took a call in the back seat.

"This is Kyle. Can I help you?"

"Hey, you, what are you still doing in the city? I thought you would be in Vegas by now." It was good to hear Yvonne's voice.

"Well, I got done early with my job, and I was wondering if you would meet me for dinner tonight?"

"You are assuming that I don't already have a date for tonight," she teased.

"I was just taking my chances, and it sounds like you might be available?"

"Yes, I would love to have dinner with you. Do you have a place in mind?"

"Yes, I hope you don't mind. I already made reservations at Scoma's Sausalito."

"You are pretty sure of yourself, aren't you?"

"Well, if you weren't going to be able to make it, I was going to have dinner there anyway. Alone." Kyle smiled. "I can have my driver pick you up around seven. Does that work for you?"

Yvonne now smiled at herself. "Yes, I am looking forward to seeing you. See you tonight."

Kyle had his driver take him back to the boat where he had been staying. He decided to rest a bit before his date with Yvonne. He was sure about having strong feelings about her in such a short period but was trying to figure out why this was happening. He didn't want a relationship after coming out of a failed marriage, but he could not stop his feelings for her. Kyle moped around, acting like a kid. He could not believe how long the time dragged while he was waiting for his date to begin.

He showered and dabbed on Lagerfeld cologne, hoping that Yvonne would like it. Not soon enough for Kyle, he was on his way to the city to pick her up and then head over to Sausalito for dinner.

He stood at her door with flowers in his hand and rang the bell.

"I am here to pick up the most beautiful girl in the city, and these are for her."

"Come on in. I love the flowers. Do you want a drink, or should we get on over there?" Yvonne said with a big smile. She looked so good.

"The driver is double-parked, so I think we should go to Scoma's."

The two of them left her apartment and locked the door, got into the limousine, champagne, and brandy available to wet their palates on the ride through the city out to the Golden Gate Bridge and then through the tunnel into Sausalito. It was a beautiful night with millions of stars lighting up the sky. Kyle asked his driver to open the sunroof above them in the back seat, so they could see the stars as they talked and laughed and nibbled on some of the best caviar. They pulled up to the restaurant, and the driver opened the door for both of them. They went in to be seated.

"Good evening, my name is Kyle Stone, and I have a reservation for seven-thirty."

The hostess looked at her reservation book.

"We are pleased to have you tonight, Mr. Stone. If you would follow me, your table is over here." Big windows showed the light reflecting on the water with the city in the background.

"Stunning," the both of them said as they walked to their table, which was discreetly situated in the corner, nowhere near the other diners.

"Michael will be your server tonight, and he will be right with you." "Thank you. We will want to have a cocktail."

"I will let him know."

Yvonne was taking in the view and smiling like an angel. Kyle felt so lucky to be out with her. He could never get tired of looking at her, and she was so darn sweet. The server came up to the table with a magnum of Dom Perignon.

"Mr. Stone, this is with the compliments of Woody and his wishes for a great evening tonight."

Kyle held the bottle.

"That is very kind of him. If he were here, we would thank him." Yvonne held on to her champagne glass while the server poured her and Kyle a glass.

"I must say, this is an impressive way to start the dinner, Kyle."

"Well, let me raise my glass to your beauty and how happy I am to be here having dinner with you with the view of the city, the beauty of the bay at night, and a lovely white candle on our table." Yvonne looked around.

"You know, if you look at the other tables, they don't have any white candles."

"That is very strange. I will ask what is up with the only candle in the restaurant being on our table, and you know, Yvonne, it seems that every time the white candle is around, there is trouble, or maybe it is just warning us of imminent evil. Anyway, back to the menu, what are you in the mood for tonight? I checked to see if they had fresh petrale, and they do if you are interested."

"That is extremely sweet of you. It sounds perfect for tonight."

The two talked about the financial business and how it was doing; they rehashed all the things that had transpired since David went crazy and stole the money, and life changed for both of them. As the night went by, a fine dinner was had, and Kyle and Yvonne were starting to get serious and not afraid to show each other their emotions, especially Yvonne. She was very touchy, and Kyle liked to have a woman touch him behind his neck and hold his hand. Shows of affection were greatly appreciated.

The limousine was waiting outside for them when they exited the restaurant. They climbed into the back, and they were on their way back to Yvonne's apartment in the city. As they started to leave Sausalito, they could see a great view of the bay and docks behind them. They were coming up upon the tunnel that led to the Golden Gate Bridge, and as they entered it, Kyle said, "Sweetheart, could you get me some ice? I am in the mood for a nightcap. How about you?"

Yvonne left his side and moved over to the center of the limo where the ice was.

"Holy shit! What the hell…" Yvonne looked back to see what the noise was. Lying next to her was a three-foot boulder covered in glass and blood. It sounded like the whole world came crashing down, the sound of shattering glass and metal parts flying all over the place, but worst of all, Kyle lay in the seat with blood gushing out of his head.

Yvonne screamed, not believing what she was seeing. The limo pulled over. She grabbed her sweater and put it on the gash on Kyle's head to try and stop the bleeding.

"What the hell happened, Yvonne? What do you see?" The driver took off, spinning his wheels, heading for the closest hospital.

"There's a large rock that came down through the skylight. Lord have mercy, he will not stop bleeding from his head, and he is unconscious. I am so scared," she said, wiping tears from her face and firmly pressing the sweater on the large gash that was soaked with Kyle's blood.

"Hurry, hurry, he can't die," she yelled desperately to the driver.

The limo sped over the bridge into the city, running lights and stop signs. The driver was doing all he could do to get Kyle to the hospital as fast as possible. A police car pulled up next to him and motioned for him to follow him with lights and sirens on. They quickly arrived at the San Francisco Memorial. Kyle was rushed in on a gurney with Yvonne and the driver running next to him.

Yvonne was flecked with blood and still crying. She could not stop herself. What happened was so unbelievably surreal. She and Driver were both asked to wait outside as they started to work on Kyle to save his life. He has lost a lot of blood. Yvonne and the driver sat in the waiting room, unable to speak at first, the effects of shock setting in.

Driver asked Yvonne, "I can't believe how shaken up I am. What the hell happened? It seemed like when I exited the tunnel, the boulder crashed through the roof."

"Kyle asked me to get some ice, and as I reached over, all hell broke loose back there. Out of nowhere, this large boulder came crashing down through the roof. The skylight shattered when the rock crashed through it, and then it hit Kyle on the right side of his head."

The driver was also shaken up but not nearly as bad. "There is something not right with what just happened. I know that tunnel area pretty well, and I can't see how a large rock falls at the same time we are passing underneath."

"What are you saying? You think that this was not an accident?

Someone was waiting for us?"

"I don't know, Yvonne, but I am going to go back up there to see if something like this could've happened. Or there possibly might be some footprints of the person who dropped the rock on us?"

Yvonne grabbed another tissue. "Okay, I will stay here and wait for some news. Do you think I should call the police?"

"No, no cops, I will handle it. You let me know. Call the car as soon as you hear anything."

"I will, and you be careful. Kyle was talking about something bad happening, a warning when we were in the restaurant."

As soon as the driver left, Mr. S came through the doors.

"Yvonne," he said, hugging her. "How is he? What the hell happened to you guys? I heard from the nurses that a boulder smashed through the roof of the limo and hit Kyle?"

"That pretty much is what happened. I was reaching for some ice that Kyle asked for, so it didn't hit me. Our driver went back out to the tunnel. He is not sure it was an accident."

"Holy shit, it might not be an accident. Wow, how bad is Kyle?"

"He was knocked unconscious and has a huge gash on the right side of his head, and he has lost a lot of blood."

The doctor saw the two of them talking and walked up to them. "I am Dr. Johnstown."

"Oh, Doctor, how is Kyle?" Yvonne asked.

"He has woken up. That is a good thing, but he has lost a lot of blood and is weak. There is also a problem with his right eye. He might lose sight in that eye, and we are closing up the gash on his head and giving him some transfusions to get his blood count up."

"Can we see him?" asked Mr. S.

"No, not yet. We will let you know as soon as possible, and I have a private waiting room for you. It's just around the corner."

As they followed the doctor, Yvonne thanked him for everything. About an hour and a half went by, and the driver came into the private waiting room. Yvonne approached him. "What did you find up there, anything?"

Mr. S now stood next to them. "I heard you thought this might not be an accident?"

"Well, I went back there and took a look, and sure enough, there were fresh footprints right where the rock came down on us."

Yvonne sat back down, and the two others moved over to the corner of the room, away from Yvonne.

Mr. S asked, "Okay, tell me what you are thinking. Who would want to do this to Kyle?"

"The only thing I can think of is we just finished a job against one of the county commissioners, and he might have done this as payback. Don't worry, Mr. S, I will get to the bottom of this, and we will do this without the cops."

"Of course, is there anything I can do to help?"

"No, just stay here, and take care of Yvonne and let me know as soon as you know anything more."

The driver left the hospital, and Mr. S sat down with Yvonne, who was still terribly upset. Another two hours went by, and Dr. Johnstown came into the waiting room.

"We have good news. It looks like he will not lose sight in his right eye, and we are cautious that he will not slide back into a coma. Go ahead and see him. Just take it slow with him. He has been through quite an ordeal."

"Thanks, Doctor, we understand." Mr. S and Yvonne went into Kyle's room, and he was lying there with bandages covering his whole head and an eye patch over his right eye. Yvonne, with more tears streaming down her cheeks, said, "Oh my God, Kyle, are you going to be alright? I am so worried."

"It looks worse than it is, and, Mr. S, how did you get here so fast?"

"I told you that I would never be far from you. Your driver doesn't think that this was an accident. You know, he went back up there and found footprints where the rock came down."

"That doesn't surprise me. Lying here, I was thinking to myself, how could a rock come down from there when there aren't any rocks in that area?"

Yvonne got into the conversation, "Do you have any idea who would have done this to you?"

"Yes, I do, and I am sure we will get to the bottom of this."

"We will find the son of a bitch," said Mr. S. "And there will be a high price to pay for whoever did this, and that is all I am going to say about that."

"You guys are starting to scare me. Is this an example of how it is going to be, Kyle?"

"There is a downside to it all, that is for sure," said Mr. S.

Yvonne sat by the bed, a look of concern on her face. "We were having a great time, partying and enjoying all the perks, but if this can happen again, and maybe next time, it is worse. I don't know, Kyle. This scares the hell out of me."

Kyle listened to all the concerns. "Well, sweetheart, I don't think we can do anything about it for now."

Mr. S jumped in. "I told you, Kyle, that if there is anything you want me to do for you, I will. I told you this after you saved my life."

"What are you talking about? Can you get him out?" Yvonne asked.

"It's just as I said, Yvonne and Kyle, you want out. I will make it happen."

"Kyle, you have to do this. Let S get you out. You must. I am starting to fall in love with you."

"I can also get you into the entertainment business with me if you wanted to," Mr. S smiled. With that, the door opened, and the doctor came in.

"I am sorry. He is going to need his rest now."

Yvonne leaned over the bed, kissed Kyle, and gave him a big hug.

CHAPTER 27

UPSIDE DOWN

They all left Kyle's room genuinely concerned about him and how this could have happened. Yvonne was on the phone with her office, and in the corner were Mr. S and the driver in a serious discussion.

Mr. S said, "We need to get to the bottom of how and who did this. I do not want Woody to hear about this. He would go crazy with an army of men ready to do some serious damage. The best way to handle it with Woody is to handle the problem before you tell him about the problem."

Driver looked out the window. "Well, I think that we have a good lead with the commissioner. There is no other person that I know of who would try to kill Kyle. I also think that you should not get any more involved in case the press gets a hold of this. They seem to know everything you do."

"I would have to agree with you. Do you know who to get to help you? I don't want you to do this by yourself, and I don't think Kyle would either."

"Yes, I do have someone who has worked with us before and can be trusted. We will have to pay him though."

"Not a problem, I will handle it. You tell me how much."

"I will. Let me set up a meeting this afternoon, and I will be in touch with you afterward."

"Sounds good. Let us get on this right away and determine if the commissioner was the one involved, or if not, then who?"

Yvonne walked up to the two men, and their discussion came to an end. "Don't let me stop you, boys, from planning whatever you are planning."

"It's okay. We are done. How about I take you to lunch?" Mr. S said. "I would love that. I am so worried about Kyle."

"I know, and we all are."

Driver wasted no time setting a meeting up with Stan Walker, whom he worked with previously on projects. Stan agreed of work with Driver, and they discussed a plan, but it would be based on getting the truth from the commissioner. About the time they talked about when to do this, Driver got a call from Mr. S.

"Hey, can you get back to the hospital? Kyle is awake, and he wants to talk to you."

"Sure, not a problem. Be there in twenty." Driver wrapped up his meeting, and they agreed to meet again after seeing Kyle.

Kyle had had a lot of sleep and was not drugged with meds. He wanted to know what was going on with this boulder coming through his window. Driver walked through the hospital door as Kyle was getting ready to have this discussion. When Driver came into Kyle's room, they were the only two in the room, and that was precisely what Kyle wanted.

"Shut the door, please, and thanks for coming back to talk with me," Kyle said as he sat up in his bed. Driver sat next to the bed.

"How are you feeling? Are you getting better?"

"Yes, I am, thanks for asking. I have some internal injuries, and as soon as they are better, I will get out of here."

"Good news. What did you want to discuss this morning?"

"I have been lying here, trying to think who would want me dead and who would know that I was going to go through the tunnel at that time. The only one I can think of would be the commissioner whom I just met. So here is what I want you to do for me. Pick him up outside his office or home and take him to the tunnel. I want you to ask him if he did this and stay with it until he confesses. Then here is what I want you to do," Kyle instructed him.

Driver got his orders and met up with his associate Stan and put their plan into action. They had staked out the Comish's house as he had quit his job with the county. Behind his house near Coit Tower was an alley, so they waited for him to drive into his garage. Then they would grab him with a bag over his head and a 9-millimeter in his side. After a little investigative work, it was determined that he would be home around two- thirty that afternoon, and that would be a good time to grab him. Driver waited in the limo with the back door open, and Stan hid in the garage, waiting to pick up the package. As predetermined, the Comish pulled up at the exact time they anticipated, got out of his car, and Stan was right there, with a gun to his side.

Stan said, "Now take it easy, and all will be okay. I will put this bag over your head, and if you don't do anything silly, my gun will go back in its holster. Got it? Slow down, dog. Don't make me use it."

"Okay, okay, what do you want?" The Comish stopped struggling. "Just come with me. There is a car in the alley waiting for us."

Stan put him in the back seat as Driver pulled out of the alley. "Leave the bag on his head until we get there."

"Get where?"

"You shut up. We will tell you what we want you to know." Driver went back to the Sausalito tunnel and parked where he had before when he first came up there to see if he could find any evidence of anyone being up there.

"Okay, Stan, I will get the pulleys out of the trunk, grab him, and let's see what he knows."

"Sure thing, leave the bag on?" "Where are you taking me?"

Stan pushed the pistol into his side again. "All you do is what I tell you. Now get out of the car and start walking up the hill, or we can leave you right here."

Driver from the back of the car said, "Yes, leave the bag on, and I will meet you up there." The three of them walked up the left side of the tunnel. A slight path seemed to be visible. At the top, Stan and Driver looked down to see all the traffic going by.

"Go ahead and take the bag off his head. I want him to see all the traffic moving by so fast down below." Stan did as he was told.

The Comish said, "What the fuck are we doing up here?"

Driver replied, "Well, we were going to ask you that question. Do you know of any reason we should be up here? And let me warn you, you might not want to lie to me, and that is a stern warning you need to heed if you know what is good for you. Stan, give me the gun and get the pulley system on the ground and let's get that set up."

"Sure thing, boss."

The Comish, a large man, looked around at all that was going on and saw all the traffic below. "What is it you want from me? Damn it!"

"What's the matter? Are you getting scared? Stan, do you have the pulleys up yet?"

"Just finishing them, not sure it can hold his weight, though."

The Comish looked up at Stan with these big eyes. "Okay, you guys are scaring the hell out of me. Tell me what you want. I want to get out of here, please."

"Well, it is like this," Driver said. "You, or someone you ordered, threw a boulder off this very spot onto my limousine with my boss in it, and now you must pay or tell us the true story and all those involved."

"I don't know what you are talking about. You have the wrong guy. I swear it—I've never even met you."

"Well, Comish, I am not in the mood for games, so here is what is going to happen. Stan will tie your hands behind your back, and we are also going to tie your legs together. Then, my friend, we are going to lower you headfirst into the tunnel; that one down there, got it?"

"You are fucking crazy. Do you know who I am?"

Driver and Stan both started cracking up. "Listen, you fucking idiot, do you know who we are?" Stan retorted.

"Listen, Stan, let's get going. He wants to be an asshole. Let's let him be an upside-down asshole." Stan tied his legs and hands and then turned to Driver, "Should I put the bag back on him?"

Driver said, "Yes, let's do that so he cannot see what is coming to hit him. Also, gag him but wait first. Dickhead, you ready to tell me who threw the boulder off this cliff?"

"Fuck you guys," spat the Commissioner.

"Okay, let's do this. Gag him, and then let's lower him down." With hands and legs tied. The two men lowered the poor bastard over the cliff so that he was hanging headfirst. "Be careful, Stan. Let's not kill him yet. We have to have some fun first."

The Comish was hanging to not interfere with the vehicles passing underneath, and they kept lowering him so that he could hear and feel the air as the cars and trucks flew by.

"Okay, Stan, let's bring him up and see what he has to say. Hopefully, he will be very talkative." Both of them pulled up the ropes. He was heavy, and both had to get involved in doing it. Once on top, they took the bag off his face and pulled his gag down under his chin.

"Holy shit, what happened to you?" Driver asked. The Comish looked like death ran over him, so pale even though he was upside down, eyes large like he had the hell scared out of him.

"Okay, let us try this again. Did you or someone you ordered throw the boulder off the cliff?"

"Yes, I did it. I am so sorry. Please believe me, please. I have a family.

I promise never to do anything like that again. Really, I am sorry." "That is enough. If you only would have told us earlier, we could

not have had to go through all this hanging around. So now, you have confessed to doing the deed and just about killing my boss, but I still have a problem, though."

"I told you what you wanted to know. Just please let me go," he pleaded.

Driver looked at Stan and carried on speaking. "You see, someone had to tell you that my limo was leaving Scoma's so that you would be ready to do your deed and try to kill my boss. So, you see, I need some more information from you. Who called you from the restaurant? Tell me now."

"I said I have already told you everything."

"Damn, this is a stubborn son of a bitch. Okay, let us do it differently this time. We are going to let him see the cars and big trucks coming at him as we lower him up and down."

They grabbed the ropes and lowered him down again. Driver held the rope with a big smile on his face. "Well, how is it down there, Comish? Do you see the cars and trucks? Well, maybe we can help you and lower you a little closer. Down, Stan. Wouldn't it be funny if a truck took his head off, and all we do is pull up a body and no head? That's funny."

The Comish was dangling and like a floundering out of water and, of course, yelling his ass off as vehicles sped beneath him.

"Look, Driver, he is giving the cars a car wash." Driver looked down to see what Stan was talking about. The Comish had peed his pants, and it was trickling down onto the traffic below. Driver still watched him.

"Okay, down some more, and then pull him up quickly when I say so." He carefully watched, so he did not have a headless body to deal with.

"Okay, now pull him up." As Stan did that, Driver watched as a truck just missed the hands and head of their dangling guest.

"Okay, Stan, bring him up. I am sure he is ready to tell all we want to know. Have you ever seen a grown man cry and weep, totally spent? Take the bag off. Comish that was awful, wasn't it? I am sure you don't want to do that again, do you? All that pee was trickling in your face."

"No, no, I don't. Please untie me, and I will tell you what you want to know."

"Stan, go ahead and untie him. I think he wants to tell us something." They untied the Comish with his pants stained in urine and his cheeks red from crying, and they put him in the limo. He could hardly walk; he was so shaken up.

"Now that you are safe and sound tell me who at the restaurant told you I was leaving in the limo?"

The Comish, totally beaten, said, "It was one of the busboys. I paid him to call me when your party left the restaurant. What are you going to do to him? Please don't hurt him."

"Give me the name of the lad. I need to pay him a visit. Now, Comish, what I do to him is none of your business. What is your business? We will drop you off, and you will never speak about this to anyone. I mean, anyone, you got it? If you do, you will think what just happened to you was like a walk in the park. Do you believe me?"

"Yes, I believe. Please let me go, please. I won't say anything."

"Okay, get out there. It has been fun, and if you want more of this fun, do not be a believer, and we will be back. Do you believe it? Tell me, Comish, do you believe?"

"Yes, yes, I am a believer," he said as he started crying. "Okay, Stan, let him out."

Now, they moved down the highway back toward the hospital.

"Driver, that was crazy. Who came up with this punishment to get to the truth? It was unbelievable," Stan said.

"When I went back to the hospital and met with Kyle, he is the one who came up with this plan. It was insane, wasn't it?"

"Insane, yes, it was. What a great plan. I don't know if I could have ever thought of that. I guess that is why he is your boss. My hat's off to him."

CHAPTER 28

DO NOT SHOOT US DOWN

The day had been worthwhile so far for Driver and Stan. They could not wait to get to the hospital and let Kyle know that they found out who had tried to kill him. Driver went through the hospital doors and headed for Kyle's room. When he got there, Mr. S was already there and talking with Kyle.

Mr. S spoke first, "Hey, Driver, any news on who did this?"

"Yes, Stan and I had a good afternoon, but it was Kyle's plan that made the difference."

"Tell us who did it, and of course, tell us how you got the information."

"Okay, I will. It was as we thought. The commissioner was the one who threw the boulder down, and someone at Scoma's tipped him off. He said the busboy called him when I left the restaurant. I will deal with him."

Kyle sat up on the bed. "Did my plan to extract the information work?

Well, I guess it did, being as you just told us who did it."

"No, you're right. Your master plan worked so well. You should have seen him after we brought him back up. He had peed all over his pants and was crying like a baby."

Mr. S said, "Damn, I wish I could stick around and hear more about this great plan initiated, but I have a production meeting I must attend. I will catch up with you later, Kyle."

"All right, S, I'll see you later. Keep dry out there. Hey, Driver, pull up a chair. Let's chat for a minute."

"Sure, Mr. Stone." Driver pulled up the chair. "What is on your mind?"

"I just wanted a chance to talk to you and learn something new about you. Tell me, how did you get involved in this establishment, and why do you go by the name 'Driver'?"

"It's a long story."

"Not a problem. I will be here for a while. I am a captive audience. Go ahead."

"I guess it started with my brother. He worked in Portland as an activist, and I think he was working for George Soros. It seems that he got hooked up with the wrong people and got into some serious problems. Our uncle was in the Family, and our mother gave him a call, and I guess it was decided to help him out with the debt, he would become a driver for my uncle."

"So that was the connection?"

"Yes, but while driving for my uncle, he got into a crash and was killed. I was just turning twenty-one and was offered to take over after my brother died."

"I am sorry to hear about your brother. That is too bad."

"So, I have been driving for a few years now, and everyone kept calling me Driver. Where is the driver? Have you seen the driver and so on. So I just took the nickname, and it stuck!"

"Did you say you spent time in the military?"

"I wanted to, Mr. Stone, but the way things happened took away my chances while I was young. What about you? I heard that you were the youngest officer to be commissioned. Is that true?"

"At the time, Driver, it was true. I don't know about now, though."

"I think I would have liked the military. Did you see any action while you were in?"

Kyle looked right at him, "Boy did I! Let me tell you about a couple of times I just about got my ass shot off. It would come after a long day on patrol in the I Corps. I had thirteen men with me, and we were heading into a valley that was known to have North Vietnamese strongholds in this region," Kyle continued to tell him. "As we made a right turn around this giant rock, small-arms fire crackled in the air as the bullets ricocheted off the rock. We immediately hit the ground to see where this was coming from so that they could return fire. Corporal Grace took two men to set up the right perimeter, and Sergeant Casey did the same for the left perimeter. The firing of 50 caliber machine guns was nonstop as the rest of the patrol hid behind the large rock they passed coming into the valley. I checked in with Sergeant Casey to see if there was any room for the patrol to move to before initiating a counterattack. As soon as he hung up the field phone, a large explosion was on the right perimeter. Sounds of screams filled the air as I made my way over there. Out of the jungle came Private Horn on fire, screaming in tremendous pain as he ran toward me and two others. The smell was horrifying. Once they reached him, they put him on the ground, put the fire out over 3/4 of his body, and administered morphine immediately to quieten his screams. I left one of his men with Horn and took the other soldier to where the men were attacked to see if they were all right.

"Moving into the jungle, they could see where the explosion of the mortar shell had hit, and fifteen feet to the left were the bodies of Corporal Grace and Private Shell. Dead. One lay without an arm and an open bloody gash to his stomach. Bodies were scattered everywhere, some bleeding, some already dead—the outcome of this horrible attack on the patrol. The small-arms fire and the mortar shells kept coming in as we were getting dog tags from those who had been killed. It was time to make a decision: back out of the valley and head to a landing zone. It was time to get the hell out of there before we were all killed. I wouldn't say I liked retreating from a fight, but we were severely outnumbered for this one, and there were no troops in the area to help in the fight. A decision had to be made, and I made it, saving the lives of all the rest, I thought. I sent the word out, spread the word that as soon as the chopper got close to the ground, start running and jump in. Do not hesitate. We didn't have a lot of time.

"Sergeant Grace shouted to me, 'Captain, are we going to make it?' Captain Kyle Stone, the youngest officer commissioned, shouted back, 'Stay strong, Grace, the men need your leadership, now just get the men on board.'

"As the order was given to run for the doors of the hovering aircraft just four feet off the ground, the smell of gunpowder filled the air. I tried so hard to get all my men in so they could get the hell out of there as fast as we could. Any more time on the ground would only mean more dead soldiers. As we lifted off, we became a bigger target for the North Vietnamese we could now see on the hill. Anxiety was so intense as we watched the ground get farther away. We tried to relax and take a deep breath the farther we got from the ground, but the bigger our smiles meant, the bigger target we became.

"Corporal Hastings spoke up, 'Captain Stone, what are you going to do when you get home?' thinking all was good and we would be home soon. Stone looked out and saw a hot missile heading their way, his stomach dropped. An explosion as the tail section was hit by an RPG causing the bird to spin out of control. Death at the chopper door, waiting to claim its subsequent victims, and the fear coming off the men could be cut with a knife. It was everywhere and on everyone's faces.

"You could hear metal being ripped away and sent flying in the cab, hitting Corporal Thomas in the eye. He screamed and covered his bloody eye. His screaming was horrible. Several tried to help him, but we were all going down, and every man was for themselves. Smoke could be seen coming from the tail section as more bullets ricocheted inside the bird, tearing holes in the metal, sending the craft into circles, out of control, and going to crash.

Capt. Stone had only a moment to decide our fate as the helicopter started to fall out of the sky. he had to decide to ride it down or wait until it was just about to hit the ground and jump and roll away from the blades and pray. He knew the boys were waiting for my decision, and there was no time at all to ponder. If you wait, you could be killed from the explosion of the fuel tanks and burn to death. If you jump, you could break your legs or be cut in half by the blades or be blown up. With that in his head, he stood in the open doorway, holding on tight as they spun in circles and watched the ground get closer and closer. Stone made the split-second decision to jump, as others were yelling, 'Captain, what are we going to do? Jump or go down?'

"'Jump!' he screamed inside the loud, smoking, burning chopper. It all happened so fast, free-falling, smoke, fire, spinning, men screaming, as Stone hit and rolled on the ground with his M16 in his hands, praying that he would roll away from the blades that could slice you in two in seconds. Kyle landed on his neck and rolled to the left, where he layed against a bloody severed leg. Corporal Ashton continually screamed, holding on to his blood-gushing stump. To the right were two others lying close, dead. They did not make it, nor the others who stayed and rode the aircraft down. Now, it was just a massive ball of fire, and black-gray smoke that acted like a blanket covering the dead threw ash and debris all over with the wounded. If that was not enough, we started to take on more fire and mortars being launched at us, an easy target as we lay there next to a burning bird.

"I knew if we stayed there, we would all be killed. Reaching for the field radio, I was able to puff smoke and call-in napalm on the VC on the ridge where they were taking mortar rounds. I then threw green smoke for them to be picked up by the next evac chopper," Kyle said covered in blood. In no time, we saw and heard the blades as they came over the hill to pick us up, along with help from a hellfire gunship laying out a continuous burst of rounds, killing them in the hills, those who were blowing up and taking the lives of the young soldiers. I was reminded not to get too excited about the evac until it was out of the way of small arms fire or, worse, an RPG. Up and over the ridge, on the way to base camp, now we could relax, and a small smile would be okay. The pure hell of war, so prevalent that afternoon, one that Captain Kyle Stone would never forget along with those who fought and died alongside him."

Driver sat wide-eyed like a little boy listening to every word Kyle said.

"That was a hell of a story, boss," Driver said, "I couldn't even imagine having to go through something like that and especially being only eighteen."

"What are we fighting and dying for? That was the question in the minds of those who were lucky enough not to die in that valley that day, Driver. I have another story of an ambush where I threw a grenade at a VC in a tree and blew him the hell up, but that story is for another day."

"What a story, boss. I feel so bad for those who died that day."

"It is a hard story to tell, Driver. The memories are burnt into my skull. The sound of screaming never leaves you once you have been through such a horrific situation."

"I am sorry, boss; I didn't mean for you to have to remember those days. Are there any other happier memories of your childhood?"

Kyle pondered the question and replied, "To lighten it up a little, there is one silly story that made an older woman very happy."

"Well, if it does lighten it up, that would be great. That was a hard story," Driver said.

Kyle took a drink of his Coke, "I agree. I didn't realize how much it still bothers me. I must say that I feel every day for my brothers who fought and now have nightmares haunting them. Okay, the lighter side. It was not long after my father had been buried that my brother and myself were going to go fishing with the baseball team we played on. We went to the Coach's house, who owned a fishing boat, and occasionally, he would invite five or six of the team members to go fishing with him and his three sons. This entailed spending the night on the living room floor of the Coach's house with sleeping bags. We were not the only ones there that night, the Coach also had a daughter, and she had her friend over, the oldest of all of them. That night found the boys playing outside, running around acting crazy. Now Pam, the Coach's daughter, and her friend Rachael were playing in Pam's room watching the boys outside– hold on a minute, Driver, I have to take this call."

Kyle was being asked to get some more information together on the Comish file for New York. "Sorry, my friend, I will have to tell you that story some other time, work calls. However, let me finish with this about my past, and then I have a job to do. You asked me about the military. I didn't think about joining the military, but things happened, and I found myself in front of recruiters. I was not interested in talking with the Navy Recruiter, being I had grown up in San Diego and always laughed at the sailors on the beach with their tight bathing suits and tee-shirts with a pack of cigarettes rolled in the sleeve. Rock, my childhood friend that I lived with for a short time in high school, decided to join the Marines; I was curious about the Army. Not sure what to do, and wondering what would happen if Rock joined the Marines, I thought it almost certain I would have to move again, where would I live, all these thoughts going through my head, including maybe joining the military. It would at least give me a home for a while.

"Anyway, Driver, I found myself in front of the Army Recruiter's desk who was working hard to excite young men to join and serve their country. The same country, whose involvement in Vietnam, with thousands of American boys shipped back to the States in body bags. Knowing this, I was not interested in joining them to fight in this war. The Recruiter was feeling my hesitation, even though I had scored very high in leadership tests showing I had what it took to be an Officer in this Army, came up with an offer that would excite me. He promised to give me a new family who would care about me and be there when I needed them. I had never thought about the military this way before. It all seemed to make sense, and what is wrong with a family who cares about you?"

Driver smiled at Kyle's stories, "Thanks for sharing that. I do feel closer now that I know more about you, and in our field of endeavors, we need to be connected in so many ways."

"There is the story of my younger life, Driver; it was crazy, but I don't know if it is crazier than my life now. You know, Driver, I have several sad stories from my adventures in Nam, but the one that still gets me is that when I returned home, I was refused the one thing I had been dreaming about.

"After a year as a Captain, fresh off the battlefield, I looked out the window at the magnificence of the city as my cab stopped at a bar. Finally, I could enjoy a moment in my life that had consumed me—taking a drink of a cold, foaming beer. The barkeep asked what I wanted to drink, and I didn't have to think about it, but before he could get the words out, he was asking for my ID. I pulled my military ID out, gave it to the bartender, and then heard the words that would nullify all my dreams."

CHAPTER 29

CAN I HAVE A COLD BEER?

"**S**orry, you must be twenty-one," the barman looked at him as he handed back Kyle's ID. Reality came over Kyle as clear as night over day: *I can fight and kill for my country, but I cannot have a cold, foaming beer. Welcome home, soldier!*

Kyle was feeling sorry for himself, sitting at the bar with no drink, staring out the window, wondering what he would do next when an older man sitting at the end of the bar spoke up.

"Captain, you said you were a captain, didn't you?"

Kyle looked over at the gentleman. "Yes, I did say that. Why?"

The older gent told the barkeep to get him two six-packs, and then he paid for them. With beer in his hands, he said, "Captain, follow me outside, would you?"

Kyle got off his barstool and walked outside as told. The gentleman made a motion, and a limousine pulled up in front of the bar.

"John, this is Captain Stone. He is just back from Vietnam. Take him wherever he wants today, and make sure he has plenty of cold, foaming beer."

Kyle just looked at him with a big smile, and the gentleman motioned to the limo. "Welcome home, Captain Stone!"

With a smile on his face from remembering that gentleman's kindness, Kyle turned to Driver, "Let us now talk about the unfinished business at the restaurant. I want you to get Stan again to help you, and this is what I want you to do to the one who placed the call."

Kyle went on to tell Driver how he wanted it done and to report back to him when completed. Driver gave Stan a call, and they met up before driving to Sausalito for their appointment with a busboy. Driver explained the plan and answered the questions he had so everything would go as planned. Once they got the busboy in the bathroom, Stan would watch the door as Driver took care of business.

"Okay, he is heading to the bathroom as he was told to do by the server," Stan said.

"Good, I want him in a stall as soon as he comes in." The server had told the busboy there was a problem in the men's room, and he was needed there to help. He entered the empty bathroom except for Stan and Driver.

Stan said, "Hey, buddy, welcome to the men's room. The problem is over here in this stall." The busboy looked concerned as he did as he was told.

Driver said, "Come on in. I have been waiting for you. We understand you like to make money on the side. Is that right?"

"Money on the side? I don't know what you are talking about," said the busboy as he looked around for an explanation.

"Did you not make a call for someone in order to make a dollar? Did you not tell someone that a man was leaving the restaurant? Was that not you?"

"Yes, I made the call, but I didn't know what it was about. I was just told that when the party on table 1 leaves, to call this number, and I did as they said. I didn't mean to cause any trouble."

"Cause any trouble? Did you know that you were setting someone up to be killed, huh? Did you know that?"

"Killed? Are you fucking kidding me? No, I am just a busboy."

"You are a stupid busboy to have made a call and not asked why you are doing that. Due to the seriousness, we need to make an example of you and make sure you do nothing stupid again.

"Stan, bring me the bag out there with our stuff in it. Now you see, you have been what we call a rat, and do you know what we do with rats?"

"No, I don't know. Maybe I do. I don't know." The busboy was looking for an exit. He knew he had messed up and was scared at this point.

"In my little bag here, I have a couple of little reminders for you. Here is the first one. Put this sign over your neck." The sign said Drowned Rat. Driver pulled the second item out and gave it to the busboy.

"This one is for you to wear on your nose. Of course, we want you to look like a rat, and this rat mask will do the trick." The busboy was now wearing the mask and the sign.

Driver filled a paper cup and proceeded to pour it over the busboy's head.

"Okay, so now you are a drowned rat, and most drowned rats don't live, but we are going to let you this time, so learn your lesson well. Now, Stan, have him go outside, and I want him to wait for his tables as he usually does until someone stops him, and then we are done. Mission accomplished."

The busboy shuffled to the door, still shaking but thankful he had escaped a worse fate.

"Stan, let's go, and I will drop you off in the city. You said Van Ness and California, right?"

"Yes, Driver, that would be great. I must ask you, though, who thought of this last plan? I could not help but laugh my ass off when he put the rat mask on. I hope you didn't mind, but I couldn't help myself."

Driver drove to the top of Sausalito to catch the 101 south back across the Golden Gate Bridge.

"I will give you three guesses about who made this one up, and they all have the initials of KS."

"Damn, this guy is good. How does he come up with this stuff so fast?"

"Well, they say he is royalty, so maybe it's in his blood, not sure, but I am enjoying being there for him."

"I guess. He has a beautiful woman and, of course, the famous Mr. S on his side. What is not to be excited about? You are one lucky guy."

Driver dropped Stan off, thanked him again for his help, and headed back to the hospital, where he gave Kyle his status report. He felt good that he had taken care of both problems in two days and was happy he could do it.

Kyle had taken some quiet time to himself, an excellent chance to reflect on his new responsibilities and think about the danger that was involved. He had determined that the perks were great, but any actions against a person or entity can have consequences, as he had just learned. He felt good, though. He knew now that he had a good team underneath him to make sure everything went well and that he was somewhat safe. It was a wake-up call. He knew now that he had to be careful and aware that these kinds of things can happen at any time and that he must be cautious.

"Come on in," Kyle saw Driver by the door. "I was just laying here, thinking about the past few days and all the excitement we've been through."

Driver said, "It has been busy, that is for sure. Let me tell you about what happened at the restaurant. It seems that the busboy was someone who was just there and did not know Comish. He was just doing what he was paid to do."

"Well, that is all well and good. His actions, innocent or not, just about got me killed, and that was the intent, maybe not his, but just the same."

"Well, we did as you instructed, and it all went well. When he came out of the stall with the rat mask on, a sign saying he was a drowned rat and dripping with water, it was hard for me not to start laughing. Stan could not help himself. He busted open when he saw him."

"That is good. Was he a little humiliated and aware of what he did and why he was receiving this punishment?"

"Yes, he knew why."

"I always want to be sure that if we initiate any punishment to anybody, I want to make sure that they know why, and our efforts are not wasted. Got it?"

"Yes, I understand and feel the same way."

"Good, and thanks, Driver, for all that you have done. You did an outstanding job. I also wanted you to know that I have decided not to keep this a secret from Woody. I don't want to start that, and I don't know the consequences of doing so."

"I am glad to hear this. I didn't want to keep this a secret either, but it was up to you, and I take my orders from you, I guess?"

"Yes, that is true. I spoke with Woody this morning, and that is one of the things he said, how we have gotten along so well and were able to contain a serious problem without any press or cops or anything else that could cause us problems."

"What did he say about your plan of making the Comish confess and tell all?"

"He cracked up when I told him about how we hung him upside down and the pee all over his pants. He gave me his compliments on a job well done, so you and I will continue to work together."

CHAPTER 30

RUSSIANS ON RUSSIAN HILL

It had been about a week since Kyle had been discharged from the hospital, and he was feeling much better. They all seemed to think that he was lucky not to have had more severe problems considering a rock had landed on his head. He was looking forward to meeting up with YL later that afternoon. They would have a light dinner in the Marina District at Perry's and then go to her place for some cocktails and quiet time. He was looking forward to some downtime, not counting the hospital. Just spending time loving Yvonne sounded like all he wanted to do.

However, Woody had another idea. He called Kyle and explained some problems with some Russians who owned a large apartment complex on Russian Hill. Kyle thought with a smile that maybe the Russians thought the only place they could live was Russian Hill. NY had contacted Woody, and one of the executives had a sister living in this complex, and there had been some weird things going on, and he wanted it investigated before she got hurt or anyone else.

"Now remember, Kyle, discretion is the law here. Don't do anything that would cause the cops to respond."

"Always understood, Woody," Kyle said. "Let me look into it and get some idea of what is going on and then let you know so you can report back to NY."

"Thanks, so far, you have made it easy working with you. How are you doing today? Those internal problems getting any better?"

"Yeah, but I'm still sore and still having headaches."

"Well, don't do anything until you feel up to it. I will wait to hear from you."

"Sounds good. I am going to crash at Yvonne's tonight. I want to curl up and be loved. That is what sounds good to me. I will then probably go back to the boat if that is alright with you?"

Woody said, "Kyle, you are certainly welcome to stay there, but if you want something nicer, check into the Mark Hopkins or Ritz-Carlton."

"Your generosity is noted." Driver had dropped Kyle and Yvonne off in front of Perry's and drove around to find a place to park and wait for them to need a ride back to her place. Kyle walked in the door and looked down at the bar.

"Why don't we move over there to the bar, in the corner by the window?"

"That sounds fine. We can watch all the people going by."

Perry's was crowded as usual. That was why Kyle had Driver get them there a little earlier so they could enjoy a good drink, good food, and of course, good conversation. There were tables in the back of the restaurant, but the bar looked good that evening. Kyle had started to become aware of maybe some people not liking him in the future if the Comish had been an example of what could happen. However, the thought of his people having his back made him feel safer as he looked out the bar window and saw Driver parked across the street, watching out for him and Yvonne.

The conversation at the bar was great and gave Kyle more time to get to know Yvonne. Driver picked them up after a few drinks and some light dinner and drove them up the hill back to Yvonne's apartment. Kyle did not know why he was so tired after lying in a hospital bed for days, but he only wanted to curl up with YL on the couch and enjoy the view of the city, shutting down for another day.

A lot had to be said for peace, Kyle thought, as he woke up to the quiet of the house and a beautiful lady lying next to him. The only other thing he wanted was his cup of coffee. He found a robe in her closet, wondering whose it might be, as he put it on and headed to the kitchen to make a pot of coffee. He thought what a lovely place she has as he looked out the big kitchen window, showing a part of the bay and the Berkeley Hills. He fumbled around, trying to be quiet, not knowing her kitchen until he found the coffee.

Sitting next to the coffee pot was a bottle of Baileys, a fine addition to a hot cup of coffee. He poured himself one and sat down at the kitchen table, again with a view. He was starting to like her place more. The sun was shining with a clear, blue sky, not a cloud in sight. It was so beautiful. He thought about giving Driver the day off, and he and Yvonne could walk down to Union Street for some lunch and shopping. Kyle thought they could just walk down Broderick Street to Union, and then, it was all there.

It was not long until Yvonne came out to the kitchen with a big smile on her face as she leaned over to kiss Kyle.

Kyle poured her a coffee, "I made some for us. It took a while, but I found where you keep most of the things. I must share with you that I am enjoying your place, feeling very peaceful, and I can tell you that it is a good feeling. Believe me, I know."

"I am glad, Kyle. It seems like your life has been changing every day.

That must be crazy."

"I don't even want to stop and think about it. It would probably give me a heart attack to relive it all again. I thought that we could, later this morning, take a walk down to Union Street for some lunch, and then we could do some shopping, maybe a cocktail or two?"

"I would love that. It looks like a beautiful day."

"It does. I was going to give Driver the day off. He has been with me from the beginning. I'm sure he could use a break."

"Does he have family around here? I don't know much about him."

"I know what you mean. There has been so much going on with me. I have not spent much downtime with him. I am sure he will find something to do with his time today."

After some coffee and a good conversation, Yvonne went to take a shower before they left for a late breakfast. Kyle looked for her keys to her place and then took the key off and put it under her mat outside her front door. He gave Driver a call and let him know that he had the morning off, and he would need him to let some folks in YL's house later that afternoon. He told him the keys would be under the mat.

When they were all dressed and ready, the two of them ventured out into the city. As they walked down the hill, the sight of the Palace of Fine Arts was gorgeous, with the sun bouncing off the dome roof. To the left, the Presidio was sprawled out for miles as it emptied its green hills into the bay. They walked along Union Street for a while, looking at the shops and the people who were out to enjoy this sunny day. With some shopping bags from several stores, they decided to go to Buena Vista for a late breakfast.

Kyle hailed them a cab, and down Lombard Street they went. It was crowded as usual. The bar was packed with patrons with white mustaches, sipping down the Irish whiskeys with cream, which made them all look like Santa. Kyle found them a seat next to a couple from Wisconsin. Everybody spoke to everyone as they also watched the barkeep line up ten empty glasses to make some more Irish coffee. He put a cube of sugar in each one, filled them three-fourths full of coffee, and passed a bottle of Jameson's Irish whiskey over each until just about filled. He then topped them off with rich cream, and there you had it, the famous Buena Vista Irish coffee. A gorgeous day full of sunshine and a great cup of coffee to wash down a plate of eggs Benedict, country potatoes, and sourdough bread. What more would the two of them want? Maybe a level walk home, but that was not going to happen. Thus, the walk was serious uphill but worth it for the incredible views, and they were both feeling it in their legs as they reached her street.

When they got close, Yvonne saw someone on her porch. "Kyle, do you see someone at my house, or is it just me?"

"Let's get closer, and then we can make a better judgment. I wouldn't worry about it."

"I don't know what to worry about or not lately. I sure wasn't worried about our dinner at Scoma's the other night, and then look what happened." She touched Kyle lightly on his face, still scarred from the injury.

"That was a fluke. Look, it is Driver. I told you nothing to worry about."

"Oh no, does he have bad news for you or something?"

"I don't think so. Let's find out. Driver, what is going on? You have Yvonne worried something is wrong."

Driver handed the keys to her apartment back to Kyle.

"On the contrary, you both have a good time and relax while enjoying the massages."

"Massages, what is he talking about?"

"Take a look inside your front room. They are all set up for us." "What, you did this while we were out? That is why Driver was here, wasn't it? Kyle, you are sneaky, in a good way."

They both fell onto their massage tables and let the two masseurs rub all their sore muscles into relaxation as they looked over the bay on this lovely day.

CHAPTER 31

HANGING AROUND

After a great day of playing tourist and getting massages, Kyle and Yvonne sat down to a bottle of Kendall-Jackson chardonnay when Kyle got a call from Mr. S. He was in the studio and wanted Kyle to come over and check out his latest project.

Kyle told him he would love to and would get Driver to take him to Berkeley, where the studio was. Kyle arrived and told the receptionist, a part-time musician, that he was looking for Mr. S. He walked around the corner to studio 7.

This was the same one that Creedence Clearwater Revival recorded their albums at, he was told. Mr. S was in the box doing some vocals when Kyle came in. An engineer was working the giant board, dialing in the sound they wanted to capture for this song. It was cool to see him working and putting his magic into the music. He sounds great, Kyle thought. In a few moments, Mr. S came out, and they all listened to his vocals as the engineer tweaked them a little. It was now time for the lead guitarist, Tilley Jackson, to come in and lay down his tracks, and when he was done, the bass and drums both came in and put it down.

It was the first time Kyle had seen how they made music. He also noticed that one song on an album could take days to get it right, depending on the sound they were going after. It was getting late, and

Kyle had some work he needed to get started on, so he said his goodbyes to Mr. S and the guys and had Driver take him to the boat to crash for the night.

"Hey, Driver, I would like you to meet me on deck tomorrow morning. I want to discuss my next assignment, see what you think of my idea on how to handle things and to accomplish tasks without any press."

"Sure, boss, what time do you want me there?"

"Let us get started around eight-thirty. I will see you in the morning then. Have a good night, Driver."

"You too, boss."

"Well, good morning, Yvonne. How are you doing? This is a nice surprise." Yvonne was in her office.

"I just wanted to call you and thank you for the beautiful flowers and wonderful day we spent shopping and lunch and, of course, the massage."

"You certainly are welcome. I found it relaxing too."

"What are you up to this morning? Are you still in the city?"

"Yes, I am getting ready for a meeting. My next assignment will be in the city, so I will be around, and I look forward to spending more time with you."

"That is good news. I will let you get on with your meeting. I hope to see you soon."

"Thanks, Yvonne. Have a good one." While Kyle was finishing up his phone call with Yvonne, he looked at the view of the estuary. The Coast Guard station was just down the waterway, and he could see the big red and white cutters floating into port. There was a naval base just to the north of the boat, but it had closed a few years ago.

Kyle had a genuine liking for the military, and being an army officer was one reason, but he thought about his father, who worked on the amphibious base in Coronado.

He used to take them to where the Navy Seal's train to watch some of the things they had to go through in their training. All the boys got a real kick out of it. Kyle was the only one to join the military. The two other brothers decided not to participate, and that was okay, as it was a volunteer army.

A new start was ahead of him back then. The recruiter offered him the chance to join special services and play baseball for the army. Kyle, a star on the ball field throughout high school, liked the offer and said, okay, he would join. He would travel throughout the world, wherever the troops were, and entertain them with America's game—baseball. Well, being only seventeen, he would need his mother's signature, and he did not feel that would be a problem, knowing she would be happy to do so. She would not have to worry about him being alone anymore and no more thinking of killing himself.

Well, his mother signed, and Kyle was going to report to basic training at Fort Ord near Monterey in a fortnight.

Kyle was excited to start his new military career and spent the next two weeks saying goodbye to his friends and girlfriend. He knew that he would be without the soft body of a young vixen in his bed for a while and was willing to make that sacrifice. He was busy consorting with his sweethearts to hold him over until he would be allowed to pursue such delights again.

But now, he would have to concentrate on being the best army soldier he could be. Before he could start playing baseball for the army, he would have to complete basic training. As his bus pulled up to the induction center, everyone seemed excited, if a little scared, not knowing what to expect in the next three months. It didn't take long to figure out what was going to happen because as soon as they entered the gate of this military installation, they saw large insignias on the cement walls holding in the fighting machine that had been trained to kill whenever it was ordered to do so.

While Kyle was admiring the grounds around the fort, a mean-looking drill sergeant with a scowl on his face had entered the bus and was yelling at them already, "You maggots need to stand up, grab your shit, and get your skinny asses off this bus. I said now, or you will get my boot up your ass!"

What a friendly welcome after a six-hour drive. Let the games begin.

Once off the bus, Kyle and his buddies stood in line as instructed and soon had another drill sergeant in their face yelling at the top of his voice, "You all don't have what it takes to be a soldier in this man's army. You are all pieces of shit, and it will be my job to make you into a soldier. I will own your ass for the next three months. I am your mother, your father, and I will make these next months the worst you ever have experienced."

Kyle stood there, shaking, watching others being taken apart. One guy was carrying too much weight. He was fat, and two DSs were busy making him feel as little as they could, bringing tears to the young man's face. Kyle waited for his turn to be yelled at and wondered what the hell had he gotten himself into.

Over the next several weeks, Kyle and his fellow privates were put through hell, day in and day out, with considerable harassment levied against all of them. He never missed his mother so much on those quiet nights when the heavens were filled with stars against a black blanket, and as Kyle looked up and thought of his mother and father, tears would begin to fall on his cheeks as his heart ached in that army cot. How could one feel so alone when living in the barracks with forty others?

It was not until six weeks into the basic training that Kyle was called to report to command and see the master sergeant. He always felt scared when he reported to command, not knowing what was up and why he needed to see him. They all were taught that you do not volunteer for anything in the army, or you would soon regret it.

As he stood in front of the master sergeant's desk at parade rest, anxious to hear why he was summoned, the master sergeant said, "Private Stone, I have some news for you and not sure you are going to like it. Are you ready for it?"

"Sir, yes, sir," was his reply.

The black man, looking so military in his uniform decked with all those stripes and ribbons, finally said, "Your orders have been changed. There is no longer a program to play baseball in the army, and you will have to decide what MOS you want to sign up for."

Kyle thought immediately that he just got the recruiter screw as it was called. They signed you up for one thing and then changed it once you were already in and had no say about it. Soon, he was yelled at to make a decision, or one would be made for him. He always liked engineering and wanted to learn about something he was interested in, and anything was better than infantry. Infantry was the one that took the most lives, out in front being the first to engage the enemy. If you liked the action, and you got off on the fear of death, then this was the place for you.

"Are you ready? We don't have all day," the question fired at him from behind the desk.

"Yes," he said. "I would like to go into and learn how to be a combat engineer."

The master sergeant looked at his desk, then back at Kyle, "That will work. I will submit your new orders and let you know when they come back. Now get your ass back out there and report to the firing range."

"Sir, yes, sir," was his answer.

It did not take long to hear something about where he was going to report to after he graduated from basic training. He was told that his request was approved, and he would be reporting to Fort Leonard Wood, Missouri, and start his training in combat engineering.

Upon opening his eyes as he lay on his bunk, looking at snowflakes falling, he had to wonder why he would be in Missouri during the winter, trying to build a bridge on a frozen river. As Kyle lay there, he thought how nice it would be to just fast-forward his life on the other side of all the misery he was going to endure and the possibility he would not come home alive.

Kyle, knowing he descended from the Knights Templar who fought for the good, made him feel important inside, and he fought hard in the Army. After months of excellence in training, he was offered the opportunity to go to Officers' School, but it would not be in engineering. He would join the infantry alongside the ones who fight the war, just like his family had always done, warriors and proud of it. He accepted this opportunity and soon was on his way to Fort Benning, Georgia, to see if he had what it took to be an infantry officer, a leader amongst men.

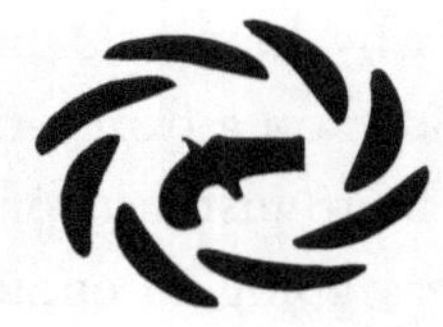

CHAPTER 32

OFFICER MATERIAL

Kyle could not believe what took place when he reached his new post. When he arrived at the Base in Georgia on a sweltering afternoon, he was told to get in the line to be processed. Standing in front of him was a Green Beret who Kyle had so much respect for. Coming down the line were two lieutenants, and they stopped at the Green Beret.

"What do we have here? You want to be an officer, Beret?" "Yes, sir," said the Green Beret sergeant.

The lieutenant said, "Outstanding, I want you to prove to me how bad you want to be an officer. I want you to take off the beret and throw it on the ground and spit on it."

Kyle, standing behind him, was watching all this and not believing what he was seeing, being this was John Wayne to him. What the hell was he getting into? He wondered. Then, slowly, the Green Beret took off his beret and threw it on the ground, and spat on it as he was told to.

Disgraceful, Kyle thought. You just threw all your integrity on the ground.

After the show was over, they continued to process in, and the Beret became his roommate. That probably was not a good thing for him, being they wanted to get Kyle out so bad. They said they did not want any snotty- nosed eighteen-year-old officers.

The instructors were after you to quit, but there was also always a competitive spirit among the different squads. When one of the squads living one floor down from Cadet Stone had a spirited day on the obstacle course, and Kyle's team won, that did not go over very well. That night, before inspection, they sneaked into the floor and went to Kyle's room. Down in the corner of the door frame, they put a cigarette butt. At five minutes to eight, the instructors came for the inspection. Kyle and the Beret's room was always immaculate and ready, but they did not see the butt placed there earlier. When it was found, they were asked which one had been smoking and put it there. Both stood to attention when being asked, and they were told that if no one admitted to it, both would be punished.

Kyle stood barefoot in his white boxers and white T-shirt and glanced over at the Beret, and whispered, "I will take the heat. No reason for both of us to be punished."

Then Kyle spoke up and admitted he had done it and forgot he put it there and that it was fine as they took him down the hallway to the staircase.

"Kyle, you love to smoke so much. I want you to go over there at the doorway and grab the trash can," the instructor yelled.

Kyle did as he was told.

"Now, I am going to be nice to you and let you smoke a cigarette. Not one but all that I have." He held out a half-full pack of Camels and said, "Now, light the cig, and then put the army green trash can over your head and finish the smoke. Once you're done, light up another until you have smoked all of them, then let me know when you're done."

Kyle said, "Yes, sir," looking a little scared, as he did not smoke at all. Kyle did as he was told. He had the can next to him, tapped out one cigarette and took a long look at it, and then started smoking one after the other with the trash can over his head, breathing it all in, turning green and coughing and choking. Water squirted out of his eyes and snot out of his nose. He stumbled in the dark until he hit the edge of the top stairs and missed his step, falling hard and rolling down each step, hitting his head on the cement, but thankfully the can saved his skull from being cracked as he stumbled and fell to the bottom.

With all the noise he was making, the other cadets came running to see if he was all right. He was spread out on the floor of the last step with the can bent and lying next to him. He looked around to see if he was all right. No broken bones, but he was shaken up. The next day, there was a lot of talk among the cadets about what had happened to Kyle when it was not even his fault, but he took credit and the punishment for it. If nothing else, he thought, he had earned the respect of his fellow cadets for what he had done.

Two weeks had gone by, and unfortunately, troubles for Kyle were not over. That was proven on Sunday night when the cadets cleaned their rooms and got their gear ready for Monday training. Kyle was walking down the hallway, unaware that the duty officer was behind him.

The duty officer said, "Get out of my way, cadet. You did not hit the wall when I walked by."

"I didn't see you, sir."

"I didn't give you permission to speak. Get down to my office immediately and wait for me."

Kyle did as he was told and was waiting in the office when the lieutenant came in. Kyle noticed two chairs and a fan in the office and wondered what that was about.

The lieutenant said, "Get in front of the chairs, face the chairs, and wait."

Kyle stood there in his government-issued white boxers and nothing else on. It was a hot and humid night, and as he waited, a young, good-looking red-haired woman wearing red lipstick with a short white skirt came in and sat in one of the chairs in front of the cool breeze of the fan.

"Okay, cadet, I want you to pick up the two grenades by your feet, and I want you to do the gorilla stomp. Crouch down and jump as high as you can while you beat the grenades against your chest until I tell you to stop."

The young woman smiled while sitting in front of him, enjoying the breeze from the fan and a cool Pepsi in her hand, and she lifted it as if to say, 'Let the good times roll.'

Kyle then started his punishment. As he jumped up and down, his dick fell up and down in his boxers. One minute into the punishment, out it, came, flopping up and down with every jump, as the red-haired woman focused her attention on his privates with a big smile on her face. It was getting to be exhausting, time after time, pounding the grenades against his chest until he fell over into the fan that was keeping them so cool. He could not help himself. His legs were so unsteady, and his chest was aching with direct, sharp pain.

"Get up, you loser. Is that what you want to be?" said the duty officer. "Sir, no, sir," Kyle responded as he got up to switch off the fan and put

it back so that the cool air would be on them. He retook his position with blood now trickling down his chest from the continual beating of the hand grenades, and as he jumped, he could see other cadets outside the office watching what he was being put through. When he was ready to collapse, the duty officer said that it was enough, and he was told to get out.

Slowly Kyle got up off the floor. His legs were wobbling, and his chest was in severe pain from the punishment, and he made his way upstairs with the help of three others. The next day, the duty officer was called in the office. The captain of the cadets stood next to the desk of the major. There was a lot of yelling, mostly the major, and the word got out that the lieutenant was relieved of command. Nobody could believe that Kyle could still be standing after such cruel, cruel punishment.

The orders came in after seven months of intense training. They started with 300 cadets, and only 189 made it through to graduate and get their commission as infantry officers.

At the graduation ceremony where the new lieutenants were sworn in, they all had their families there to share their incredible accomplishments. Well, everyone except Kyle. His dad was dead, and his mother and brothers did not bother to show up. His orders were to report to Fort Bragg, where the Ninth Infantry Division was stationed. There was a lot of talk in the command about Kyle because he was the youngest officer ever to receive a commission.

He was assigned to command headquarters, and while signing in, he met the Colonel's Secretary, Suzette. Kyle liked what he saw and had been in training for over a year, so it was nice to smell and be around a beautiful woman. They started to date right away, and it was not long before they were engaged.

One day, when Kyle came into command during his lunch, and he walked into the office and found the Sergeant Major, standing about six feet tall with a heavy build, all packaged in his green camouflage uniform, with his hands all over his fiancée. Knowing he was new to the Command and outranked the Sergeant Major, Kyle stood there for a minute, unsure what he should do. It was starting to bother him, so he decided he had to do something.

Instead of discussing it calmly, Kyle reacted the wrong way when he said, "Sergeant Major, take your hands -off Suzette!"

The Sergeant Major said, "Are you talking to me, Lieutenant?"

"Yes, I am, Sergeant Major, and when you talk to me, lock your heels!" "You are making a big mistake, Lieutenant."

The Sergeant Major was right, it was a big mistake, and it did not take long to be called into the Colonel's office for a reaming out, and at the end of the day, he got orders to ship out to Vietnam, and with that, Kyle was sent packing for a long trip across the ocean.

Kyle was back at his barracks, packing his gear and talking to everyone he could get a hold of to let them know he was leaving for Vietnam. There was a lot to do before shipping out. It was just about time to leave for the airfield when he heard a knock at his door.

"Lieutenant Stone, it's Lieutenant Robinson from Headquarters, and I have new orders for you."

"Yes, I am Lieutenant Stone. You must be kidding me. I am already packed and ready to go. Who changed my orders?" Kyle asked.

"They came from Colonel Edwards. That is why I rushed over here to tell you. I hope they are where you want to go."

The orders were for him to stand down from Vietnam and wait for future instructions to come. That was good news for him. He just dodged a bullet, he thought.

It did not take long for the instructions to arrive. He was to work with a Senator, Chairman of the Armed Service Committee, on some hush-hush personnel situation involving a Colonel who was up for his first Star as a Brigadier General. Kyle would work undercover, getting any dirt he could on the Colonel with the objective to limit him from becoming a flag officer. These activities continued for many months, and Kyle was pleased with his duties, basically left alone to do what he was ordered to do.

Until one day, when he got called into the Senator's office and was instructed to get ready to deploy to Vietnam. The Colonel he had been following had received orders to Nam, and Kyle had to follow him there as ordered. There was a significant problem with that. He could not tell anyone he was going to Nam, a war zone. He only hoped he did not get killed; nobody would know what happened to him.

Kyle got assigned to an infantry unit that the Colonel was going to command. He was to act like any other infantry officer and go on patrol every day or when ordered. He was not to tell anyone the real reason for being there.

The thoughts going through Kyle's mind were scary as he sat in the third row of a 721-Airliner heading over the ocean toward what he was hoping would not be his final resting place. Would he ever see his family again? He tried hard not to overthink this but looking around at other members of the unit just showed how somber a moment this was. It seemed as if all the others had the same thoughts by the expressions on their faces and tears coming down their cheeks as they wrote their first letter back to those they just left behind. He thought they all were probably hoping like he was, that this would be the longest flight ever, but in no time, it was time to exit the aircraft and enter the war. Left on the floor of the 721, personal thoughts, written on a napkin:

War, what is it, and is it for the right reasons? My life is worth a lot, and why should I risk it for some people I have never met or seen? I do not want to die or be a cripple for the rest of my life when I am so young and have so much to do in my life. My life, and why should I have to command those under me to kill strangers they have never met and strangers that are women? Why? Do we have the correct answer to these questions? The answers will fill my heart after it breaks from watching my friends being killed and shot with bullets that rip through their flesh, leaving them lying in blood with gaping holes, screaming for help. My thoughts are flowing through me. I must get it together, but the body bags I have seen scare the hell out of me and the reality of what can happen, as it did to those dead in the bag and now, they are only a number on a tag on their big toe.

CHAPTER 33

TIME TO GET SERIOUS

The morning sunshine was so warm and inviting. It was great to be sitting on the deck for a meeting. The ship steward approached Kyle.

"Would you like more coffee, Mr. Stone?"

"I think I have had enough coffee, Jimmy. Could you bring me one of your spicy Bloody Mary's? Also, I will be expecting Driver. Have him come up and join me."

There was an area that was set up on the bow of the ship. It had tables and chairs under a cover with a bamboo rug, good enough to relax under or have a meeting. Being the ship was an old one did not bother anyone because the service was five stars, and that was what mattered, Kyle thought as he waited for Driver.

He sipped on his drink and overlooked the estuary as he thought about his life and where he was now. He wondered what he could have done in his short life that would have eliminated the mess he was in. He only wished he had this talk with himself many years ago. Maybe if he stayed in the military, he was already a Captain at 20, could have been a Colonel by now, and who knows, he might even have been General Stone. How about choosing a different wife? That would have made a big difference in his success and the future of financial independence.

But wait, he thought, I would not have my beautiful girls. When you think about all of this, it only confuses you when you look at the big picture. Kyle pondered—taking another drink of his bloody Mary, looking out over the blue water. What about the elephant in the room? What if my father did not kill himself? What difference would this have had on me and my approach to life? Kyle continued to stare over the railings of his boat as a tear came to his eye. He could not shake the sadness and hole in his heart.

"Sir, Driver is here. Should I send him over?"

"Yes, Jimmy, could be the reason I told you he was coming," Kyle said, smiling.

Kyle was trying to get in a good mood and was looking forward to an extended stay in the city when Driver joined him. "Good morning, Mr. Stone. Had a good night's sleep?"

"Yes, Driver, and good morning to you. Do you want Jimmy to bring you anything?"

"I already took care of it. I am all yours."

Kyle took a sip of his Bloody Mary. "You caught me in a melancholy mood. Have you ever taken the time to assess your life and wonder what you could have done differently to have affected your outcome?"

Driver replied, "Well, it seems you are in a blimp and floating over your life, seeing where you could have done something different. Boss, we all have taken that ride in the blimp; however, the problem is, you can't change it, you have to embrace your past and be positive as you concentrate on the present, and that will take care of your future."

"Doctor Driver, well, that was good, thanks for the pep talk, you know how complicated my life is, and your knowledge is limited. Someday I will write a book about my life; nobody will believe everything I have gone through. It is crazy."

"I would like to hear more someday. You are right. Your life has been crazy. If you do write a book, be sure and sign a copy for me."

Kyle smiled. "Well, that was fun. We must have a drink soon. I have a lot more to tell you, however now I must bring you back to today. We have a problem. There seems to be trouble in a complex on Russian Hill. One of our execs has a family member; I do not think it is his sister or mother, probably more like his aunt. I can check my notes, but it doesn't matter. The problem is there is a problem over there on how they have been treating the residents."

"Do we know who is causing it or how bad it is?" Driver asked.

"Yes, it seems that there are two Russian brothers who own the complex, and they are treating everyone with disdain and contempt. If anyone complains about a problem with their unit, they will send the super over, and I guess he disrespects the tenant and makes them sorry that they ever complained. There have also been reports of physically handling some of the older tenants, and one reported a broken leg."

"Okay, there are some rotten apples on Russian Hill then."

"Yes, there are, but that's not all. A couple of them have disappeared, I am being told, possibly foul play. Anyway, I am being asked to investigate it and report back with the problem and the fix. That is where you come in. I want you to go over there and snoop around. Be discreet, as usual, but get me how many live there, how many total units in the building, and get me the layout of the building also. See if you can find the original plans. Also, see if there is any chatter among the residents about something that is not right, let them know you are on their side."

"I will go over there today and start putting together a report for you." "Yes, thanks, remember, we must be open to all you hear about and do not rule out anything. Get a hold of me when you have it. I will then initiate a plan for all of us, and we will take care of those involved."

Yvonne was busy at work after a great weekend with Kyle, who she was starting to fall for. She was not sure about his job ever since they had their little talk. She was thinking about her conversation with Kyle when they were in her condo. She was sitting on the couch with a glass of wine, and Kyle was sitting in the chair facing her. He had his favorite cocktail on the end table as he brought up their relationship and the possible difficulties.

"It is apparent that we are starting to like each other. Is that right, or am I too presumptuous?" Kyle asked her.

"No, I don't think you are. I certainly like spending time with you, and hopefully, you enjoy my company also. Why are you asking?"

"Well, it is not a secret YL that I now have a new job, and this one is a little different, to say the least."

Yvonne listened carefully.

"Let us address the elephant in the room. I will not be able to confirm my whereabouts or when I get back, or when I leave anywhere. Knowing this going in, and if you still want to see me, I do not want to be questioned. It will be a given that I will see you when I see you, not to put it too harshly."

"Kyle, I understand what you are saying," Yvonne said. "I have already dealt with this in my mind, and yes, I still want to see you."

With a smile on his face, Kyle opened up his arms for a big hug and kiss.

Yvonne had to move to the new office that Kyle got for her. This was necessary because she was to take over for Kyle while he had to smooth things out with his new employer. There was a lot to smooth out. YL knew that Kyle had an idea, and she knew he would take care of it. There was also David and all that he had done to try and destroy Kyle at all levels of his life. Yvonne was not a hundred percent in, especially when she went over all that had happened in her life since she met Kyle.

All this muddled inside her head when she had so much to do at work. Being she just moved into her new office just west of Lombard Street on Francisco Street, near the Marina District, there was a lot to do. She had a real nice view of the bay and the large park out of her office window. It was a little pricey, but Kyle said it was okay. They were making so much money before all this trouble started to take place. Kyle said she would not even believe the attorney's fees he had to pay.

Yvonne spent her days supporting the staff who still worked there, keeping up on the business relationships, taking care of customers, and selling to new customers. She was a very busy person, and she loved it. Especially with Kyle's new job, it was good now that he was in the city working, but that was not going to be the case in the future. She thought she would deal with all that later. Besides her business keeping her busy, she had her girlfriends, all professional women that had stayed in contact with each other throughout the years. And that is what makes for good friends, Yvonne thought. One of her friends was her roommate before getting her place. She never had her own residence. She always needed roommates to help with the rent. This time, she could afford her own home because of her salary and bonuses, and she liked it.

She knew Kyle had no choice. What would he do with his business if it were not for her? And it was an excellent opportunity for a young single woman. YL had dated quite a few men before dating Kyle, and she often wondered if she wanted to date someone else in addition to Kyle, but she felt that she was pretty busy with work and did not feel a need to go out with anyone else for the time being. She and her girlfriends had talked about the whole dating idea, and it was agreed that not all guys were good dates and sometimes a complete waste of time. How much time do you want to spend chasing someone who would make you happy and checks all the boxes, and how many do you have to go through to find the right one? Kyle was safe for the time being, but if he did not treat her right, she was way too pretty to sit on the sidelines.

CHAPTER 34

THE RUSSIANS DID IT

Kyle had been on the boat for a day while he caught up on some expense reports he needed to get in. They had been so good to him; he did not want them to think he was taking any type of advantage of them. After all, they were the Family. He had talked with Driver, and he was on his way over this morning with the information Kyle had asked for.

"Jimmy, Driver is on the way over to meet with me. Allow him to board, and then send him up here."

Kyle was sitting on the bow of the boat where he was set up for having meetings. He liked having meetings there because he had the five-star crew of the vessel to serve whatever the guest wanted—a nice touch.

"Good morning, Driver. Have a seat. How are you today?"

"Just fine, Kyle. The weather is great today. It is beautiful up here."
"It is. I never get tired of the view. Plus, it is always changing. How

good is that?"

Jimmy approached. "Another one for you, Mr. Stone?" Kyle nodded. "And you, Mr. Driver?"

Driver ordered a vanilla latte and then told Kyle what he found, "I have what you asked for, boss, and it is worse than we thought. They

220

are not nice people. They have everyone scared to death. It seems they manage by fear, and if you say something, you might not be there the next day."

Kyle sipped on his coffee. "That bad, huh? I had an idea, Driver, that this is a hugely dangerous situation affecting a lot of older residents."

"Well, that is not the worst. It seems, Kyle, that these guys, three of them are from Russia as we suspected, are arms dealers working out of that apartment building as a front for the gun-running business."

"Holy shit, Driver, this is now an international crime wave. I must let my People know; I don't think they have any idea that there is a gun-running operation. Well, that is worse than stealing from a lemonade stand now, isn't it?" Kyle joked.

"I thought that they were going to be some mean bastards from my conversation with Woody. However, with this new news, we might have to bring in the FBI to take a look at the gun-running. It will take some doing, but I think it is necessary to bring some big-time fear into their world, give them a little bit of their own medicine. I am talking about hitting them so hard it will make them change their mind about owning this apartment building, knowing that someone knows what they are doing. Maybe they will go back to Russia. Either way, we will have solved the problem. I want you to give this envelope to Stan. We might want to use him again, and you have already been taken care of."

"Yes, I have. Thank you."

Kyle and Driver spent time going over Kyle's plan, taking care of the details, never wanting something to go wrong because of sloppy work.

Kyle laid out the plan, "Okay, Driver, we are going to start with one incident. It will be followed by one more and then the last one. This should do it, but if not, we will reevaluate our situation."

"Sounds good. What will be the first event for them?"

"I want you to watch them and find out which of the cars belong to them. Get some help, and then I want you to set it up so that we blow up one of their cars, but only after we slip them a written message to stop dealing in fear with the tenants, or fear will be on their back door. I want you to wait ten minutes from when they read the note and then blow up one of the cars. Make sure they see it."

Driver had his notepad out. "What about the second incident? When do we do that?"

"It will probably be right after; I mean the next day. We will hit them again. This time, I want you to set the car up so that there will be an explosion in the car when the key is turned, consisting of mainly smoke and a loud sound. I want them to think that the car is blowing up after starting it, but not this time, only smoke and noise to mess up their heads and hopefully scare the hell out of them."

"Got it, boss. When do you want me to start?"

"Get on it now. It will take you time to get the supplies you will need." Kyle was beginning to like his lieutenant status. It was just like in the army, commanding men to complete a mission, especially this job, which came with all the perks.

Driver was busy getting all the necessary tools to complete this mission and also hooking up with Stan. He had an envelope for him, and they needed to go over all the details and execution. It was necessary to scout them out first, see what habits they had about the cars they used. Was there a specific time any one of them left the apartment?

Driver sat down with Stan at the Washington Bar and Grill at Washington Square.

"It is important, Stan, that they see the car explosion. Kyle wants it to go off two minutes after the note is read. That is something else we need to make sure of, that they read the note."

Stan, with a large beer in his hand, said, "It seems this job has a lot to do with timing. I understand, Driver, and when you see Kyle, tell him thanks, and I appreciate his generosity."

The two sat for a while longer, putting all the finishing touches on the job, and then left the Washbag to finish up getting the supplies. It took three days for Driver and Stan to develop a schedule that they could use for the bombing. They decided to call the Russians—Russian #1, and #2, and #3—for the sake of simplicity.

Driver said, "Boss, Russian #2 left the apartments at eight forty-five on each of the three days we watched and always took the same car. That makes it easier."

Kyle said with a serious expression, "That will work for the first bombing to take place. You will have to do the same for the second bombing, but no C-4, and you will wait again till morning but still dark.

But on this first bombing, place the C-4 in the car, and use only enough to do the job. Don't blow up any other vehicles, nor Russian #2."

"Don't worry, boss. We will be careful, but the hard part is the timing of the note being read and the bombing, but we can do it. I will let you know when it is done."

"Thanks, Driver. I await your call." Kyle gave it his blessing, and the boys went to work. It would all go down the following day. Making sure that the note was read before the bombing was the tricky part, but they said they had it handled. Kyle was okay with that. He always believed that if you give someone a job to do, let them do it, and then you can criticize if necessary or praise if they did a good job.

CHAPTER 35

WOLFGANG PUCK'S

Kyle was still staying on the boat. The comforts were incredible, and the chef was out of this world with his cuisine. He had not contacted Yvonne. He did not like to mix pleasure with business, especially when he was new and being watched. Right now, he had a job to do, and doing it well was the only way.

Kyle received a phone call from Yvonne. He could not take it. He was in the middle of dealing with some gun-running Russians. She would understand. He felt that she got this gig and would be able to deal with it.

As he waited, he spoke with his children to see if they were all right and needed anything. One would never know with the mother they had what could take place at any time. Kyle just hoped that she did not do anything stupid as she had in the past, not now that he was with the Family. They do not play. She better keep it real.

A quiet night went by, and Kyle was up early as now it was time to execute the first bombing. He would not get involved, but he would be ready for anything that came up.

"Good morning, Mr. Stone. I know it is early, but did you want any breakfast or just coffee?" Kyle sat in the main cabin.

"Good morning, Jimmy. No breakfast, but I would like some orange juice with my coffee."

"Sure thing, Mr. Stone, be right back with it." Being up so early gave him time to call New York and check-in. It was always good to keep in touch with the big, big boss. As eight-thirty approached, Kyle knew they were getting close. If the same pattern was held, it all should go down at eight forty-seven.

"Hey, Jimmy, I am tired of this coffee. Bring me one of your special Bloody Mary's." Jimmy shuffled over to the kitchen to get Kyle what he wanted. Kyle was ready, and at eight forty-nine, his phone rang.

"Boss, the first bombing is done, and it went just as you wanted it to." Kyle had a smile on his face.

"That is good news. Good job. Tell me how it went down."

"Stan had the hard part. He waited until Russian #2 was ready to leave, and he slipped the note under the door. The Russian picked it up and then looked around cautiously. Seeing nothing out of place, he crumpled it up and threw it on the floor. He proceeded to walk outside just before eight forty-five. I hit the button to blow up his car when he was in full view of it. The explosion was loud and took the car out."

"Great, what about the Russian's reaction?"

"He just about jumped out of his shoes, fell to the ground, and looked around to see who did this, and then quickly went back into his apartment."

Kyle was ready with the next note.

"Write this: *'How does fear feel? If you did not feel fear like you are spreading to the tenants, we will wait next time until you are in the car. We are telling you again, vacate the premises, or this will happen again.'* Do you have that, Driver? Read it back to me. Here is the deal, Driver. What we just did will make no difference to them. We will hit them again in two days, just like I said, smoke and explosion but no C-4."

Driver was glad that Kyle was pleased. "Did you need me to come over to the boat?"

"Yes, I do. I want to go out to see my kids. See you in a little bit."

A day had gone by, and Kyle was back from visiting the children. He loved seeing them. He hoped they knew how much he loved them. It was time for the second bombing. This time just smoke and explosion, but the kicker was that it would go off when someone turned the key, just like the note promised.

Same as the first one, Kyle was ready to hear from Driver. This time, it was Russian #3. He had a van he used, and they were ready for him to turn the key. They had delivered the note a day before, so they would know what was coming if they did not leave. Create fear was what Kyle told them. Around the time expected, Driver called with his report of how things went.

Kyle said, "Let me know. How did it go?"

"We know that they read the second note, and Russian #3 got into his van, turned the key, and we could hear the sound effects and the smoke- filled van. He got out of the van and ran into the house. He was visibly shaken."

"Good to hear, Driver. I will let you know about the third one. You and Stan take some time off. You deserve it."

"Thanks, boss, we both appreciate it." Kyle felt good about giving them some time off. The way they executed his plans, no complaints, no mistakes, just the way he liked it.

Kyle felt that he needed to spend some time with Yvonne while he thought about the third bombing or something similar. He needed to give the Russians the time to evaluate their situation, especially after two attacks. Are they prepared for another? Did they think it was coming, or had Kyle gotten through to them?

Kyle would give them some more time before he decided to act again or not. Kyle had called Yvonne back and explained that he was in the middle of something, and they discussed getting back together and going to dinner. Kyle told her that he would book the restaurant, and he would pick her up at seven-thirty.

Yvonne was looking forward to seeing Kyle again. She was feeling happy these days, with a good job, a fabulous apartment looking over the bay, and a great boyfriend who had a limousine, a private jet at his disposal, a lot of money to spend on her, and of course, being good-looking. What could be better?

Driver went to the door to get her; Kyle was in the back on the phone. Yvonne was so pretty. She had on a gold lame jacket with a satin pantsuit.

She looked good, thought Kyle, as he watched her walk to the limousine. Driver opened the door and let her in.

"Hi, Kyle, good to see you. I have missed you."

"Yvonne, you are looking very fashionista this evening. I love your jacket."

"Thank you, Kyle. You are as handsome as ever."

"Thanks. Have you wondered where we are going tonight?" "I have given some thought. Yes."

"We are going over to the Asian buffet. They have some new entrées." Yvonne smiled. "Well, I am glad I dressed up then."

"No, we are going to go to Wolfgang Puck's new restaurant, Postrio, as his guest. He said he would have something made special for us. I am excited."

"That sounds so good. I am glad I dressed up, really this time. I read about his restaurant in the Chronicle. They say it will be a big hit and that reservations were hard to come by. Well, for some people," she said as she smiled at him.

"Well, there have to be some perks to this job, and tonight, you get to share those with me." Driver pulled the limo up to Postrio's, and they walked in for a night of sumptuous cuisine.

"Good evening, welcome to Postrio. Do you have a reservation?"

Kyle stood next to Yvonne. "Good evening. Yes, we do. It is under Kyle Stone."

The maître d' smiled at Kyle.

"Mr. Stone, we were told to expect you. I think Wolfgang has prepared something just for you. Please follow me to your table."

"I have never been with anyone who is recognized as he walks in. Kyle, this is crazy, the respect you get wherever you go." Yvonne took Kyle's arm.

Kyle smiled back at her as they walked toward their table.

"I know, YL. It is still a surprise to me, but I will say that I kind of like it."

"This table was reserved for you, Mr. Stone. Is it to your liking? Please enjoy your dinner. I think Wolfgang will be out to see you soon."

"Thank you. We look forward to a nice experience tonight," Kyle responded. The waiter was there in no time.

"Welcome to Postrio. May I get you a cocktail?"

Kyle asked, "What are you in the mood for, YL." He looked over the drinks menu.

"I can't decide between a cocktail or champagne."

Kyle looked at the waiter. "Bring us a bottle of a new champagne, Veuve Cloquet Brut, please, and anything else you wanted, Yvonne?"

"No, the champagne will be great. Thanks."

"What are you in the mood for? Maybe you want to wait until we get a special visit?"

"You are right. I will wait. It is so nice in here. I am so glad you chose this restaurant."

After a couple of sips of champagne, Wolfgang walked up to the table. "Mr. Stone, I am so happy that you decided to try out my newest restaurant. May I be introduced to this beautiful woman you brought with you? You must be Yvonne?" Yvonne looked over at Kyle with a puzzled face. Kyle just shrugged.

"Yes, I am," she said.

"I am delighted to meet you, Mr. Puck."

"Call me Wolfgang, and I will cook you a very nice meal." "You have it, Wolfgang. I look forward to whatever you create."

Wolfgang said, "I am pleased. I will be back with your dinner. Relax and enjoy the ambiance."

Yvonne sat there with a big smile on her face. "I am so excited. This is so special tonight."

Kyle raised his glass in the air, "I toast you, YL, for what you have done for me in my business. You have done such a good job of keeping it going and with a nice profit. I could not have done it without you. Cheers."

"Thank you, Kyle. It has been quite a ride since I was hired a few months ago. A lot has happened. Who would have known?"

It was not long until the waiter approached the table with a lobster bisque to start with. He then followed it up with a baked Maine lobster, and to finish, crème Brule for dessert. A fantastic night was had in the city, the city by the bay until Kyle had to get serious at the table.

"Did you enjoy your evening? I know I enjoy being around you?" Kyle asked softly.

"I have to thank you. It has been very relaxing and enjoyable. Did you enjoy it?"

"Of course, but I have something to tell you."

"What is it?" Yvonne asked with concern in her voice.

"I have discussed with you my business and how I cannot speak to you of things," Kyle replied. "Well, I have been given my next assignment, and I will say it is a mountain to climb. I want you to take this."

He handed her a brown envelope. "There is enough money in there to sustain you for a while, and here is a number to call in the event I do not come back."

Yvonne's face went pale, "You are scaring me, Kyle. I don't like this at all."

"I know, but it is necessary. Not to worry, I will be back, but just in case I am not, do as I say and take the money. We will get through this." They both leaned over the table and hugged each other, expressing their love and concern for each other, not knowing what the future would hold.

Early the next morning, Kyle got a phone call from Driver.

"Here is the latest on the Russians. There has been a lot of activity that has previously not taken place, but they have not vacated, nor have I seen any trucks."

"That is what I was expecting. I did not think the two incidents would urge them to leave. So let us initiate the third one." Kyle said.

"What is it you would like to do this time?" Driver asked.

"Well, Driver, I think until there is imminent danger, they won't be pushed over the cliff, sort of speaking. How many cars or trucks are left at the place?"

"They have two vehicles left. They have moved them to another location in the complex, and they use the other van most."

"Can you still get to them?" "Yes, we will take care of it."

"Okay, I want you to cut the brake lines so that they lose their brakes on the downhill of where they live. I want it to be so damn scary to them. We do not have to do anything else to get rid of them. Suppose there is a good crash, the better. I just don't want anyone else hurt."

"You got it, boss. When do you want this to go down, and is there a third note?"

"We will wait a day after the third note. The note will read, *'We have asked twice for you to vacate. We will ask only one more time, and if you have not left, it will not be the three of you leaving. One will have left earlier and not on their own. Vacate now!'*"

A couple of days passed, and Driver was on the boat. "I have the latest news for you, boss."

"Have a seat. I will be right with you. I need to finish this."

Driver walked over to the galley and got himself a cold Heineken. Kyle was now through with his morning task.

"Driver, come on over. No, wait, that beer looks awful good. Get me one, please."

"Sure, boss." They both sat down and started to discuss the mission they had been on and how it stood today.

"I am anxious to hear how our friends are doing on Russian Hill after the third incident."

"We did as you asked, and we cut the brake line so that it would happen after they left the complex and where there were not a lot of pedestrians around. We also took care of it so they were going to use the van at a time that they would not run into anyone."

Kyle looked intent. "That sounds great. How did it go?"

"We got lucky. All three got into the van we fixed, and they drove it out of the complex and onto the main road. We followed them to see what happened, and when they made the last turn before the on-ramp, they lost their brakes on the downhill. We could tell they were struggling with the van, a lot of movement inside. As they tried to make that last turn, they ran through the street sign, over the median, and into a drainage area. The van hit hard. The speed was pretty good. We could see the two front-seat Russians were draped over the dash, but we could not see the third one."

"Did they move?"

"Yes, it took a minute, but both in the front sat back, shaking their heads. The third got off the floor back onto the seat."

"Good, let me know how the activity is at the complex, so I can plan my next move if I have to."

"Will do, boss. I will let you know as soon as I have something to report to you."

It took a couple of days, but Driver was back at the boat.

"Boss, I think we got them this time. There are two moving vans there now, and they are at the Russians' apartment and the office. We are watching them closely, but I think it is them that are moving out." Kyle sat at his desk in the main cabin.

"Good news, Driver. Let me know when you can confirm. I will let Woody know when I hear from you, so make sure you are sure that they have left."

"There is one more thing. They left a note in an envelope. Here it is." "Thanks, let me have it." He opened the envelope and read the note.

"You are right. We got to them. They are moving out and selling the apartment complex, but they also want us to know that they will find those responsible and cause bodily harm. I do not think that they know it is us but let us watch our backs. We know they are out there and looking."

Kyle had gotten the confirmation he was waiting for and was ready to call Woody and report not only the progress they made on the problem but that they had successfully completed the mission, and it was a big mistake. The Russians came there to run guns, and in doing so, they hurt a lot of people who lived at the complex and kept the rest in fear. Now the problematic Russians had left, and the complex was up for sale. It was time to call Woody, Kyle decided.

"Hello, Woody. How are things in Las Vegas?"

"Doing well, Kyle. How are things in San Francisco, more directly, Russian Hill?"

"I must say, Woody, this was a tough one, dealing with the Russians. However, I was able to determine the problem. They were running guns and treating everyone around them like shit and threatening them all. It took a while, but we were able to get them to vacate and put the complex up for sale. You can let those affected by them know that things will be different there, and they can start to enjoy their lives again."

Woody smiled like a proud papa. "Kyle, I would have to say that you have done it again. This time, you did not ask me how to exterminate the problem. You just took care of it and then came back to me with success. I can now let my people know that it is handled."

"Yes, Woody, but there is a note to deal with. They left a note before they went. It is a warning that they will find out who did this and make them pay."

Woody said, "That is not good but sometimes part of the business. I would caution you not to be too visible out there. Use your people to watch your back."

"That is a good idea. I was wondering what might happen next after the last attempt on my life. I will be careful, and let me say, the work of Driver and Stan on this has been great. I appreciate what they have done."

"That is great. From my perspective, you were given the problem. You solved it. Good job again, Kyle."

"Thanks, Woody. What do you have next?" Woody smiled.

"I am running out of problems. You solve them so fast. Hang there in the city, and I will be back with you."

Kyle smiled.

"Thanks, Woody. That's what family is for. Let me know when you need me. Take care."

CHAPTER 36

YVONNE ON FIRE

Kyle was not sure what to do with his time off. It had been a while since he had time to relax. He thought he could go over and surprise Yvonne at her office. He had not been there since they first moved all the office furniture and supplies to the new office after the fire made them move.

It was crazy over there as Kyle thought about all that had happened in that office. On the good side, he built a multimillion-dollar empire, even though it was taken from him by Howard and the courts.

Howard left and went back to Chicago to start his empire with all that he stole from Kyle. Then he burned up in a fire in his apartment. They said it was caused by a white candle burning which fell onto the floor, catching the drapes alight.

David, his best friend, turned on him and tried to kill him and rape his neighbor's wife.

The janitor refused to clean the offices anymore because of the evil spirits that lived there. The bad spirits took over the office, wrote threatening words in blood on the walls, and made the candles explode.

Kyle was getting depressed thinking about the negative energy in that office, how it changed the lives of those who got caught up in it all. After losing his company, his marriage, and most of his millions, Kyle wondered about the curse the witch put on the candles. Was it the curse causing all the bad things to happen to those involved? He felt uneasy thinking about it.

He had been smart and put some away when he saw that things were starting to go sideways at work. Also, thank God for Yvonne, who jumped in and started to run the company and, with hard work, had built it back up. The good thing for her was that she got a new office in San Francisco, Marina District, and it came with a nice view of the bay.

He was happy that Yvonne was not hurt from all the bad energy and the curse if it were real. He wondered if his life could ever get back to normal, or maybe, this was the new normal. After visiting Yvonne for a little while, she suggested that he come over after work and barbecue a couple of steaks and kick it at her house. That sounded good to Kyle. He went across the street to the Safeway and picked up the necessary items for a good dinner with a pretty lady. He felt like a lucky guy.

Yvonne gave him the key to her condo so that he could put the groceries away and get things ready for the grill. When YL pulled up and came into the house, Kyle had a cold cocktail prepared for her and some fresh flowers to lighten up the kitchen. He was busy getting the steaks marinated and some mushrooms to sauté, throw in some loaded baked potatoes, a fine bottle of wine; the perfect ingredients for a fine dinner. It was a lovely night for grilling as he looked out over the bay with ships coming back into the port for the evening. He had a fine cigar and a fresh cocktail. Things were good. Were things going to remain good? Could he quit worrying and just enjoy all the good things in life?

They sat around her dining room table and enjoyed two medium-rare steaks with the mushrooms she loved so much. A fine dinner was had, and then to the couch to just relax for the night. They had both decided that they wanted to stay in after Yvonne asked Kyle to spend the night with her. Kyle notified the ship that he would not be there and gave the steward and the chef the night off. They both just kicked back and watched television.

Yvonne smiled over at Kyle, "I wanted to ask you about your family. You don't talk much about them." "What do you want to know?"

"Everything, start with your mother and father."

The conversation went on for hours, it seemed. Kyle did not talk much about them, but he had a story to tell when he did.

For Kyle's family, it all started on an island south of San Diego where his dad had a job working for the navy as a firefighter. His father came from an affluent family in the Pacific Northwest, where his family had flourished in the founding of a town. His dad had left the security of prominence to go on his own, even though his grandfather had founded the town and pleaded with him not to leave what was to become his fortune in the future. Still, he wanted to do it his way and took his family and headed south to a beach town far, far away. This decision would turn out to be the wrong one, and if he could do it over, Kyle was sure his dad would have stayed and raised his family among all who loved them and had great respect for the family.

On the other hand, Kyle's mother came from a family that worked the waterfront of a young city. His mother never got to know her own mother; it seemed she had disappeared, leaving very young siblings behind. With such a messed-up life for his mother when she was young and having to grow up without her mother being around, her father, who worked at the Boatworks in Coronado, the city where Kyle was born, did not have the time to raise three children, his mother, and her two brothers.

To make his life easier, her father took her to a mission in Oceanside to be raised by the nuns. His mother was devastated to be taken away from her brothers and the only family she had ever known. How unfair this was, she thought as she cried her eyes out, feeling loneliness in her heart and that empty feeling of fear that hurt in so many ways. This was not easy because her father was so strict and never believed his children when they told him about their lives, or he just did not care. He was immersed in his own problems at a time in history when children were to be seen and not heard. Kyle never understood the stories he heard about her father being so strict with his children because he was a loving grandfather to his grandchildren.

Kyle always enjoyed hearing the stories of his mother's family and how they were significant in the founding and leadership of a young city growing along the waterfront. The waterfront of bridges being built, boatyards busy building boats of all sizes for those who lived along the shores with businesses springing up everywhere. Those who worked so hard and went through so many hardships were all so excited and full of hope to be part of a young nation. One could hear the noise of saws and hammers along with seagulls singing their praise.

Her grandfather Benjamin was a fur trader hunter from Connecticut, and in the early 1800s, he left New England in one of those big sailing ships with the large masts blowing in the air. He had spent childhood watching them come into the Boston harbor in all their glory of sails in full bloom, the wind blowing them in and out of this very picturesque beauty of the mix of water and land. Those that sailed away left to a world that was little known about. It was men like Benjamin who opened the wilderness to all the rest of them. He boarded one of those magnificent ships he dreamed of, and now those dreams of an adventurous young boy were to come true.

Kyle admired his great-grandfather; they did not make many men like him. He traveled from Connecticut to San Diego, trading his furs along the way and seeing things others only dreamed about. He reached the coast of Southern California after months of exploring and gathering his wealth, and he was instrumental in the founding and the growth of this small coastal town. Kyle always thought back proudly of his family's history and his great-grandfather, who also fought in the Mexican American War.

The federal government had brought in troops on the Texas-Mexico border after tempers were reported flaring between the two countries, leading the United States to declare war on Mexico. Within one month, California became the Republic of California, and the bear flag was raised in Sonoma. Benjamin's bravery and leadership were noticed by those in rank and awarded him four thousand rolling acres in the region where he would build his ranch for his family. He set up a blacksmith shop in San Diego and built the first wagon using spoked wheels instead of the solid wooden wheels that were used at the time. It was there in San Diego on those beautiful hills and valleys that he would build his ranch and raise his family.

As Kyle's mother would tell him and his brothers the story, there always had to be a box of Kleenex on the table because she would always start crying as she remembered her great-grandmother. As the story goes, her grandmother was pregnant and needing a doctor, so her grandfather, running out of solutions, put her in the wagon and got two of his most dependable mares and hooked them up to the wagon, and they headed to the city, San Diego. It was a rainy, dark afternoon. The sky blackened with clouds and wind blowing over the hills as they started their three-hour trip to the city on a dirt road with wagon tracks dug deep into the well-traveled dirt road. The rains had flooded it, and they could not have picked a more miserable afternoon to travel.

Benjamin moved his pregnant wife down the bumpy road, giving her positive affirmations that everything would be okay as soon as they got to the city and reached the doctor. It was not much longer when Benjamin found his wagon wheel stuck in a muddy hole, and his horses could not pull them out. Benjamin climbed out from under the tarp he made to keep them dry. Her great-grandfather Benjamin, who had sailed thousands of miles, went where no others had gone, lived off the land, was now stuck in the mud with his pregnant wife in need of immediate medical attention.

Knowing he had to do something to get the wagon unstuck, he got out to push the back of the wagon, but it would not move, so he went to the wheel and was pushing on the spokes when it started to roll back. As it did, it caught his pants. The heavy wheel rolled over his chest, killing him there, in the rain and dirt, his wife in shock and severe pain bent over the wagon.

Such a tragedy that afternoon devastated the family. Kyle's great-grandmother went on to live a long life, one filled with a lot of work and love, running the ranch and taking care of the large family. Kyle was very proud of his family and all that they had accomplished in the early 1800s, including Benjamin, being one of the founding members of San Diego.

After such a tearful story, they were ready for a good night's sleep.

Kyle and Yvonne had been asleep for a couple of hours when there was a noise at the kitchen door. It was just after one in the morning, and someone was trying to break in. Still asleep in the bedroom, the intruder was now in the kitchen. He had a gas can and threw things around in the dining room, working his way back to the kitchen. When he made it to the back door, he threw a match into the kitchen area and watched as it all went up in flames before he bolted out the door and away from the condo. The inside was now all on fire, spreading to the front room when suddenly there was a crash in the bedroom. Jumping up out of sleep, the two of them looked around the room.

Kyle asked, "Did you hear that crashing noise?" as he wiped the sleep from his eyes.

Yvonne was on her way to the bathroom to see what had fallen.

"Kyle, it was the candle on the back of the toilet. It had slipped off and crashed on the floor."

Kyle looked concerned, "Hey, do you smell smoke?"

"Yes, I do." Yvonne started to walk over to the closed bedroom door.

Kyle yelled at her, "Do not open the door! Get away from it!" He got out of bed and went over to the door. He put his hand on the door to see how hot it was before he opened it.

"My dad taught us this. Let us see what is going on." He opened the bedroom door a crack and investigated the front room.

"Holy shit! The whole room is on fire. We will not be able to get out that way."

There were no windows in the condo. Both looked at each other. Kyle looked around the room as the smell of smoke worsened and started to come under the door. Yvonne was now noticeably shaken up, looking at Kyle, hoping he came up with some way to get them out. He spotted a floor light pole behind the nightstand. He grabbed it and tore off the light as Yvonne watched.

"What are you going to do with that?"

Kyle, with the pole in his hands, said, "Stand back. I am going to break through this wall."

He started swinging the pole into the drywall repeatedly as the fire was getting hotter and spreading fast. The door was beginning to smolder. Yvonne was alarmed and counting on Kyle. If he were wrong, they would both burn up and die. He kept smashing the wall with all his strength and was now through one layer of the wall, working on the other one. He was not sure if he would have enough time but kept swinging as fast and hard as he could.

"Hell yes!" he screamed as he broke through to the other side.

"Come on, Yvonne. Follow me as I clear the wall." Kyle was now in the bedroom of the couple who lived in the other unit. He climbed on his belly as he pulled himself through the hole.

"What the fuck is going on?" said Larry, laying on his bed and watching two people come through his wall.

Kyle got to his feet and helped Yvonne through the hole.

"Sorry to meet you this way, but there is a fire in her condo, and we all need to get out of here. Wake her up," Kyle said, pointing at the person asleep next to Larry.

"And get the hell out of here. I am going to call 911."

Yvonne and her two neighbors grabbed their coats and ran outside as the whole condo went up in flames. Kyle met the other three out in the street as the San Francisco Fire Department raced around the corner. The fire was lighting the whole night up as several more fire trucks arrived to get the blaze under control. Kyle had Driver come over to get Yvonne.

"So, you called your girlfriend? Everything okay for you to stay there for a while?" He checked with Yvonne.

"Oh, of course. She is ready for me."

"I will have Driver take you there. I will stay here and talk with the fire inspector. Then I will go to the ship. I just want to make sure that you are all right. I am sick over this, Yvonne. All that matters to me is that you are okay. You have lost everything, and I want to find out how the fire started. Driver, take Yvonne over to Sarah's and then come back for me. I should be done soon, and thanks for the clothes."

"No problem, boss. Be right back. Are you ready, Yvonne?"

The fire had just burned out, thanks to all the trucks and men that showed up to put it out. There was nothing salvageable from it, just a smoldering mess. The fire inspector walked up to Kyle.

"It is too early to say anything, but you both are lucky to be alive. It looks like gasoline or something like that was used to start the fire. We found a gas can in the kitchen. Mr. Stone, someone tried to kill you."

That was not the news he wanted to hear. What was he going to tell Yvonne? She just lost everything due to him. Kyle was sick to his stomach.

Back on the boat, Kyle emerged from what had happened the night before. Who was trying to kill him? The Russians were front and center in his mind, but there could be others before he blamed them. He was mainly concerned about Yvonne and her life; they could've just burned up. He had been on the phone with Woody, going over everything, and they were going to wait until the investigation was complete before they would decide on what action would be necessary to take.

Woody agreed with him about Yvonne, and that made Kyle happy. He made a couple of phone calls and was ready to leave. He decided to go over to Sarah's apartment, where Yvonne was staying. She was not going to work, being so shaken. Driver pulled up to Sarah's, and they went to the door. Sarah opened the door.

"Oh, Kyle, please come in," she said as she looked at him and the other two individuals, he had with him.

"Hello, Sarah, is Yvonne around?"

"Yes, I will get her. Please, you can all have a seat."

They sat on the couch as she went in the back to get Yvonne. Yvonne came out, and Kyle could see that she had been crying, her eyes were watering, and her nose was light pink. She had just gotten out of the shower to get the smoke out of her hair. Kyle stood up to hug her as they shared what they both just went through. Kyle was ready to introduce the two he brought with him.

"Yvonne, I want you to meet some special people I brought over to meet with you. I know it is just after the horrible fire, but that is why they are here. I know you just lost everything, so Maryanne is your new real estate agent. Yvonne, we will replace your home. We will buy you a new one. When you are ready, Jackie can take you house shopping in what area you want to live in, and we will buy the home for you."

Yvonne now sat in the chair. A smile came over her crying face as Kyle shared the good news with her.

Kyle said, "Besides, I know you lost all your clothes and belongings. I want you to meet Cathy. She will be your personal shopper. She will help you purchase all the clothes you need as well as furniture and everything else you will need. I am so sorry this happened. I will do anything it takes to make you feel happy and safe again."

They both hugged each other. Yvonne started to cry again as Sarah hugged her, but this time, it was happy tears. "Kyle, I cannot believe you have done this and taken care of this all so fast. I don't know what to say."

"You don't have to say anything. I just want to make this all up to you, make it right." Kyle had not told her that the inspector thought it was set on fire, not an accident. He would tell her, but this was not the time. He needed to fix it all first and then tell her later. He still wanted to wait for the final report. Kyle addressed the two he brought in.

"Okay, you guys share contact info, and then we need to go," he said as he reached his hand for Yvonne's. The agent and personal shopper left the apartment, and Kyle hugged Yvonne.

"I am going to stay on the boat. You just rest and take care of yourself.

I will call you later."

They shared a kiss. Kyle left and went to the boat, not telling her that he was probably the target.

CHAPTER 37

SEND IN THE ARMY

river dropped Kyle off at the boat. He was pretty messed up, worrying about Yvonne and not thinking about what this might all mean to him. With Yvonne taken care of, he thought that he would try and relax in the beautiful sunshine of which there was plenty today. He had Jimmy make him one of those special Bloody Mary's so he could relax on the chaise lounge and pillow. Time to kickback.

As he lay on the bow of the boat, he had a view of the estuary as it wound around Coast Guard Island, with the hills of Oakland to the east. It was all so tranquil, with a gentle breeze washing over him. What a peaceful day to be had. Kyle could use a down day; it was good for his sanity. After doing what he said he wanted for a long time, relaxing, and now waiting for his dinner from the chef and sipping on a nice glass of cabernet, he gave Yvonne a call.

Yvonne, who was still at Sarah's, had gone over to the wine rack to get her a bottle of merlot as the phone rang.

"Hello, Kyle, how are you?"

"Hello, I am fine. I just wanted to call and see how you are doing."
"Well, it will be better when I get this bottle of wine opened and put

this crystal glass to my lips."

"Oh, maybe the whole bottle would be a good idea?"

"I hear you. Can you believe what we just went through?"

Kyle was very concerned.

"I had to call you. Are you doing all right?"

"Yes, I am, Kyle, but you don't have to act like it is your fault. You saved our lives. I stood there and watched you beat your way through the wall while the fire got closer. I was so scared."

"I know, I was looking around to see how we could get out of there, and that was the only thing I could think of. I was determined to break through. Not to make light of it, but you should have seen the face on Larry as I crawled out of his wall. It was so special."

"My goodness, I bet he couldn't believe what he was seeing. However, it ended up saving his life and, Kyle, talking about saving our lives. What about the candle slipping off my toilet and crashing on the tile? If that had not happened, we would not have woken to the fire and probably would not be here now."

Kyle wished he could just hug her. He felt her pain as acutely as his own.

"I guess you are right. It is just that the candle keeps showing up at different times in my life, going back to the curse." "Well, if there is a curse, it is a good curse for you." "I guess so. I just want to have everything slow down and be normal.

I have had enough stressful events happen around me."

Yvonne wished he were there to hold. "I want to thank you for Maryanne and Cathy. It means so much to me to know that I can put my life back together."

"Yes, they will be great, and the house you get will be bigger, and you will love it. Do not worry about money. Do what the girls say and be sure to get everything you want. It is important to me."

Yvonne answered him. "I am worried about you." Yvonne now sat on her couch, looking over the bay. "So much has taken place in your life. I was getting worried about you and how you could handle your problems, much less the new problems your employer gives you to solve, and before you say anything, I don't know what you do, and I am totally in the dark."

Kyle sat at the dining table in the main cabin. "I am glad you added that last part. It would be best if you weren't involved in anything other than your business, and remember, I am starting to be very grateful for this position. It has been rewarding, and I am starting to feel very safe."

"Don't worry about me, Kyle. I see nothing. I know nothing. What are you going to do tonight? Do you want to come over?"

"Chief is ready to bring me my dinner so that I will stay here tonight. Maybe go to bed early and read a good book. I will call you tomorrow. I am thinking of taking off for Mexico for a few days. Do you know anyone who might want to go, especially after last night?"

"You know you don't have to ask me twice. Have a good night, and I will talk with you tomorrow."

"Enjoy your evening. Good night."

The timing was good. The chef put his dinner in front of him, and this fine meal needed to be eaten while it was hot. Kyle saw Jimmy doing the dishes as the sun set in the west and darkness came over the Bay Area.

"Jimmy, I am going to shut it down early tonight. I think a good book sounds good, and I happen to have one I have been longing to get into. Please get my room ready, and a shot of tequila would also be nice. Use the 1940."

Jimmy got his room ready as asked, and being it was now dark, he brought in a candle and lit it for Kyle to have some more reading light. The room was now ready. Kyle was impressed with the way Jimmy got his room ready. The personal touches did not go unnoticed, and Kyle really appreciated them.

As he waited, he flipped his new book open and started to go to another world, a world of some other guy's problems, where they had nothing to do with him. How nice. As the night wore on, he could hardly keep his eyes open as he moved through the first chapters of his book, and soon, he was fast asleep. He didn't know how many hours he had been asleep when the candle next to his bed fell off the table and crashed on the floor, waking him up. As he opened his eyes and smelt the smoke from the candle, he sat up and looked around, but darkness was all he could see.

Still feeling uneasy about everything these days, Kyle put on his robe and slippers, walked over to the door of his room on the officer deck, just outside the bridge. He looked down at the stern of the boat and then to the bow, saw nothing, turned around, and then he heard someone or something coming up the stairs. Kyle put his back to the outside wall of his room, looking at the stairs, trying to see who it could be, but he could not see anyone.

Listening carefully, he picked up the voice of someone who was speaking Russian. He quietly turned around to go to the bridge in front of his room when two Russians suddenly opened fire with their AK-47s. It sounded like a warzone.

Kyle hit the deck and started to crawl from his room, knowing if they got him in there trapped, he would have nowhere to go. He crawled to the bridge, the weapons firing fast and furious around him. All the windows on the bridge smashed as bullets rang in his ears and passed right over his head. The shells bounced around the inside of the bridge, and the air filled with the smell of gunpowder.

As he crawled on his belly, Kyle felt a burning sensation on his right arm as the bullet had seared through and taken part of his arm. The blood started to run heavily down his arm to his stomach. As he lay on the floor, waiting for the shooting to stop the pool of his blood got larger. Kyle knew that if he just stayed there, they would find him and kill him. He started to crawl to the doorway, where they obviously knew he was hiding. Kyle crawled through his blood to the door and pulled himself up with his good arm so that he could try and get a look at what the hell was going on. He needed to put a plan together quickly, or he'd be dead.

He could see two armed men in front of the bridge and one over to the right. The two in front were standing there with their AK-47s on full fire mode as they rested their weapons on their stomachs and kept emptying magazines, hoping to kill anybody or anything. The third seemed to be the lookout for his two Russian killers. It did not look good for him, and he knew it. They were only a few feet away from filling his chest with deadly lead.

Kyle heard someone else yelling from the port side, and then he heard gunshots coming from that direction. He pulled himself up again, and he saw Jimmy with an M16 with fire coming out of it.

Then, to the starboard side, he heard the same thing, and it was the chef emptying his magazine at the Russians. Hitting the two in the back and side, they went down. The third started to run past the bridge. Kyle reached his good arm out the doorway and grabbed his leg as he ran by, sending him down the stairs. Jimmy took aim and waited until he hit the next level, and then bam! Down went the third Russian. The Russian on the stairs was killed with a headshot, but the two others were still alive and would be interrogated or tortured until they talked. Kyle did not care if it was torture, not after what he just went through. He was thinking that they should get a helicopter and take these two up. *If they won't talk, throw one out. Believe me. The other one will talk.*

Still shaking, Jimmy and the chef came over to see if he was alright. Jimmy left to get the first aid kit to take care of Kyle's gunshot wound on his arm. They stopped the bleeding, but it would require some stitches. Kyle held his arm with a blood-soaked cloth on it.,

Chief said, "Good thinking, Kyle tripping that Russian up gave me a chance for a clear shot."

"Well, I was not sure what to do, but I did not want him coming into the Bridge. That would have been the end of me. However, as I am bleeding all over, who is going to take me to the hospital?" he asked the two standing there.

Chief said, "Oh no, we don't go to the hospital. We do not want any cops to get involved in this."

Kyle looked worried.

"Really? What about my arm?" he said as he looked at the wound still bleeding.

"Don't worry. We have all it takes to do the job and keep your arm from falling off," Chief laughed.

"I am glad you think it is funny. I am bleeding all over myself, and I have a dead Russian on the stairs without a head."

What a mess on the ship. Blood all over the deck. The fire hoses were brought out to wash the sea of red overboard. The two Russians, still alive, were taken down into the ship. The third, the dead one, had been removed from the stairs, and his head was found two levels down. Kyle was so glad that he did not have any visitors. It would have been a different story. He had a question for Jimmy, who was cleaning up the bloody mess.

"Jimmy, first, let me say thank you for showing up when you did and taking care of business, and eliminating the threats. I would not be here if you did not show up when you did."

With a hose in his hand, Jimmy said, "Boss, I am just glad you're alright. That was gnarly. I can't remember when I emptied so many magazines."

"You know, Jimmy, this is a night we won't forget soon. It scared the hell out of me. Hey, I did have a question, though. You put the candle in my room. Why did you do that? It is not a regular piece for the rooms?"

"I was walking out of the supply room, and it was sitting right by the door. I never saw it there before. I don't know who put it there, but I knew you were going to read, so I grabbed it. Why?"

"I will tell you why. I was sound asleep with my book on my chest when I heard a bang and crash, and the candle had fallen off my night table, waking me up. Let me say this Jimmy, had you not put that candle in my room, I would not have woken up, and they would have had me where they wanted me, dead! Here is the kicker, if you look at my nightstand, you will see the sign of a crocked X, this is the sign of my forefathers, the Knight Templars. They knocked the candle off the table to wake me up. You see Jimmy, I am still being looked after and very appreciative. That candle saved my life, and of course, you did too when you shot the perpetrators."

"That is crazy Kyle, the Knights Templars were here last night, this blows my mind. It kind of spooks me. Anyway don't worry about this mess we will clean it all up and handle all the details. You do not have to get involved."

"Okay, thanks, Jimmy. I will make contact, and by the way, do you want to keep the candle?" "Oh no, Boss, I don't like any kind of black magic or anything to do with a witch or any curse. I am still trying to process the Knight Templars and the mark on the table. I will tell you Boss, there is nothing boring in your life, that is for sure."

Kyle had a complex expression on his face. He thought about the candle again and what Jimmy said. What was it with the candle? If the curse was real, maybe he needed to embrace it instead of running from it. When he thought about the crocked X mark on the table and just had to smile, he was now feeling love.

As soon as Woody was in his office, Kyle gave him a call.

"Hi, Woody. I presume you have heard about our visitors on the ship early this morning?"

"Yes, I have. Are you all alright? I heard you got shot in the arm?" Woody sounded concerned.

"Yes, I did, and, Woody, I am lucky that is all that happened to me. I was lying on the bridge floor while two crazy Russians emptied at least three magazines into the bridge, sending bullets everywhere. Pretty scary, to be honest with you. When I was in Nam with the Senator, it was nothing like this. I thought they had me and were ready to come in for the kill when Jimmy and Chef showed up blazing."

Woody said, "Do you remember when we talked about this just the other day?"

"Yes, I do. It crossed my mind when all I saw was the fire of the barrels.

That will get one's attention real fast."

"Well, here is the deal. It is too hot where you are. I want you to get out of there for the time being. Let us come in and clean this up. We now know from the Russians who did this, who ordered the hit. I do not want you involved. We have people who handle such situations, and they will eradicate the problem, and I want you to know for sure that this will be taken care of, and when you come back, there will not be any problems or people you have to worry about. Also, Kyle, I cannot promise that this will not happen to you again. When you shake the tree, you never know what might fall out of it."

Kyle was happy that this would be handled.

"Well, boss, I might lie low in Mexico, somewhere warm. I will let you know when I decide shortly."

"Okay, I am glad you are all right. We will talk soon."

CHAPTER 38

THE END AND THE BEGINNING

He was ready to check out of his room, and he thought he should run by Yvonne's and let her know that he was going to leave for a short while.

He walked into her office. "Is Yvonne in? Tell her Kyle is here, please." The receptionist spoke to Yvonne. "Mr. Stone, please go in."

Yvonne got up from her desk with a smile on her face. "Kyle, I was not expecting to see you today."

"Well, I thought it was necessary to let you know that I will be leaving for a short period. All I can tell you is that someone tried to kill me again. I won't go into any details, but I can say that this is very serious and probably not over. My company will handle the problem or problems. That is why they need me out of the way. I will be back as soon as it is safe for all."

"This sounds serious. Is there anything I can do?" Yvonne looked concerned.

"No, just go along with your daily business. Take care of things with Maryanne and Cathy. I will contact you when I return. It must be done this way. I don't want you to get hurt."

With a sad expression, Yvonne said, "I will miss you so much. How long will it be, or can't you tell me that?"

"I don't know, but I think it will not be that long, but I want you to know Yvonne, you have brought me love again in my heart. You have stood by me in the most difficult time in my life, worse than war. You do not know how much that means to me. You taught me that I could trust someone, get close to someone again, and share what surprises come along. So during my absence, my heart will be full of love for you, and stay safe. I will call you. I will miss you too."

With that, there was a big hug and kiss as tears ran down YL's face, and then they parted ways.

Yvonne stood by the door and watched the man she was falling in love with walk away. She wiped the tears off her cheek. Certainly not liking this part of the job, the one she loved was the target of someone who wanted to kill him. This was something she could not fathom. She had never met a man like Kyle. He was so unique and so kind and full of the truth. All she could do was stand there and wave goodbye while she broke out crying, wiping her tears as she went back into her office.

Kyle walked back to the limousine.

"Driver, take me out to my children. I have to let them know I won't be around for a little while."

Driver steered the car toward the suburbs. "I meant to ask you about the other night. I wish I were on board that night."

"I'm glad you weren't there. You might not be here now!" Kyle said.

"It sounds to me that you got lucky. What woke you up, the Russians?" Driver said with a smirk on his face.

"I don't know about being lucky, but it was a weird thing. Jimmy had put a candle on my nightstand so I could read, and later that night, it fell off and crashed on the floor. That is what woke me up. It is several times since a candle was present and remember me I told you about Howard. He came into my company and acted like a franchisor but only wanted to gain enough information to initiate a takeover? Well, he died in his apartment when a candle by his bed fell on the floor and burned his apartment down, burning him to death. And then the candle on my nightstand falls on the floor, wakes me up, but saves my life. Weird."

Driver listened prudently. "Did you not see a candle or flame, or was it a light when you were underwater?"

"Yes, I did, and it sent me to the surface, but remember that David, my old VP, had us meet with a witch and get these candles, four black ones and one white one, and put them in our offices. And you know, Driver, ever since, everyone there has been affected adversely by what took place afterward, except me. It seems to be there whenever I need help, over and over again. If it hadn't fallen off the table and alerted me, like before, the Russians would have been able to sneak into my cabin, and that would have been the end of me. I think that is what they were counting on, but it was not to be the case, and now there is one dead Russian and two shot-up Russians."

Driver said, "Well, boss, I will say it again. You got lucky!" "Okay, you are right. I got lucky."

On their way to his kids' house, Driver asked a question, "Did you call your wife and let her know that you are on your way there?"

"Yes, I did, but no one answered, so I have no choice but to go there and try and see my kids. You have met my wife, so you know what we might get into."

"Yeah, I met her, boss, a very difficult woman to live with. Aren't you separated now?"

"We are, but it is still difficult to watch your past fade away and new relationships made. It's hard doing the right thing for the kids. If you don't do it right, it can affect them for the rest of their life. I know. Are you going to be involved in the Russian caper, or is that altogether a different segment of the Family?"

"No, I am not involved. I will be going back to Las Vegas until I hear from you that you're back, and then I will be back."

"Okay, I don't know how long I will be gone. It depends on the situation with the Russians and how long it takes to get to the bottom of who tried to kill me, and how long to eradicate the poison. I am not letting anyone know where I'm going for security reasons, but I know I will be anxious to get back."

As they drove up to Kyle's old house, there was a cop car in front, and Kyle hesitated to go to the door, but maybe he needed to see what was going on, hoping it was not the kids in trouble or, worst yet, hurt. Kyle got out and walked up to the door and knocked, then waited. A black cop opened the door with only his pants on.

"What do you want?" he asked. Kyle stepped back for a moment as he didn't expect this.

"I'll tell you what I want. I want to see my kids." "They are up the street," the cop said.

"Great, is Suzette around, or have you taken over the house?" "What are you, a wise guy? Why don't you tell me who you are?" "When I asked for my kids, I thought that might be a giveaway."

The cop turned around and started to walk to the bedroom. "I will get Suzette."

"Who was that?" Kyle heard Suzette ask as she was lying in bed.

"Some guy in a limousine who says he is your husband. He was in a limo. I thought you were divorced, and he was not around?"

Suzette, irritated now, said, "We are getting a divorce, and he should have called first. I am sorry, you forgive me?"

"I don't know. Why don't we go back to bed, and then we both can receive forgiveness?"

Kyle left the house and got back in the car. He didn't know that she was dating and bringing strange men into the house. He told Driver that it was not worth the fight and had him take him up the street to see his kids. Kyle felt guilty that he must leave his children. It was kind of hard to take when he thought of some other man influencing them or, even worse, if a continual flow of different men were coming out of their mother's bedroom.

Nothing he could do about it now. It would have to wait until he got back, and then he would have a discussion with Suzette on how to date and still be a good mother. It was funny he thought that because he got a call from her just about that. Still upset that he had shown up at her house unexpectedly, he could tell she needed a favor, so she decided to play nicely. She asked Kyle to watch the kids that weekend. He felt it was strange as she had never asked before. Instead, she did all she could to keep them away from him.

As it turned out, this was to be the first time she would be out of town with a boyfriend. She said they were going to go skiing in Tahoe. Kyle did not care. It was an opportunity to be with his kids without her being around. He decided to take them to Disneyland. How special, he and his two girls all to himself. Kyle was happy.

They started out in Oakland, where he boarded his girls onto the private jet, waiting to take them to Los Angeles. This was the first time the girls had been on a plane. He hoped he did not ruin it for later years when they would have to fly coach. It was a short flight, but they loved it all the same as they took off over the ocean, and the jet took a steep bank to the west, then south, as they headed for Disneyland. This was starting to be something special for the three of them.

Upon landing at LAX, the limo was waiting, and shortly they were off to the Disneyland Hotel, where magic was waiting. The girls waited on a couch in the lobby while their dad took care of the room. They noticed that he was in an earnest conversation with the hotel clerk or manager. They could not tell, but it was serious, and the two gave all their attention to the counter. The conversation was over. The clerk or manager put his hand on their dad's shoulder and said something to him, and they saw their dad with his head down, as if in shock or something. It was deadly serious.

Kyle's mind was spinning. How could he tell the kids? How would he tell them what he had just been described? They were only a foot away. He needed time. So many thoughts were going through his head and heart. He had the room key in his hand. He looked down at it and decided to take them to the room and not say anything. Once in the room, he introduced them to the minibar, and as they were going through the goodies, the hotel phone rang. Kyle answered the phone, and it was Suzette's parents. They wanted to know if he had heard yet that Suzette was dead.

She had been in a car crash. Kyle gave his condolences and said that he had just found out in the Disneyland Hotel lobby, checking in for a fabulous fun weekend. They asked if the girls knew yet, and he told them no, but he was just about to tell them if he could find a way to do it. They all decided that maybe it would be better if they were there when they were told. Kyle agreed and said that he would fly the girls up to Napa, where they lived, and then they could altogether deliver the devastating news. They were on the way to the airport after telling the kids that they had to leave after just getting there. That was not easy.

Kyle told Driver to find out how Suzette was killed and let him know. The kids did not seem to mind if they could get back on that jet and have more flying fun. Once in the air, his driver called and explained that Suzette was driving her boyfriend's Porsche, speeding through the windy country road when they came upon a sharp curve, and an older man was standing by his truck, which was parked on the side of the road. He was trying to clean up some boxes that fell from the back of his truck.

Kyle could hear something strange in Driver's voice as he told him, "Boss, you won't believe this, but the contents of the boxes were white candles."

Kyle's jaw dropped open in disbelief upon hearing this.

"When Suzette came around the corner, she pulled the car to the right to avoid the candles but lost control, and they went over a seventy-five-foot cliff. Both were pronounced dead at the scene."

Kyle, still in disbelief about the candles in the road, thanked the driver for the information as he looked over at his smiling girls. How could he ruin all that was good with them and deliver such horrible news? Thank God for grandparents, was all Kyle could say. He did not know what he would have done without them helping the children get through what probably would be the worst news they ever got. Kyle certainly hoped so.

The grandparents would take care of the kids for a little while, and then Kyle would fly them down to Mexico, where he would be staying until things settled. Kyle, still feeling sad over his ex's death, headed straight for the airport, where his plane was gassed up and ready to go. Puerto Vallarta was the destination. There in the sun, he would rest.

Kyle looked out the window as the jet thundered down the runway, wheels up, and he was on his way. The sunset appeared in the window, and he wondered what tomorrow would bring. He was so ready for tomorrow, he thought, as he was given his tequila and tonic. Kyle took a sip of it and thought back at what had just happened in his life that changed everything and everyone.

He wondered if the witch stuff had anything to do with all the crazy things that had happened. David was now divorced and in jail at San Quentin for fraud. Howard had an accident in his room and burned to death in a fire. Suzette, the third person to betray him, drove off a seventy- five-foot cliff to her death. Only one person came out of the madness okay, and that was Yvonne, who deserved all the good that came her way. The financial corporation had gone from a multi-million dollar enterprise to a small insurance boutique that Yvonne now ran.

This was part of the story that bothered Kyle a lot. He built something that no one else had thought of. He made it huge, giving so many the sort of lifestyle they only dreamed of. He knew he had helped so many families make it in this world. He could not help feeling so sad about how it all went down, with greedy people and selfish, stupid ones taking it all apart, one brick at a time. All the while, Kyle was trying to keep it alive and finally giving up when it all caved in on him. With it all being said and done, Kyle felt more protected than he had ever felt in his life. Was he with those who cared about him, or was he being set up for more falls?

He certainly hoped not. He could stand for some happiness and closure. Well, the rest was pretty much how it was told, and now Kyle felt like he had a clean slate to come back and start his new life, one of peace and love. One could only hope.

The Streamline jet was on the way to twenty-five thousand feet flying over the California coast then the Mexico coast before heading inland to reach their destination. Kyle felt at peace as he looked out the window seeing nothing but storm gathering around them and smiling to himself over all that had happened. As he reflected on the crazy things that he had to go through, he thought maybe while he relaxed in Mexico, he should write a book about his life, then he thought, nobody would believe him, so why do it?

"Mr. Stone," the stewardess called to him. "Yes," Kyle answered.

"This fell out of your suitcase in the overhead. I thought you would want it?" She handed Kyle a white candle. Kyle was in shock as he grabbed the candle. He could not believe what just happened.

He immediately called the stewardess, "Come back, please, before handing me this candle. Had you seen it before?"

"No, Mr. Stone, I saw it for the first time a few minutes ago. Is there something wrong?"

Kyle still with a blank face, "No, it's fine, thank you."

He placed the candle on the seat next to him as the jet pushed through the storm clouds. He sat there trying to figure out how the candle had got there. Who knew he was going to fly today? Who had put the candle where he was going to sit? He was duped and a little worried. He remembered all the times the candle had shown up and from where it came from, but he still couldn't figure it out.

"Please fasten your seatbelts if not already fastened in. We are passing through some rough weather. It should smooth out soon," said the redheaded air stewardess after talking with the Captain.

The plane was shaking as she spoke. Kyle thought this one was getting nasty quickly, and he knew because he had been on many flights without smooth air. He looked over at the white candle on the seat next to him and hoped it would make him feel better because he was starting to worry as the plane was really in the heart of a massive storm. It was like it had grabbed the plane and was shaking it.

The pilot's voice came over the sound system, "I am sorry, but this is pretty bad. I will try —Oh shit, we lost oil pressure in engine two!"

Kyle held on to his seat, now more worried than ever. Everyone looked scared as the shaking got worse. The plane dropped a couple of hundred feet, and the candle fell onto the floor.

"I cannot hold her up. We are dropping too fast. Please take emergency procedures," the captain said in a profoundly serious voice. But the passengers could also hear the fear coming from his message.

Stewardesses called out, "Go to emergency measures. Everyone put your head between your legs, it will be okay, but this is a great time to pray."

Kyle leaned over to get the candle before it rolled away. He was taking in the announcements and grabbed his ankles, a position no flier ever wanted to do. Just as he reached for the candle and the tips of his fingers found it, the plane took another big bounce and moved sideways, rocking back and forth. The candle rolled to the back of the aircraft. Kyle felt a gentle hand on his shoulders with his head now between his legs and his eyes closed.

He did not bother to look up. He knew nobody was sitting there. It must just be nerves, he thought. In a matter of seconds, which felt like an hour, he reached again for the candle as loving thoughts of his family was going through his mind as it might be the last time to have seen them all, sad, sad emotions and thoughts pulling on his heart, as the plane plummeted.

He thought about his children. How could they deal with another death, the death of their father after just losing their mother? This cannot happen! It was only days ago that she swerved off the road and plunged down a 75ft ravine. What would the kids do now? He prayed hard for them to be spared from a life of pain and hurt or having an emotional anchor pulling them down. Kyle knew he had been living with it for over 30 years. It never ended.

Kyle had been torn up over losing his dad. He did not know if he took it harder than his other brothers. It was hard to believe they felt this much pain. Remembering all the times he grew up, he wished his dad were there to share it all with him. The birth of his babies to be shared with Grandpa, his marriage, his graduation from Officers Candidate School, so many instances where he had the hell scared out of him that he wished his dad were there. Speaking of having the hell scared out of him, he knew his dad wouldn't have approved of him going along with the witch to get revenge. In cases like this, he needed his dad.

A lot of praying to God was going on on the plane. Most were asking for their lives to be spared or praying for their loved ones as Kyle was doing. He prayed for his girls and that Jesus would look after them and protect them.

As he prayed, he felt the hand on his shoulder again. It was stronger this time and comforting as he glanced up to see if anyone was there. He looked out the window, and all he could see were black clouds streaming by as the plane continued its quick descent. He was only hoping that the pilot was trying like crazy to pull the nose up as he was sure he was.

It was YL's turn to now be in his head as he thought of all he was going to miss, the soft touch, love in her eyes and heart, and unselfish love and respect for him. He just met her, and now it was going to be over. Life wasn't fair, he thought. He needed to find love and peace before it would be his time. He was wishing. A strong emotion of loneliness came over him as death came closer. From the depths, he remembered the war and how he was so scared at times, but nothing felt like this, not being able to do anything to stop it.

Kyle opened his eyes, felt he was being lifted, looked at the seat, and felt someone sitting next to him. It felt peaceful.

Suddenly, he heard a soothing voice, *"You are not alone, my son. You have never been alone,"* the voice said calmly.

Kyle was surprised at hearing the voice so clearly, and then again, it said, *"You were not alone when you had to jump out of a burning chopper. I was right there with you. I had you. You were not alone when you were pushed out the window. I was hanging there with you; I had you. When you found yourself underneath a yacht while saving someone else, I was there in the darkness and pushed you up to the surface; I had you. You were not alone in the limousine when the rock came through the roof; I had you. You were not alone when you were attacked on the ship. It was me who knocked the candle over so that you would wake up; I had you. You see, son, I have always protected you and always loved and cherished you."*

Kyle was so full of emotion, hearing all that was being said, tears filling his eyes with a hand on his shoulder.

As Kyle wiped the tears from his eyes, the plane continued speeding down to a fiery grave. He turned and looked at the seat next to him where the indentation as if someone was sitting there had been. Only this time, there was someone there as he felt this tremendous warmth in his heart. Sitting there, looking as young as when he left this world, but now with an aura around him was his dad! In total surprise, with a smile as wide as his face. It was his dad saying all those things, his dad who saved his life all those times. So much love took him over. His heart was starting to overflow.

His dad smiled at him, "I want you to know how much I love you and know you are not alone and will never be, know that you are loved and keep on loving others, we will be together again, and most importantly, son, I am sorry for what I did and how much I hurt you. I am sorry, son, with all my heart, I will make it up to you soon. Stay blessed."

With that, his dad faded away, and the plane's nose continued its fast descent. Kyle could tell it was way too fast. The pilot was steering the plane over the desolate valley heading to a hill with the airport still miles away.

The passengers had no idea what was happening in the cockpit and how fear took over the pilot and copilot. Not being able to pull the aircraft over the hill, inside the shaking was something no one on the plane had experienced before.

Kyle, scared to death, suddenly thought of all of his loved ones. They flashed through his mind so fast, his daughters who just lost their mother. Kyle had no control of his life now. Fear and sorrow flooded over him as the plane hit the hill, taking the right wing off. They were flung sideways, throwing passengers about inside, bones being broken, blood splattered on the seats, luggage dislodged from overhead lockers, and so much crying and screaming.

Kyle held his ankles, head down as he was thrown out of his seat, the plane upside down as it continued to crash into the hill. After being thrown several rows, he looked up from the floor between the seats, and smoke filled the plane, flames licking in the back as the plane broke apart.

Kyle checked his legs and realized he might have broken his neck or injured it seriously. The pain was unbearable. He stood up, but the pain was something he had not felt before in his life. A lady and her seven-year-old daughter were between the seats across the aisle, crying in fear. Kyle knew he had to get them out, or they would burn to death.

Not able to hold his neck up, pain burning through his body, he clutched the daughter with one hand, grabbed the mother's jacket with his other hand, and pulled them as hard as he could to release them from the seat on top of them. Once up, Kyle could see the forward exit lights. He moved them through the smoke, getting them as close as he could, not being able to move forward, dizziness taking him over. He pushed them forward out of the smoke into the doorway to the exit as he fell on the floor, holding his neck. Now left only with his mind and soul, consumed in his love for his daughters and those who loved him, confusion as he heard the sirens coming closer and the firemen grab their hoses and run to the fire in the cockpit and scattered wreckage over the hill.

Upon the plane's powerful impact on the hill, both pilots were thrown from the cockpit. As First Responders tried to save them, their injuries were not sustainable, they died.

Kyle could hear passengers screaming, sirens blaring and firemen yelling as he laid on the floor with more explosions around him. Gasping for any air he could get from the thick deadly smoke; he felt a fire within, his chest ready to explode in choking and burning pain overwhelming him, all the while the flames are jumping closer. In defeat of life, Kyle was closing his eyes for the last time, anticipating a horrible death by fire.

"Kyle reach for me, I am here," Kyle confused, did he really hear a voice, as his eyes continue to be closed. More direct, "Kyle, Kyle Stone, you must reach for me now, feel my Love." Opening his eyes, and feeling an overwhelming pulse of Love, he reaches out into the thick wall of smoke with all the strength his heart and soul can give in his last attempt for life. A firm hand grasps his as an amazing flow of Love runs through him. The Love he had always searched for. How beautiful it felt immersing his soul and giving him the strength to get up on his knees.

Another explosion, tearing the fuselage open causing Kyle to fall out of the burning plane, rolling to the ground.

As Kyle sat near the ambulance, clothes torn, leg bleeding, chest full of smoke, he stared at the fiery mess of metal, he felt complete for the first time in his life, knowing that Love and Faith had saved him.

After a disaster of immense proportions, a life of emptiness, Kyle Stone finally, finally finds the true Meaning and Power of Love.

END

www.ingramcontent.com/pod-product-compliance
Lightning Source LLC
Chambersburg PA
CBHW061619190726
48288CB00007B/2390